WHIRLPOOL
OF
SHADOWS

Jaya Ganga, In Search of the River Goddess
(Penguin Books, 1990)

WHIRLPOOL
OF
SHADOWS

VIJAY SINGH

JONATHAN CAPE
LONDON

First published 1992
© Vijay Singh 1992
Jonathan Cape, 20 Vauxhall Bridge Road, London SW1V 2SA

Vijay Singh has asserted his right
under the Copyright, Designs and Patents Act, 1988
to be identified as the author of this work

Lines quoted on pp. 43 and 44 are by Robert Desnos, 'J'ai tant rêvé detoi', from
The Poetry of Surrealism, transl. Michael Benedikt, Little Brown & Co., 1974. Lines
on p. 79 are from 'Toujours pour la première fois', by André Breton, from the same
anthology. On p. 215 lines are quoted from 'Le Poisson Soluble' by André Breton,
Manifestos of Surrealism, transl. Richard Seaver and Helen R. Lane, Ann Arbor,
1977. The poem quoted on pp. 187, 188, 189 is a traditional Indian one,
translated by William Knighton, from *The Private Life of an Indian King*, Oxford
University Press, 1921.

A CIP catalogue record for this book
is available from the British Library

ISBN 0-224-03309-3

Printed in Great Britain by
Butler & Tanner Ltd, Frome and London

For Mandakini

"The King himself is a profligate and a sot, devoid of sense, who thinks of nothing but his own licentious pleasures . . . He is surrounded by a host of sycophants of all shades, English, Native and East Indian, who prompt him to every species of extravagance by which they hope to gain anything for themselves."

F J Shore, 1835, in Michael Edwards,
The Orchid House, London, 1960

This novel was partly inspired by the life of King Nasiruddin Haider who ruled the British Indian state of Awadh from 1827-37. But the situations developed here are a work of fiction.

ONE

I WOKE UP

a little earlier than usual. From somewhere came the sound of
a dog licking a bowl. A dog? In this place? Perhaps it was just
my imagination. I felt empty, cheated, as if my sleep had betrayed me just when something pleasant was about to happen
inside my mind. As often before, I tried to search the labyrinth
of dreams, but there was nothing — no images, no shapes, just
a formless feeling.

A pigeon flew into the room through the open side window.
He alighted on the lampshade and then, cocking his head, flew
upwards, settling on the corner of a picture frame which, ironically, held a print of Rene Magritte's painting of *a flying pigeon*.
He started cooing, at the painting it seemed, as if awaiting an
answer from the framed bird. The deep-belly gurgling of the
pigeon was soothing. I got up to wash.

On my return I noticed that the pigeon had undergone a
profound change. It had grown bigger, almost double its size.
The head, the belly, the feet, the eyes, the feathers, everything
had magnified with amazing symmetry. Now the colours began
to change. Grey gave way to green, green to a leafy pale yellow
and then, the head turned deep yellow, the beak white and
the feathers started to brown, some deep brown, some red,
some rust. Kicking the Magritte print contemptuously, the
pigeon flew out of the window, and perched on an overhead
wire. Slowly, with both wings outstretched and a claw firmly

clutching the wire, he revolved like an acrobat. The revolutions became faster and faster, as indeed did his cooing, and he started to shed feathers, yellow, red, violet, rust, thousands and thousands of them. I got up to take a closer look at him. His cooing gave way to loud, unpigeonlike hissing, and the spray of feathers turned into a storm, so wild that within seconds they filled the entire space. All that could be seen were his two eerie eyes, peering through frantically spinning wheels of colour. As the feathers advanced towards me, I rushed to shut the window but it slammed back open. The feathers burst past me, flooding the room, as if to attack me from behind.

I shut my eyes and cried out, 'Help! Help! Maggie!'

'Yes, what is it, Valerie?' asked the nurse, rushing into the room. 'What is it, Valerie?'

'Nothing. Nothing really,' I said, removing my hands from my face. I opened and shut my eyes several times. The feathers had disappeared.

'Didn't you call out for me?'

'I'm sorry, Maggie. It was nothing. Just a passing . . . '

'But you look disturbed.'

'Yes, I am a bit.'

'Come, come. What happened?'

'It was these feathers . . . '

'Feathers? Oh you saw some feathers, did you?' Maggie asked, as though she too had seen them.

'Did you see them too?'

'What?'

'Feathers.'

'No, I didn't see any. What did you see?'

'Feathers, pigeon feathers. Millions of them.'

'Come, come. That's your cinematic imagination, Valerie! Even in hospital, you can't forget your work, you see,' Maggie joked. 'But what exactly did you see?'

'Feathers. Millions and millions of them swarming the room. Like locusts. Till I felt asphyxiated, and I called out for you.'

'Interesting. I must put that down on record for Dr Jungman. It's probably the Pedlolin.'

2

'You mean Pedlolin gives feathers?'

'It has been found to induce optical hallucinations in some cases. But I wouldn't worry about it.'

Maggie helped me back to bed and then, pressing me gently down, said, 'You're doing rather well, in fact. The doctor sounded quite pleased with your progress at the conference yesterday.'

'But did you ask him about what I asked you?'

'Ah, your diary. I forgot to tell you about that. Sorry. Yes, Dr Jungman was of the opinion that you could start writing. In fact, he felt that might assist you in psychic reconstitution.'

'Great!' I exclaimed, 'Something to do at last.'

'Yes, but remember he hasn't asked you to tire yourself out.'

Maggie jotted down something on the daily report, and then, spotting the Magritte painting on the wall, exclaimed self-reprovingly, 'Ooolala! What is that surrealist pigeon doing in your room?' She climbed a chair to take down the painting. With Magritte's pigeon dangling from one hand, she left the room.

I took out my diary and started writing.

Convalescence is a state of absolute helplessness. It's like being in a war-torn village where the inhabitants have been glued to the radio-sets for months. Just as their fates hang on the generals ordering the bombs, I feel equally helpless in the hands of my doctor. His smiles make me want to sing and dance, his consternations make me think of graveyards. The doctor changes form – at times he has the touch of a mother; at others, of a grave-digger. Never before had I thought that life could depend on the verdict of one man. And when I realise how often not even the doctor knows what is happening inside a body or a mind – does Pedlolin give feathers or Mandolin crocodiles? – it makes me want to laugh. Anyway, Maggie says I am much better now, and if this is true, I shall be back to life soon. To life? To what?

The closer you get to death the more your childhood comes to mind. I was still at school when my teacher said to me, with a flirtatious glint in his eye, 'You have the poise and talent of an actress and the soul of a writer. It's going to be a difficult choice for you, Valerie – seduction or solitude.' Actually, it could have been neither, but chance intervened and there was a time when the doors to cinema and theatre were open to me. Sadly, I ended up being seduced by my own youth, and chose to become an actress. Ironically, my first film was called *Wrong Choice*.

In the beginning, acting was my passion and I often thought of Bernard Shaw's words: happy was the man who made a living from his hobby. Acting was a way of externalising my inner needs. I spent hours every day, trying to discover a language which could do justice to emotions – anger, jealousy, happiness. There was something magical about taking up ordinary natural gestures, and reshaping them in a way that made them more genuine than nature itself. It was like experimenting with teaching nature, Nature and honesty, Honesty.

Then came success, too easily perhaps. The first film did well, and my performance earned me an award. The films that followed confirmed my initial success, and soon my passion became a profession. Shaw would have loved this. But a peculiar mechanicity set in, and the nights I had spent pondering over the purity of human gestures now simply transformed themselves into a feverish insomnia. Lured by the purple-winged fantasies of cinema, passion disappeared. Creative revolt gave way to habit. Then the press entered my life and with that the worst. Television interviews, newspaper articles, tantalising bill-boards – they hurled me high into a distant, star-speckled space where only creatures of a similar breed lived. It was quite like earth, the perfumes smelt the same, the clothes looked much the same, people even claimed to have lived great fairy-tale romances, but what made this world different was that everything – eating, sleeping, loving – had to be done with a mask. Removing it was taboo. And so people lived an entire life, with little time on their hands to look down and measure the distance they had travelled from the umbilical cord. I became increasingly disillusioned with my life, and one day thought of quitting it.

4

Around that time a young producer contacted me with a script. The film revolved around the life of an actress, a diva, who lived in a mythical kingdom. Every subject of this kingdom knew the secret of its success, but was bound by an oath never to disclose it. One day Diva saw through the hypocrisy and decided to break the oath and give the secret away. Her 'divine betrayal' destroyed the kingdom. Stars, producers, mediamen and their lackeys suffered destruction one by one. Although the script sounded a little too sensational and melodramatic, it was nonetheless a bold critique of the film world. The idea behind it tempted me, and I decided to do it.

Then came Cannes. I had some idea of the reception the film would get, but the actual screening turned out to be a disaster. The press picked me, not the director or the producer, as their target. 'Better Star than Anti-Star', said the first paper. 'Better Figure than Mind', scoffed a macho journalist, suggesting that women good in bed often made bad thinkers. The *London Pun* announced in big bold letters: 'Sex-bomb gives birth to a Saint', and lashed out at my 'fake morality', distorting every detail of my personal life it could lay its hands on. The article ended with: 'Having gobbled all the mice, the cat is now setting off on a pilgrimage'. They ignored the film and concentrated on me. When the press could not find anything in my past to talk about, they invented juicy little details. That I was on drugs, that I had been forced to have an abortion following an affair with my psychoanalyst, that I was suffering from an incurable disease – oh, I could go on and on about those vampires . . .

Depressed I inevitably was, on seeing how the press had treated me, but what made me really vulnerable was that I was two months pregnant. I spent most of the day in my hotel room, without seeing anyone or receiving any calls. A mounting feeling of loneliness suffocated me. Loneliness? Is that the word for it? It was a peculiar sentiment, a mixture of solitude, death, defeat, nausea, all rolled into one, the feeling that life had now turned full circle. In the afternoon, I called Alain, the man I was sharing my life with, and asked him to come down from Paris. With his arrival the pot boiled over. I don't know

how we drove ourselves into a discussion over my pregnancy. I
wanted the child I was carrying. He did not. Alain felt that a
child chains freedom, and refused to be saddled with fatherly
responsibilities. But I desperately wanted the child. I was the
only survivor of my family – my mother had abandoned the
world many years before, my father had never really existed.
My gods had died with my adolescence. There were no sisters,
no brothers, no uncles, no aunts. Just me and my freedom, lost
in the orphaned woods. I needed the family that fate had denied
me. The argument, after the morning's press, turned wilder and
wilder. Alain fumed and fretted, cursed, called me names, then
picked up his bags, screaming from the door, 'If you want the
child then let his real father look after it.'

I can't recall what happened immediately after his departure,
though I remember going for a long interminable shower which
almost felt holy. It seemed as though water ran over my body for
years, for decades, for centuries, until, seeping through the pores
of my body, it purified my bones, my heart, my soul. When I
came out of the bathroom I felt divinely serene. I decided to wear
my best evening dress, and called Room Service to ask for two
whiskies, one tomato juice and a Poire Belle Hélène. The order
arrived. I tipped the waiter, poured the whiskies, the juice and
the ice-cream into a tall glass, and stirred them all with the
fifty Somnolon pills I always kept handy in my bag. Once the
concoction was well mixed into a creamy paste, I swallowed it,
and lay back on the bed, taking the receiver off the hook.

I came back to my senses with the creepy sensation of a
reptile crawling up my breast. I shrieked with fright but soon
realised that it was a hospital drip. I lay for a long while, trying
hard to remember what had brought me there. Then suddenly,
as though some lamp inside had been switched on, everything
came back, and I recalled Cannes. I ripped the drip from my
arm, jumped out of bed, opened the cupboard, found a pair of
jeans, and dashed out of the hospital.

It was night, and raining, and quiet. Raindrops tapped
gently on lime leaves. A dog barked in the distance. The boule-
vard was deserted, silvery wet. In the driveway an ambulance

was parked. I started running down the road. At one point I turned into a dark lane, banged into something solid, and fell into a puddle. Finding me struggling, a passer-by stopped and helped me up. I asked him, 'Where on earth are we, Monsieur?' 'Still on earth, Madame,' he answered. 'But is this Cannes?' He chuckled, 'The beaches of Cannes are for the rich, Madame. I regret to say, you're still in Paris.' Thinking me drunk, he wished me 'bonne soirée', and left. It began to pour heavily. I walked under a porch and stretched out on the steps, wiping the mud from my clothes with a newspaper. To know that I was in Paris was reassuring, and I began to recognise the roads and the boulevards. The run and the fall had left me terribly weak. A road sign pointed towards Cimitière de Montparnasse. I thought of my mother who lay asleep there. I got up and started walking again, without any precise destination in mind, until I reached an intersection with two cafés. One of them was called Le Bistro Venitien, and the other, Café de la Renaissance. Paying homage to an undesired rebirth, I walked into the latter.

The café was crowded, noisy. Wading through to the back, I found myself an isolated table. The waiter peered at me.

'Good God! Hope it wasn't a bad fall.'

I was surprised. 'How did you guess I fell?'

'You don't have to guess, Madame. Your clothes speak for you. There's mud all over your hair. You could wash it off in the toilet.'

'No, thank you. I think I'd just end up even wetter. It'll dry out on its own'. I checked my pocket for money and ordered a coffee.

'But I think you need a cognac,' said the waiter, with a late-night sparkle in his eye. 'Are you sure you wouldn't like a cognac to warm you up?'

'No, thanks. A hot cup of coffee would be fine.'

'Have an Irish coffee then. That'll keep you warm. Come on, it's on the house.' He winked at me, and left, swinging around on his heels like a tango dancer.

Just then, someone whispered behind me.

'Did you notice her walk in?'

'Notice who?' asked the other, in a squeakish, needle-sharp voice.

'Shh! Not so loud, twit! The woman behind you. Don't look back now.'

'Why? What about her? Do you know her?'

'I think she's Valerie Scott.'

'What!' shrieked the other. I pretended not to have heard anything.

'Take it easy, take it easy. You don't have to get excited just at her name.'

'But it can't be. The newspapers this morning said she was in a hospital. She's a real mess, you know.'

'I still think it's her — the same blue eyes, a beauty spot on the edge of her lips. And did you hear her speak to the waiter? Remember the slight English accent, and that grainy voice. I'm sure it's her.'

'Stop dreaming, will you?' said the other, still far from convinced. 'You can't tell an actress from beauty spots and eyes. They change with every film. But we can always check it out, if you like.'

A minute later, one of the two got up to go to the toilet. On his way back, he came to me with an unlit cigarette in his mouth:

'Do you have a light, please?'

'Sorry, I've left my cigarettes and lighter behind,' I replied.

'Could I offer you a cigarette then?'

'Yes, thank you so much.' The waiter helped us both light our cigarettes.

The man went back and whispered to his friend:

'Hard luck. It's not her. She's pretty, but not her.'

'Are you sure you'd recognise Valerie Scott?'

'Of course, yes. I may not have counted the beauty spots on her face, but I've seen her films, seen her on TV. Believe me, it's not her'.

He managed to convince his friend, and the two started talking less self-consciously.

'What a horrible situation she's been pushed into!' said one, with a tinge of concern in his voice.

'But she can only blame herself for it, Claude.'

'Why do you say that?'

'Why not? If I had her kind of money and fame, I would try and live two lives. Stupid! I really can't understand why people want to commit suicide.'

Claude slurped his drink.

'I think the press should be held responsible. It murdered her.'

'Rubbish! The film deserved the kind of reviews it got. You can't make a film on who screwed who to get what.'

'But the whole purpose of the film was to expose the hypocrisy of the film world, Pascal,' retorted Claude, taking up my defence. 'Whoever exposes hypocrisy deserves a pat on the back.'

'Aren't you being just too naïve for words now? You really thought this sexy girl had turned into a saint, and wanted to destroy the whole world of stars? Bullshit! This was just another mini-star trying to become a megastar. So, why do you think she tried to kill herself? What do the papers say?'

'Some say her suicide had to do with a man. She wanted a child, and he didn't.'

'Whatever it is,' remarked the man with the thin voice, 'I am convinced that all these bloody stars, big or small, are shady – egocentric, self-indulgent, full of themselves. Their births, their deaths, their love-affairs are all tricks to become what they are . . . '

The nurse barged into the room unannounced. Finding me still at the desk, she frowned. 'No, no, no, no, Val. Remember what Dr Jungman said – you can write, but not a fat autobiography. Don't overtax yourself, Valerie. Now have some dinner and go to bed.'

It was late evening by the time I finished my dinner. Night was beginning to set in, and over the garden a crescent moon glowed in a deep blue sky. After many weeks at the hospital, I felt a balmy calm within me. Writing had indeed done me some good. I turned off the light.

I awoke with a dream. An unusually pleasant dream; quite different, at any rate, from the ones I had been used to of late. I was shooting in some forlorn city. It was quite a ramshackle set – poorly lit, dingy, muggy, like an abandoned foundry. Hundreds of bits and pieces of electric cables and coils littered the place. It was so hot that most of the lighting men on the set had taken their shirts off. Beads of sweat shone on their bodies. The smell of sweat pervaded the set. There was some problem with the shot. The director wanted me to pronounce a word in a certain way which, being a foreigner, I couldn't easily manage. And each time I got it right, the spotlight towards which I was supposed to be looking while speaking my lines, blew out. We did umpteen retakes of the same shot, so many that I ended up taking a fancy to the man behind the faulty spotlight. Of a brownish complexion, firmly built, not too tall, he had thick dusty black hair and an enchanting half-mouthed smile. The next thing I recalled in the dream he was making love to me, his sweating body on top of mine, and my fingers tightly plugged into two curious dips behind his shoulders. Funnily enough, the dream was replayable – like a video. I remembered playing the love-making scene over and over again, until it got stuck, and I woke up.

A rather curious and pleasant dream, I thought, and the promptness with which my subconscious was back to mischief, amused me. I hadn't quite fathomed who my dream-lover could have been, when a nurse called to say that Paul Katuszewski had come to visit me.

Paul had been my agent for nearly ten years. He was also a trusted friend. In fact, he was the only one from my world who was allowed to visit me at the hospital. Everyone else was banned, as the doctor put it, for fear of reactivating my dormant anxieties. But finding films for actors and actresses was far from being Paul's only activity. The Parisian film circles knew him better for his encyclopaedic knowledge of cats and dogs. Some years ago, Paul founded a new science that he named *chatastrologie*. To begin with, his science related only to cats, but over time, Paul broadened its scope to meet the needs of dog-lovers. His scientific genius consisted in drawing astrological charts for pets, based on their dates of birth and a close reading of their nose-tips. For a while, his business really flourished, and it became fashionable for film stars to own Paul Katuszewski's hand-drawn astrological charts. But Paul discovered the hazards of his science the day a doddering semi-hibernating Dobermann pounced at his face, nearly pulling out his eye. That made Paul rethink his profession – he gave up his close-quarter prying at dog-noses, though retaining his love for the animal world.

Paul walked in with a gorgeous bouquet. He was juggling with a vase when I asked him:

'So how are the dogs doing, Paul?'

'Not bad, not bad at all. I am back to nose-reading again. You know, next year is going to be the Year of the Dog.'

'Wonderful! First the Year of Women, then the Year of Children. And now, the Year of Dogs. Hope they don't lump them all as one and the same breed.'

'Oh! You and your dogged cynicism, Valerie,' Paul laughed. 'But how are you? Any better?'

'Much better. They say I'll get out soon.'

'And your stomach? Has it settled down now?'

'Yes, that's fine.'

'The last time I saw you, you'd asked the doctor if you could read and do some writing. Was that okay?'

'Yes. In fact, I've spent the whole day writing. He also said I should try and talk about my inner world as much as possible. Things seem to be shaping up, Paul. It seems I've come to terms with my suicide attempt and the miscarriage.'

'I must say you look much better,' said Paul, pulling up a chair.

'I feel better. Much clearer about things.'

'Have you decided to start working again?'

'In a way. But not in France, somewhere else. Let's see. I had an amazing dream last night, Paul.'

'Not a bad one, I hope.'

'On the contrary. A rather pleasant one, in fact. And very curious indeed.'

First I hesitated about recounting my erotic dream to Paul but then, since he knew virtually everything about my life there was little point in being prudish. I related as much of it as I could remember, but Paul's inquisitiveness puzzled me. He asked me to repeat the dream over again, asking questions every now and then, trying to identify the country and the people. I was amazed at his persistent probing.

'Since when did you take up psychoanalysis, Paul? Not another science!'

'Don't joke,' Paul cut in. 'You really can't tell if it was Asia, Africa or Latin America? Think, Valerie.' Paul's enraptured seriousness was amusing.

'No. That's it,' I said. 'Telling more will be inventing another. That's all I can recall.'

Perplexed, Paul got up from his chair and walked a couple of paces towards the door.

'Incredible, this is absolutely incredible!' he exclaimed.

'Why? What is incredible?' His reaction was beginning to disturb me.

'You see, there's an Indian producer from Bombay who has been after me for days. He's hell-bent on casting you for his next film. And isn't it amazing that you should have dreamt of such a place the night before?'

'Who are you talking about?'

'You don't know him — a new chap.'

'When did he get in touch with you?'

'A couple of months ago. He's called several times since and has even sent the scenario, and a book.'

'What is it about?'

'I haven't looked at it yet.'

'Do you have it with you?' I asked.

'Hey! Wait a minute. You're not going to jump into things.'

'Why not? The doctor has allowed me to read.'

Paul opened his brief-case, shuffled around the papers

and pulled out a book. 'Well, I don't have the scenario on me right now but I have this book from which the film has been adapted. It's an autobiography. I can leave it with you, if you like.'

Paul left, and I started reading.

TWO

THE KING WAS OBSESSED

with his hair. Nature had bestowed on him a robust growth of shiny black hair, but what upset him intensely was that it was flat and straight, like the fringe of a silken tapestry. As a young boy, he had tried virtually everything in the repertoire of the royal apothecaries and hakims to lend his hair a curl or two, but nothing seemed to work and the anxious heir's hair remained as lank as ever. When nothing on earth could satisfy his fantasy, Nasiruddin turned to common sense and gave up washing or combing his hair. As a result the unkempt and scraggly hair gave birth to the first curls. Nasir was indeed overjoyed, and quickly set about consolidating his gains by applying to his hair a gelatinous mixture of bones, hides, glue and sand, an invention of his own experiments with alchemy. But Nasir's attempt at immortalising his curls only lasted until the day his father Ghaziuddin Haider, the reigning ruler, organised a banquet for the new British Resident of Lucknow. Nasir came prancing into the banquet hall, dressed in a frocklike brocade tunic, playing a violin, his hair resembling a glue-soaked broom. His father threw a fit of anger. 'Enough, enough of this bastard's eccentricities! Throw him out of here!' That put a rather unceremonious end to a ceremonious coiffure, and the jubilant prince was back to square one, left with the only option of putting up with his natural straight hair.

When Ghaziuddin Haider died, people thought that would

14

put an end to Nasiruddin's problems, for the new crown on his
head would also bury beneath it both the hair and its lankness.
But no, said the new King, refusing to let the crown descend
on his head until he had had his hides, his sand and his curls
back, and so returned the curlicues on his temples, like two
incurable question marks flanking the crown. Cynics laughed at
and mocked the eccentric Nasiruddin but the new King refused
to budge, and wore his muculent curls until the day a stranger
wandered into his court, and relieved him forever of all the dust
and glue and scum beneath the crown, and bestowed upon him
instead a new coiffure. Nobody in the state could ever fathom the
secret formula by which a lank-haired Nasir turned into a curly-
haired and side-whiskered Scotsman, and yet everyone knew that
the stranger who had worked wonders with the King's hair was
someone called Samuel de Russet, a barber of dubious British
descent whose curling-tongs and scissors had become the most
fearsome instruments of power in the State of Awadh. When the
barber fled Lucknow twenty years before the Sepoy Mutiny with a
million pounds in his bags, he was already a legend for the British
in India, a yardstick by which each free-lancing English racketeer
in the colony could measure the degree of his success or failure.

Many years ago, Samuel de Russet ran a small hair-dressing
salon in Spitalfields, a working-class suburb of London. Having
started off as a one-man outfit, the salon had indeed done well
for itself for at the end of the third year, de Russet employed
three barbers and a masseur, offering a wide range of services to
his customers. But born ambitious and brought up by an even
more ambitious mother who spent her time chasing the rich
customers at the salon, de Russet was hardly the kind to be
satisfied with making money from people's hair. Just as he was
busy thinking of business alternatives, one of his old customers
came to the salon after a long trip to India. Impressed with the
salon's success, he remarked, 'Dear me! What progress you have
made, Samuel. But if I were you, I'd go and make my fortune
in the colonies. That's where the money is for a businessman
like you. Oh dear! I'm told the kings there give away bagfuls
of jewels to the British!'

On his next visit to the salon, the customer might well have wondered what had happened to the prosperous barber but de Russet knew exactly what he wanted. He sold off his business, picked up a few local curios and took the first ship out of England to India. Once in Calcutta, he tried selling English frames, clocks, vases, swords and even whips to the local nobility. But the going was tougher than the barber had first imagined. Faced with dozens of English businessmen already in the colony peddling everything from opium to ladies' underclothing, de Russet was disheartened, and wondered if disposing of his hair-dressing salon so hastily had not really been a mistake. One day as he was sitting at the Fort William Army Club, drowning his sorrows in Scotch, he ran into a friendly army officer. As alcohol soldered a new bond of friendship, each recounted to the other his life story. De Russet discovered that the army officer was a mine of information on India, and indeed seemed more suitable to being an opium trader than a soldier. De Russet told him all about his business anxieties, and asked him for advice. The officer promptly suggested, 'First advice: Don't tell anyone here you were a barber. Say you're a businessman. Simple principle – more respectful your profession, more respect you get. Second advice: Calcutta is full of the kind of stuff you want to sell. I reckon Awadh would be a better bet. That's where the money is. That's the land of wine, women and wealth.'

Samuel de Russet left Calcutta for Lucknow, the capital of Awadh. When he arrived at the British Resident's house the fashionable curly-haired officer looked all set to leave for a hunt. Noticing the Resident's obvious hurry to jump into his waiting carriage, de Russet introduced himself as a businessman, and briefly explained the purpose of his visit to Lucknow. The Resident was quite unimpressed with the visitor's credentials, and remarked curtly, 'You'll appreciate the Resident cannot be expected to help every Tom, Dick and Harry wanting to sell all kinds of things. Advising businessmen is not his job. Anyway, show me the stuff, and I'll tell you what I think of it.' The Resident's quick harum-scarum look into de Russet's trunk made him even less sympathetic. 'Such curios, Mr de Russet, are thirty years behind the times for these parts of the world. Pardon my asking – have you been in business long?'

De Russet first tried to sell the story that he actually belonged to a family of businessmen, but when the Resident probed dangerously deep into his visitor's background, he gave up, muttering, 'I'm also a trained hair-dresser.' That seemed to ring some bell in the Resident's head, for he actually managed to produce a smile, as though at meeting someone who had the same profession as his own forefathers. With each second, the Resident became friendlier, his authoritarian tone now melting into an amicable manner. Asking his visitor into his drawing room, the Resident ordered a cup of tea, and sent for his wife. The barber was still wondering what hidden charms his old profession could possibly hold for an officer of the East India Company, when the Resident lifted his right hand up to his head, and hooking his finger into one of the curls, peeled a wig off his head. 'How lucky of me indeed to run into a London hair-dresser in Lucknow!' said the Resident, covering his wife's embarrassment with his friendly tone. 'Look what the heat and dust of India have done to a lovely Park Street wig! Do you think something could be done to reset it?' If that was the price of happiness in Lucknow, the barber had a better bait to offer. 'But why not a new wig, Sir? I have everything in my trunk to make you another.' The Resident was overjoyed with the barber's offer and when a few days later, a beautiful curly wig crowned his turnip-bald head, the British officer thought the time was right to introduce de Russet to King Nasiruddin Haider, whose experiments with curls, and glue and sand and bones and hides, had by now substantially enriched Awadh's theatre of the burlesque.

A faint-hearted Samuel de Russet appeared before Nasiruddin Haider, the wealthiest man in the land, thinking it was now or never. The barber quickly made out that the King was indeed the more nervous of the two. For the glue-laden Nasiruddin, de Russet was less a barber than some renowned physician or magician, who, by chance, had stumbled into his court. The

17

King felt so weak and overawed by de Russet's presence that no sooner had the barber felt his hair, than he opened his heart before him, pouring out his countless childhood hair-fantasies and unfulfilled dreams. Samuel de Russet listened to the King with due tact, a question here, a question there, till the meeting seemed more like the King consulting a mind physician. By the end of the day, the barber understood what the King needed. Touching the King's hair, he said, 'How about two rolling curls up in front, Your Majesty?' Nasir let out a jubilant cry, 'Just what the King couldn't get . . . ' 'Now your humble servant will get them for you, Your Majesty. Another light curl here, just above the ear. And hot tongs should be able to give us two curly side-whiskers.' 'Side-whiskers!' The King jumped in ecstasy, 'Did you say curly side-whiskers! What the King of England has! Oh! that's a dream come true!' In the barber's honour, the King ordered two days of state celebration.

The King was overjoyed with the barber's presence at his court, but de Russet was not the kind to be satisfied with dregs of royal honour: he had set out in search of diamonds and emeralds and sapphires. Just as the barber's gold-dust dreams were beginning to tarnish, the King, sensing his disappointment, awarded him a sprawling jagir on the outskirts of Lucknow. Status followed property, and de Russet now became Sarfaraz Khan – 'the illustrious chief'.

Although the barber's authority grew each day and ministers and nobles vied with each other to humour him, de Russet's most valuable asset was his close association with the King. Nasiruddin and Khan, as de Russet came to be called, spent hours together every morning at the Coiffure Mahal, scrutinising every single detail of the royal hair. When the King's hair did not call for Khan's services, his flair for chess did, and the two spent days on the banks of the Gomti, playing chess. The only rule of the game the barber knew was that the King must never lose. It was at one of these chess games that the King confided in Khan his other problem since childhood – his fear of being poisoned. Whatever the mind physicians might have made of the King's phobia, Khan diagnosed it as a golden opportunity for gaining a hold over the King's mind, and he was convinced that if he could protect the King from this fear, he could get from the Kingdom of Awadh whatever he wished. Khan said, 'If I may make a suggestion with your permission, Your Majesty, you must never disclose this fear to anyone. It could be dangerous for your well-being.' The King replied meekly. 'But I have just confided in you, Khan.' The barber came closer, conspiringly. 'Now, if we can screen all the food, alcohol and water supplies to the palace, we should be safe.' 'Don't bother with water,' whispered the King, 'I have locked a whole well for myself, and I wear its keys round my neck. I draw my own water at night.' As for the rest, Khan knew what to do. He made the King dictate an order that from now on all food, wine, beer and champagne supplies to the palace be made by the barber, and that no food or drinks be served to the King unless personally cleared by Khan. Thus Khan won two things from the chess games — he became the King's protector, and the sole supplier to the palace stores, where lay the millions.

But Khan had another extraordinary quality: he was a prophetic dreamer. In a country of countless legends, the barber-legend went that Khan's dreams were clairvoyant, and that anyone's machinations against the King could be tracked down on his nocturnal screen. Moreover, Khan was said to speak out his dreams with such lucidity that had an English-speaking clerk been posted on the slumbering spy, he could actually have taken down notes straight from the horse's mouth — which is what gave the clairvoyant's dreams a deadly edge. Especially after one of his prophetic dreams led to the uncovering of a plot to kill the King, Nasiruddin took the barber-legend more seriously, and had one of his European clerks permanently posted by Khan's bed, with standing instructions to wake the barber at the slightest sign of danger. The barber did not mind this loss of privacy. What mattered to him was power and money, and the knowledge that his nights were as crucial to the King's life as his days, only made him happier.

One night Khan and Malika Zamani, the King's favourite consort at that time, differed over something, and the evening ended with Khan being snubbed by the Begum in public. For a man who loved boasting that 'of Begums there are many but of Khan there is but one', this was no mean insult, though Khan preferred restraint to a hasty reaction, and walked back to his bungalow, perturbed. Refusing the dinner which was already on the table, he headed straight for his sleeping chamber, followed by the khwabdar, the dream-attendant, who by now had become part and parcel of the barber's bedding. Khan changed into his night-shirt and went to bed, the attendant by his side, shifting his weight sleepily from one leg to the other. It must have been very late for not a soul stirred around the palace when the attendant heard some noisy crackling from the barber's mouth. Alerted, the attendant tilted his head towards the barber's face, and heard an indecipherable burst of sounds. 'Caca, ca-ca, caca-ca, caca-caca-ca, ca-ca-cacaca, cau-cau-cau . . . ' The attendant was most perplexed since, of all the sounds he had heard the barber produce, this indeed was the strangest, and by far the most incomprehensible. The attendant stooped lower over Khan's face, whose mouth had now begun to foam, and through the fizzing foam, the barber, in all likelihood, was struggling to make more sense, 'Ca-cau, cau-caucaucau . . . ' The attendant moved closer, and the barber burst forth, 'Caught you, caught you, a red-handed catch, Dulari. Dulari. Caught you in the act . . . ' The attendant at once vigorously shook Khan, who leapt out of the bed, as if being attacked.

'What happened? What happened?' the barber asked feverishly. 'What did I say?' asked Khan again, who always needed a cue to recollect his dream.

'You called out Begum Sahiba's name, Sir', the attendant uttered nervously.

'Which Begum?'

'Begum Sahiba, Sir.'

'Which Begum Sahiba?'

'The Begum Sahiba, Sir.'

'Idiot! Which one? There are hundreds of them in the harem.'

'Malika Zamani, Sir. You called her by her maiden name.'

'You mean Dulari,' which was Malika Zamani's name before

she became the chief consort of the King. 'Come on, come on, out with the whole thing. Now what did I say about Dulari? That wretched sweeper's daughter who calls herself a queen!' The barber hadn't forgotten the last night's snub.

The dream-attendant mumbled reluctantly, 'You said, caught you, caught you red-handed, Dulari.'

The barber needed no more prompting. He knew exactly what was happening. 'Summon Mumtaz Mahal immediately,' Khan ordered, going to the next room to fetch his hukka. He had barely managed to get his hukka going when Mumtaz, the most loyal eunuch at the court, arrived panting, anticipating the urgency of Khan's midnight calls. Khan asked:

'Mumtaz, where were you posted tonight?'

'At the palace gate, Huzoor.'

'Any idea where Dulari is?'

'You mean Malika Zamani, Huzoor?' Mumtaz noticed Khan had chosen to address the Begum by her maiden name.

'But where is she?' Khan ranted.

'Back at her palace, Huzoor.'

'Sure?'

'Yes, I am, Huzoor. She left the King's palace late last night.'

'I see. I see,' uttered the barber thoughtfully. He walked away, looking unusually preoccupied. He called the eunuch into a corner and recounted the dream.

'I think she's up to her tricks again,' stated Khan, a shade vindictively.

'You mean Begum Sahiba, Huzoor?'

'Who else? I suspect she's being unfaithful to the King.' Khan sounded as triumphant as afraid.

'And now, Huzoor?' asked the eunuch, pleadingly.

'Why? Are you scared?'

'She is a dangerous woman, Huzoor.'

'But we have to investigate.'

'If she finds out, Huzoor?'

'I owe my loyalty to the King more than to his Begums, Mumtaz. We are here to defend the King.'

'Yes, Huzoor,' the eunuch concurred obediently. 'But she can be vicious, Huzoor.'

'You reckon?'

'Without a doubt, Huzoor. She can be really dangerous. And you know her hold on the King.'

'Yes. I do.' Khan turned away, and sighed. 'What a marvellous destiny God has bestowed on a sweeper's daughter!'

Gradually, Khan, who until now had sounded indecisive, mustered up courage, and asserted, 'Let's see what happens. For the King's happiness, we have no choice but to investigate the matter. Mumtaz, go straight to her palace and check what's going on. And if you find that fellow there, have him immediately locked up. My orders.'

The eunuch left, but Khan became more and more restless, wondering if he had really not overstepped the reach of his authority by casting aspersions on the most powerful woman in the state. Would the King believe him, or Dulari? Would she seek revenge? Would Dulari be his Waterloo? Many a doubt weakened Khan's resolve and yet, his deep faith in his clairvoyant dreams convinced him that the 'low-breed nymphomaniac', as he privately called her, was out to fool the King and betray the royal trust placed in her. Every now and then, Khan popped out of bed, frantically pacing up and down the room, calling Dulari names, and then going back to bed, taking long puffs at his hukka. Seeing clouds of smoke spiral out of Khan's mouth, nose and ears, the dream-attendant thought it was perhaps best to leave the master to his nerves. 'May I go away, Sir?' murmured the attendant into Khan's ear. 'Stay where you are, you idiot,' thundered Khan, trembling at the edge of his bed. 'And don't you move. Daft! A disgrace to the race of Anglo-Saxons! Couldn't you find a better job for yourself in a kingdom where whores and sweepers have become queens?' The statuesque dream-attendant philosophised, 'Never thought of that really. But you'll concede, Sir, it's easier for a woman to become a queen than for a man to become a King. If I had been a woman, who knows, I too might have become a legend like Dulari . . .'

*

Dulari indeed had come a long way since her birth. She was born to a poor sweeper who had once borrowed sixty rupees from a pawn-broker. Her father died, leaving behind a pauperised wife, a beautiful daughter, and the debt. The creditor's sister, a professional match-maker, knew the worth of good looks in the Kingdom of Awadh, and asked her brother to buy Dulari off against the debt. Thus Dulari left her mother and came to the new house. She grew up to be a genuine beauty, eyed by everyone in the village. Just when the harvest was ready, and the creditor and his sister were all set to make a fortune out of the sixty rupees they had bought Dulari off for, Rustom, the handsome but penuried former husband of the third wife of the creditor, arrived on the scene, and eloped with Dulari's virginity which by now had upset many a secret fancy in the village. As the creditor and his match-maker sister tried desperately to find Dulari, the penniless couple fled, finding refuge with Beebi Mullati, a tutor at a noble's court.

Dulari's anxieties about money came to an end when Rustom, her husband, found a job in the King's cavalry, but she soon discovered there were other things to life than money. While her husband travelled far and wide, quelling riots, chasing bandits, Dulari spent her time being seduced by her own adolescence, and ran a virtual riot with her youth. Rustom returned from the King's battle-fields to find that his own battle had only begun. Dulari had given birth to a child, but who was the father – the elephant-keeper, the goldsmith or him? He was still busy comparing the child's features with the prospective fathers when a royal messenger came to Beebi Mullati's house, looking for a wet-nurse for the newly-born prince. Beebi at once recommended Dulari for the job – less perhaps for her promiscuous qualifications than for getting rid of the tantrums and the flying pots and pans at home. Dulari picked up her child and left for Lucknow. No sooner had she stepped into the prince's room than the King caught a glimpse of her, and exclaimed, 'What an angel! What an angel indeed!' Gently raising the veil over Dulari's face, the King turned

23

towards his chess partner, Khan-the-barber, and mused. 'But wouldn't the King be wasting a woman of such celestial charm on a two-month-old child?' Knowing the King's admiration for the King of England, Khan knew exactly what to answer, 'Her beauty would do honour even to the King of England, your Majesty.' 'Would it, Khan? Then let her join the royal harem.' Thus Dulari walked into the King's chamber. The next day she was titled Malika Zamani, Queen of the Age.

Khan, a confirmed bachelor who slept uncomplainingly under the eyes of the dream-attendant, was hardly the kind to meddle in the King's personal affairs. Had Dulari confined herself to the world of the King's pleasures, Khan could not have been happier than to see the King lost in a new love, whilst he made his millions, selling Burgundy, Sancerre and Möet to the royal household. What worried Khan about Dulari though, was her ambition and her lust for power. Watching her conduct herself at the palace, he was convinced Dulari saw the King's bed not as the proverbial love-nest, but as a stepping-stone to the throne. Within the first week, Dulari managed to acquire for herself one of the richest jagirs of Awadh. Not content with property alone, she slowly began to place her relatives and friends in positions of influence and authority. Her future began to look more threatening as her son's marriage was settled within the royal family, and she managed to charm the King into declaring to the British Resident that Kaiwan Jah, Dulari's son, was not the disputed son, as popular gossip held, of an elephant-keeper or a blacksmith or a cavalryman, but indeed the King's very own, and his likely successor. Dulari's influence indeed confirmed the local saying that the power of the State of Awadh lay between the thighs of a woman.

The storm unleashed by Dulari's arrival at the palace had managed to overturn prime ministers, army chiefs and head eunuchs, but the only flower it could not destroy, and which still bloomed and secreted the same perfume, was the barber. The showdown with him came the day Dulari claimed to have written proof that Khan had robbed the royal exchequer of stupendous quantities of wealth. She wanted him replaced by one of her men. That shook Khan, whose private coffers had indeed much to fear from Dulari's prying glances. Just when Khan was soaked wet with nightmares of life-imprisonment and public execution, his clairvoyant dreams produced the check-mate – 'Ca-cau, cau-caucau, caucaucau . . . caught you, Dulari! Caught you in the act!'

Dawn was about to break over Lucknow and the birds were chirping inside the bungalow when Khan, hearing the sound of hasty footsteps, rushed out of the room, and saw Mumtaz-the-eunuch, grinning from ear to ear.

'What news, Mumtaz?' Khan-the-barber enquired.

'Caught him, Huzoor. He's caught,' the eunuch giggled with eunuch-like femininity.

'Caught him? You've trapped the bastard, have you?'

'Yes, Huzoor.'

'Shabash! Shabash! Bravo!' Delighted, the barber couldn't believe his ears and even less, his infallible clairvoyance.

'Caught her being unfaithful to the King, did you?'

'Yes, Huzoor, I did. I saw it with my own eyes.'

'What?'

'The act, Huzoo.'

'You mean the very act, Mumtaz.'

'Yes, I do.'

'Unbelievable! Incredible, this race of eunuchs!' exclaimed Khan, titillated as only a fifty-year-old bachelor discovering the world of sex could be. 'You mean you saw them in the act?'

'Yes, I did.'

'Wonderful. Now we have that slut by her neck. But tell me, how did you go about it, Mumtaz?'

'I went straight to her palace and said I had to see the Begum Sahiba. The guard said she was with a visitor. I said never mind. I have an urgent message from Khan Sahib.'

'Why did you use my name, Mumtaz?' asked Khan, alarmed.

'You said they were your orders, Huzoor.'

'Orders to catch her lover, not to sneak into her sleeping chamber.' Khan looked preoccupied for a while, and then said,

'Now that he is caught, it doesn't matter but that was really close, Mumtaz. And then?'

'I went in. Not a soul in sight. I slipped quietly into the spy cellar, peeped in, made sure she was with someone, and came out and waited for the man to leave.'

'And then?'

'He came out, disguised as a woman. With a long veil, right down to the toes. I followed him till he was well past the harem courtyard. Then I asked him who she was, pretending I didn't know she was a man. He didn't answer, and started hurrying towards the back-gate. I followed him right up to the gate, asking — who are you? who are you? He squeaked and squirmed, but didn't utter a word. When the guard saw me questioning her, he said don't bother with the Begum's visitor, he is dumb. But I swear I had seen him talking to the Begum.'

'And then?'

'I think the guard is hand in glove with the Begum, Huzoor.'

'Obvious. But what happened after that?'

'As I was talking to the guard, the man turned into the Kababwali Street.'

'Never mind all these details. Come to how you had him locked up.'

'Locked up? Did I say he was locked up, Huzoor?' The eunuch looked puzzled.

'You mean he's not locked up?' Khan screamed.

'No, Huzoor, he just dissolved into the dark. By the time I finished with the guard, he was gone.'

'But you said you'd caught him.'

'Yes, I did. I saw the whole thing with my own eyes.'

'To hell with your goddamned eyes, Mumtaz,' Khan raged. 'Where is he? The man, his body, where is he physically?'

'Can't say, Huzoor.'

'Then why did you come here grinning to say he was caught?'

'Forgive me, Huzoor, but I don't recall saying he was locked up. I swear on God. I caught them both in the room. If I may add, without any clothes on.'

'To hell with that. But proof, proof, where's the proof of this.'

'My eyes, Huzoor.'

'Stop this rubbish, will you? You really think the King will believe your bloody eyes, and not Dulari. For all you know the King will have your eyes put out for that. And probably mine too.'

Khan wandered off into the garden, visibly disturbed. The eunuch came after him, and pleaded on his knees:

'One more chance. Give me one more chance, Huzoor. I think I can still catch him.'

'How?'

'I think I can, Huzoor. I know where he might be.'

'You're not going to make another mess of it, are you?'

'No, Huzoor. I won't leave him this time. But I must rush.'

'Go ahead, Mumtaz. But for heaven's sake don't forget the risks involved. She can be vicious.'

By the time the eunuch left, accompanied by two other guards, the sun was well above the Gomti temple, rapidly dissolving the morning mist. The palace guards were beginning to change duties and the mehris, holding brooms taller than themselves, were sweeping the gardens, raising a pall of dust that mingled with the wintery mist. Night's fatigue and tension had left Khan anxiety-ridden, but he knew that the answer to moments of anguish seldom lay in despair and indecisiveness, and what he most needed at this time was a counter-strategy to rebuff Dulari's charges against him. Being late for his daily rendezvous with the King's coiffure, Khan skipped his bath, quickly changed his clothes, and left for the palace. On his arrival, he was surprised to find the King already dressed, curls intact. 'Sorry for my lateness, Your Majesty,' said Khan, apologetically. 'On the contrary, Khan. It's the King who is early. You see the King doesn't need you any more. He can manage his hair by himself.' That startled Khan – was the King suggesting the end of his career? He came closer to the King, touched the front of his hair, and intoned flatteringly, 'Isn't that marvellous, Your Majesty! You've even got the little lock on the temple just where it should be.' The King burst out laughing, 'Look what you've done, Khan. You've turned the King of Awadh into an English barber. But tell me, Khan, what would you do if the King didn't need your hair-dressing talents any more?' Khan shuddered, convinced Dulari had worked this mischief. Bowing low, he muttered, 'I will do what His Majesty wishes his servant to do. With your orders, I will perhaps continue attending to His Majesty's well-being — the water well, food, wine . . . ' Now it was the King's turn to shudder. He suddenly became pensive, as fear of being poisoned rose to his head. 'But why talk of such morbid things, Khan. How about a game of chess?'

The King and Khan climbed up to the Shatranj Chakri, the filigree canopy on the terrace under which generations of Awadh Kings had played chess and cards, watching the Gomti flow and the wheat-fields bathe in the sun. The gold and ivory chess-board arrived, and the game began. The King made a disastrous start, losing four pieces in a row. As Khan was carefully contemplating openings to let his opponent win, the King said, 'Hurry up, Khan. Don't tell me you've forgotten your chess since I last beat you.' Khan, leaning his head on his hand, pleaded, 'Your Majesty perhaps cannot realise how much it takes for an English barber to play against a chess wizard. Chess runs in your blood. There, I move the horse . . . ' Khan gradually managed to swing the game against himself, and the King, looking more and more satisfied, said:

'Guess what, Khan.'

'Checkmate, is it?'

'No, no. I was thinking of something else. Did I tell you the King of England has sent me a gift?'

'No, you didn't, Your Majesty.'

'It came through the Governor-General the other day. An exquisite bust — a Roman nymph.'

'How marvellous, Your Majesty! It will go down so well at the Hall of Ceremonies.'

'Indeed it will. I'm so touched with the King of England's gesture.'

'I am sure he wants to keep you in good humour, Your Majesty.'

'Yes, but a gracious gesture all the same. Khan, any idea what England would like from Awadh?'

'A Khajurao temple statue perhaps . . . '

'Oh no! Can't send a bust for a bust. Something more imaginative.' The King took a long puff at his hukka, 'How about a Lucknow masseur? You can't beat him at his art.'

'Great idea, Your Majesty. Though it might be a bit too personal for the conservative English taste.'

'But don't you see, Khan, I do want to make a personal gesture. Or how about one of our dancing girls from Awadh. Does he fancy dancing?'

'Indeed he does. He loves ballet.'

'Then I know what to send. We'll send him a Khajurao statue, carried by a dancing girl. How does that sound? Now let's see what he sends in return.'

'Since he knows Your Majesty's artistic taste so well, he may well send back the same – an English dancer.'

'Splendid! Splendid, indeed! I've been dreaming of an English girl in my harem for ages. That'll lend it so much more charm.'

The clue came the moment the King mentioned the English girl. Khan knew he had found the answer to Dulari's machinations. After the chess session was over, Khan rushed back home to check if Mumtaz-the-eunuch had returned from his mission of apprehending Dulari's lover. Indeed he had, but without any luck. Khan took him aside and said:

'You once mentioned an English girl to me, Mumtaz. Is she still around?'

'Yes, Huzoor. In Kanpur. She lives with her family.'

'How do you know them?'

'My cousin, Rashid, works as their coachman, Huzoor.'

'Is this girl English or Anglo-Indian?'

'Absolutely white – white-as-a-bedsheet, Huzoor. But her father's dead.'

'Have you ever seen her?'

'Yes, Huzoor. Who doesn't know her in Kanpur! A very pretty girl — about sixteen years old, fair, has learnt Indian dances, speaks Urdu, Persian . . . '

'But what matters is her English, Mumtaz. Does she speak English like the English?'

'Yes, Huzoor. As I said, she is white-as-a-bedsheet.'

'Do you know her name?'

'Yes, Huzoor — Ann Walters.'

Khan placed his hand on Mumtaz's shoulder, and whispered. 'I am thinking of bringing her over for the King.'

'Great idea, Huzoor. King will love her.'

'And if that works . . . ' Both laughed. 'Yes, if that works, Dulari's days at the palace are numbered. Come, Mumtaz, make off to Cawnpore tomorrow. And be sure you bring her back!'

The English girl they had in mind was me . . .

THREE

IT WAS FOUR IN THE MORNING,

and I had not slept a wink. Nothing since my arrival in Bombay a few days ago could explain my sleeplessness and yet, my mind was like a pot of oil on the boil — stray thoughts, unknown faces, macabre odours, cold spiralling sensations. Each time I sat up in bed to smoke a cigarette, something within me implored: one last time, just one tablet, it can't do that much harm, can it? My hand would stealthily creep towards the bottle of Mogadon sleeping pills, but as I opened it, my doctor's parting words would ring in my ear, 'You must stop this dependence on drugs, Valerie. You can't kill yourself to sleep, can you?' I put the bottle away, and slipped down under the blanket.

What about Maggie's sleep-therapy? At the hospital it had proved quite useful. So why not in Bombay? Maggie's principle was simple: shut your eyes, and concentrate on the blank, blackboardlike space, effacing all stray thoughts and images until you fall asleep. I decided to try her therapy again. After a few minutes of concentration, the relentless fight between the foot-loose thoughts and the mental blackboard duster began to resemble a game of snakes and ladders. Each time I mounted the ladder towards the top, a thought raised its hood, stung me, and I was back to square one, wide awake as an owl. The game recommenced, erasing a thought here, shooing a face there, focusing hard on the black space and, just when I was high on the ladder, close to the kingdom of sleep, a snake stuck its fangs out and stung again, and I was back to where I had begun. I tried again and again, until the whole exercise looked absurd and futile and I gave up, lighting another cigarette.

It was five, and I was watching the morning glow slowly colour the objects inside the room when the air-conditioner produced a strange sound, unusually pleasant for a machine – resonant, thick, like that of the aboriginal instrument, the djiridoo. It was probably the air-conditioner overheating, but it didn't quite sound like a mechanical fault. The sound of the djiridoo became louder and more regular, punctuating the flat gurgle with cyclical musicality, and the sequence began to sound like a proper recital. Fascinated, I decided to sit back and relish the music, and make the best of an insomniac night. A while later, it seemed the lone djiridoo had found a partner, and a duet started. That only seemed to signal others to join in: two, three, four, the djiridoos multiplied, and their symphony transformed the air-conditioner into an orchestra. Taking it to be the last gasps of the dying air-conditioner, I jumped out of bed, and switched it off – the sound stopped. Barely had I turned around when the sound came up again – I bent before the air-conditioner and listened. I just needed to listen to the sound once more to know exactly what it was – the cooing of a pigeon. Was this the return of my pigeon hallucinations? I began to sweat and advanced slowly towards my bottle of Trapolin in the medicine chest. I popped a pill to be on the safe side, although I was not too panicked by the cooing which, ironically, was still quite pleasant and harmonious. As the cooing became louder and louder, I picked up my dressing gown, and swiftly walked out of the room on to the terrace.

'Aie-aie-yo. Aie-aie-yo,' whined Lingappa, the guest-house cook, visibly stunned by my unexpected, half-naked entry onto the terrace. Lingappa stood gaping at my legs, his mouth half-open, his nostrils twitching, cigarette smoke spiralling out of his moustache, until in a flash, he grabbed the floor mop, made an about turn and dashed off into the room behind. I put my gown on and sat down in a chair, shutting my eyes.

32

The Trapolin began to work almost immediately, sprinkling its powdery calm over my head. The pigeons stopped cooing in my ears and when I looked down at the fishermen returning to the shore, I noticed my eyes were recovering their focus. The Arabian sea was calm and soundless, on its wrinkled face patches of oil spills twinkled.

I was still striving to fathom how my pigeon hallucinations had returned, when Lingappa twittered from the drawing room behind me. 'Madam. Bed tea. Bed tea ready, Madam?' I turned towards him, and saw Lingappa standing — head down, looking at his toes, too frightened to catch another glimpse of my legs. 'Yes, bring it in please.' But he stuck to his posture. I repeated myself. He still didn't budge. I had to call him three times before he agreed to lift his head, and when he saw my body embalmed to my toes, he broke into a full-mouthed, black and white smile, sending out a whiff of reassurance. Greeting, 'Madam, good morning. Good morning, Madam,' as was his manner, always placing Madam once at the beginning and then at the end of a sentence, Lingappa capered in, placing the tray on the table. Wanting to make up for the shock of my nightie, I said, paying him a compliment: 'Where did you learn your English, Linga? You speak it so well.' He was the only one among the guest-house staff who spoke English.

'From my father, Madam. He fought in the war you know.'

'Was he a soldier in the British Indian Army?'

'No, no, not soldier. He was Lance Naik.'

'And what's a Lance Naik?'

'You don't know Lance Naik? NCO.'

'NCO, what's an NCO?'

'Non-commissioned officer, Madam.'

'So he was an officer. And he taught you English you say. That's not bad for someone who has learnt his English at home.'

'But no, Madam. Madam, no. I went to school also. Till middle only.'

'Till when?'

'Middle.'

'Middle of what?'

'Middle of school.'

'I see. So they still teach English at junor levels, do they?'

'Yes, yes, Madam. Madam, yes. But I speak many other languages you know, Tamil, Kannada, Malyalam, now Marathi. And you, Madam? Madam, and you? How many languages you speak?'

Lingappa was getting too curious for my liking, and before his polyglottism could embarrass my patchy bilingualism, I removed the tea-cosy from the pot, and poured myself a cup of tea. Just then, the pigeons burst out cooing and flapping in my ears.

'What's that!' I exclaimed.

'Nothing Madam,' said Lingappa, reassuring. 'It's the pigeon pouja today.'

'What's that now?'

'Pigeon pouja, Madam. Madam, prayer before the pigeon deity.'

'Pigeon deity?'

'Yes, Madam. We worship pigeons in our community.' Lingappa walked up to the end of the terrace, looked right and beckoned, 'It is on, it is on, it is still going on. You are lucky. Come, come, Madam, you can see the pigeon pouja.'

The pigeon pouja indeed solved all my psychic riddles better than any psychoanalyst could, and when I looked where Lingappa pointed, I saw four women, presumably the wives of the guest-house staff, grouped around the rear part of the air-conditioner. They were chanting a hymn — hands folded, eyes shut, holding an aluminium platter on which were ceremoniously arranged a coconut, a lump of jaggery, a red thread, some bird feed and rose petals around a picture of a pigeon. 'Inside, inside.' Lingappa pointed towards the air-conditioner. 'The pigeon deity is inside.' One of the women struck a matchstick and lit an oil lamp, the flame reaching the compressor. I was terrified:

'Gosh! That'll set the air-conditioner on fire.'

'No problem, Madam. Madam, no problem,' reassured

Lingappa. 'Holy flame, just holy flame.' Thinking now I knew why the air-conditioners in Bombay short-circuited so frequently, I asked Lingappa discreetly:

'But how did the pigeon reach there in the first place?'

'Our good luck.'

'But how?'

'They live there, Madam.'

'In the air-conditioner?'

'Yes, it is a sign of very good luck.'

'What?'

'Pigeons coming home.'

'But there are pigeons all over.'

'Yes, but if they make a nest at home just before the pigeon pouja festival, it is very auspicious.' Lingappa pointed to a hole in the air-conditioner's insulation, and murmured into my ear, 'See, see. You can see the pigeon mother now. She came here just two weeks ago. To hatch eggs. To make more pigeons. We are lucky.'

The prayer ended, and the woman with the platter in her hand came towards us. Lingappa folded his hands, and bowed before the pigeon paper-deity which by now looked half asphyxiated by the clouds of smoke enveloping it. The woman dipped her finger into a claylike white powder, and drew two horizontal lines on Lingappa's forehead. Anointed, Lingappa turned towards me, prompting, 'Try, try, Madam. It brings good luck.' I bowed and the woman gleefully put a dot on my forehead, and blessed me. The ceremony ended with Lingappa reincarnating as a space-age professional. Looking at his electronic watch, he announced:

'It is one minute and thirty seconds past seven. Breakfast at what time, Madam?'

'What breakfast?'

'Big breakfast I have prepared for you, Madam.'

'But first tell me, how long does it take to get to the Filmwala Studio?'

'Full one hour, Madam.'

'Oh! I'd better be hurrying then.'

'Yes, yes, Madam. I know. Shooting begins today.'

The air-conditioned pigeon pouja made me feel calm, as though after a sound sleep. I returned to my room. The pigeons were still fluttering and cooing in the air-conditioner, but their presence didn't bother me at all, and it was quite unbelievable to see how one of the most terrifying hallucinations of my recent life had simply vanished in the face of a curious pigeon prayer. I had a quick shower, got dressed and sat down to write my 'shooting diary' which, by now, had become something of a ritual of my cinema career. I had begun writing it ten years ago, on the first day of *Wrong Choice* and ever since, I have jotted down my thoughts, reveries and fears each morning before shooting. At the end of the first entry, I had slipped a rose petal into the book. The life of this rose petal, moving from one day to another, is also a measure of my own life. When I opened the book on its last page and saw the arterial transparency of the rose, so delicate and childlike, I was overcome with emotion. I had neither expected nor wished to open this book after Cannes. The diary was supposed to have ended on its last page, page 1000, written at the Carlton Hotel, the day I had decided to end my life. I reread the last page, sadly amused to read something that looked like a leaf from another life. To contrast with the morose thoughts of that day, I wrote, 'If I died in Cannes, I was reborn in Bombay. Reborn in the role of the English Queen of an Indian King. I can't wait to get into the costume of Miss Ann Walters.'

Deboo, the director, arrived on the dot, and we immediately set off for the studio. Sunshine, clear pale blue sky, a gentle sea breeze, transistor music in the streets – Bombay seemed to set the pace for an ideal beginning to my first film in India. We didn't have to drive too long before I was struck by the astonishing popularity of cinema in the city. That the Indian film industry produced nearly two films a day was common knowledge in the West, but to observe the Bombay cinephilia in flesh and blood was quite a revelation even for a well-informed eye. Walls, buses, local trains, overhead bridges, pavements, lamp-posts, letter-boxes, tree trunks, virtually every patch of empty space on the roads was coloured with cinema posters and handbills. I was merrily savouring the great variety of film publicity on the billboards, when I suddenly remembered something I had meant to ask Deboo:

'I can't quite figure out why we are shooting in Bombay at all. Weren't we meant to shoot the entire film in Lucknow?'

'Indeed we were,' replied Deboo, grinning. 'But only if these wonderful stars of Bombay would allow us to do that.'

'What do you mean?'

'You see, our schedule for shooting in Lucknow was all worked out, when Vikram, our male lead, said that he had some problem with his dates. He had to be back in Bombay to wrap up an earlier film which he hadn't been able to complete. So he couldn't give me the time he had initially promised, and I had no option but to shoot a scene on a special set in Bombay.'

'Sounds quite complicated, doesn't it? Won't you have problems matching the two different decors?'

'I'll try and harmonise things, but that's another issue. The star system here is a real pain in the neck,' said Deboo with disgust. 'And all because our stars are allowed to shoot three films a day. One tiny shot goes wrong somewhere, and several shootings are upset all the way down the line. You won't believe the hilarious situations this system has led to at times. There was this producer here in Bombay whose hero wouldn't give him any dates. For a while he waited, but when there was no sign of him showing up, he said enough is enough, and had the hero killed off in an accident, and shot the rest of the film with shots of his dead body! Another incident – a top regional hero suddenly found himself the Chief Minister of his state, leaving ten unfinished films behind. He later managed to complete two of them – shooting between cabinet meetings! Oh! you can't imagine what nuisances this system has created.'

Deboo had not fully finished recounting his problems with the star system, when the driver took a sharp turn, and entered the studio gate. Spotting Shyam's white Ambassador on the driveway, one of his assistants ran up to him, and said, 'The shot's ready, and Vikram is already on the set.' Deboo turned towards me, and said, 'I better rush before I start having problems with my star. I'll finish with him while you get into your clothes.' 'Great,' I answered, 'and will you remember to send my dialogue assistant in, please?'

My schedule for the day was very light. Action takes place on the palace terrace where the King and the barber are playing chess. They are discussing how best to organise a banquet for an English officer who is carrying a gift from the King of England for the King of Awadh. Miss Walters, the Begum of Awadh, who is to accompany the King to the banquet, appears before him, as though to seek his approval for the costume she is to wear. Looking at her, the King frowns, and asks her to put on something more ceremonial. The Begum bows obediently, 'Your orders, Shehansha,' and leaves. While Vikram, playing King Nasiruddin Haider in the film, and the barber had six fairly complicated shots, with long dialogues and different cameras and travellings, I had just two – simple and straight. What worried me about my shot was not so much my lines for I had just one, but the pronunciation of an Urdu word which, Deboo insisted, had to be flawless and Miss Walterslike. To make sure all went off well with my pronunciation, I had been given a full-time dialogue assistant.

Lilly, the makeup girl, was putting the last touches to the diamond coronet on my head when someone knocked at the door. 'This is Awaara, Madam, your dialogue assistant.' Through the half-open door, a young man discreetly appeared, bowed and found himself an edge of the sofa behind me. Catching a glimpse of me in the mirror, he bowed again, 'Good morning, Madam.' 'Please remain seated. I won't be a moment.' He sat down again, reading a notice on the side wall. Something about him looked very familiar – light eyes, curly jet black hair, a birth mark on the nose.

'We've met before, haven't we?' I said, extending my hand to the dialogue assistant.

'We? Before? No, no, Madam.' My familiarity seemed to have taken him by surprise.

'Are you sure?'

'Positive, Madam.'

'At the producer's party last weekend? Couldn't we have met there?'

'No, Madam.'

'You were at the party, weren't you?'

'Yes, Madam. But I was at the back. And you were with the stars.' Unconsciously, tongue in cheek.

'I might have been with the stars as you say, but I am certainly not one.'

'Isn't that being too modest now, Madam? I hope you are not going to call yourself – as stars here do – a public servant!'

'Believe me, I have never been that kind of a star. I am sure we must have met there. You look so familiar.'

'Common faces look familiar, Madam,' he muttered, and then immediately looked down, as if embarrassed by his own wit. I got up and pulled the script out of my bag.

'Sorry. I didn't quite catch your name.'

'Awaara.'

'Awa-ra. Is that how it is pronounced?'

'No. Aa-wa-ra.' Then spelling it out for me. 'A-w-a-a-r-a.'

'I see. Aa-wa-ra,' I added, 'I better get that right since we'll have a lot to do with each other during this film. And my name is Valerie.'

'Yes, I know, Madam,' he said coyly.

'Dear me, you're not going to be calling me Madam on the set, are you? Call me Valerie.' I spelt it out. 'V-a-l-e-r-i-e.'

'But isn't it spelt V-a-l-e-r-y?'

'Yes, that's in English.'

'But I thought you were English.'

'Yes, I am. But,' I said, with a deliberately theatrical overtone, 'to be more precise, shall we say half-English half-French. And if you want the rest of the story, half-Protestant, half-Jew.'

'Good God! Sounds more complicated than the caste system here,' he exclaimed, looking away. He had a wicked half-mouthed smile I noticed.

39

'Shall we do those Urdu words now?' I suggested.

'I thought there was just one.'

'That's cheeky, isn't it?' I remarked jokingly. 'Quite right. Just one word today. Now how does it go?'

'*Shehansha*. Pronounced as shai-hun-sha.' He articulated each syllable.

'It means the King, is that right?'

'Not quite. Ruler of the World.'

'Just come once again. How did it go? Shaihun-sha . . . ' He corrected me, and I wrote it down, splitting it into syllables.

Awaara made me rehearse the word over and over again. Since writing and splitting the word up into English syllables only ended in confusion, he insisted I work purely through the ear. After several attempts, I managed to underplay my Anglo-Saxon 'sh's and 'aa's, and Awaara slapped the script book shut. 'Great. I think we can go for the shot now, unless you want to ask something else.'

'Like what?'

'It's up to you to say that. I don't know if you have any questions on the historical background? On Miss Walters?'

'No one told me you were also a historian.'

'Not really, but I know the period fairly well,' Awaara said. 'Well, a bit. Didn't Deboo tell you that?'

'What?'

'I thought he did. Doesn't matter.'

'About what?'

'Nothing important. But I thought he might have mentioned it to you.'

'About what?'

'My relationship with *Twilight of a Begum* – the book from which the screenplay has been adapted.'

'No, not a word. You mean you are the author of the book?'

'No, no. Miss Walters wrote the book, but I put it together.'

'Hang on. I'm getting mixed up. What did you put together?'

'You see, Miss Walters left behind a set of writings on her life.'

40

'I know. Her autobiography – *Twilight of a Begum*. I'm reading it.'

'But to start with, it wasn't a book at all. It was more like a diary, odd jottings, which I put together on the basis of family records.'

'What family records?'

'Well . . . well.' Awaara hesitated, stumbled, and then added, 'Family records, her family records. So Deboo really hasn't told you anything about me and the book.'

'Not that I can recall. I was told Miss Walters left an autobiography behind. So you're the author of the book.'

'Half the author I imagine,' Awaara looked at his watch. 'We'd better rush. I don't want to get on Deboo's wrong side on the first day.'

I asked Awaara to stay around just in case I needed his help for the dialogue, and walked onto the set. In contrast to the bright, air-conditioned makeup room, the set was dark and dingy and hot – a smell of sweat filled the air. I was still trying to spot Deboo on the set, when he flashed a torch at my face, and remarked teasingly, 'Just look at you, Val. Seems you've walked right out of a sauna!' Lilly immediately raised herself on her toes, and patted the sweat off my makeup with a face tissue. I walked up to the position from which I was supposed to enter the shot.

It was beginning to swelter, and the reflectors above made the atmosphere humid and stuffy. Feeling a bead of sweat tingle down my neck, I turned to Awaara and asked him to wipe it off with my hanky. Just then, Deboo charged at Awaara and snatched the hanky from his hand, 'Here, give it to me,' he snapped. Confused, Awaara retreated, and Deboo wiped off the sweat, very gently, perhaps too gently, whispering, 'If you continue sweating like this, sweetheart, you're soon going to be fit for a shower sequence. We'd better get this done before I'm forced to call this shot off.' He went back to the camera, and I turned to Awaara, smiling appeasingly, 'Shai-hun-sha, shai-hun-sha . . .'

The clap-boy clapped off the shot. I entered. Vikram gazed

at me fondly. Then, slowly, he frowned, 'Is the King's Begum going to receive a British officer in such demeaning clothes?' I bowed in apology, 'Your orders, Shahanshaa . . . '

'Cut,' said Deboo, pulling himself away from the camera, 'Shai-hun-sha. Get that sharp and clear. Valerie. Don't forget the King's Begum spoke flawless Urdu. Shai-hun-sha. Good. Silence . . . ' The next take went off impeccably until I turned towards the spot in front, and puff, it fused. Another retake. Vikram faltered with his lines. Retake 4. Cut, sound started off late. Deboo ordered the next retake. Vikram delivered his lines perfectly, as did the barber. My entry was well-timed, and just as I raised my eyes slowly towards the spot in front, there was a loud blast, and total black-out. Deboo grunted in the dark, 'God! If this is anything to go by on the first day, I don't see them lasting through the film.'

One of the lightsmen on the scaffolding lit a kerosene lamp. The entire set suddenly turned dreamlike. Waves of dim brown light floated about the room. Beneath a tall, grey shadow, dream-walking on the wall, I noticed Awaara, his own shadow fawning at his feet like a dog. 'Coo-coo, coo-coo,' I tried to attract his attention, but Awaara looked too engrossed in his muse. Statuesque, thoughtful, a cigarette hanging from his mouth, he stood gazing into a distant world. 'Coo-coo,' he didn't react. Approaching him surreptitiously from the back, I tapped him on the shoulder. He jumped:

'Oh! Madam, Madam.'

'Madam? I beg your pardon, Sire.' I said, playsomely. 'They call me Valerie.'

'Excuse me. Just a little, a little . . . '

'Hope you didn't take Deboo's rude remark seriously.'

'Doesn't matter – a director's prerogative, I guess.'

'I think it was just tension.'

'So do I. At least, I hope so.' Looking up at the shadows on the wall, Awaara mused, 'Fascinating, aren't they?'

'Like a dream.'

'Don't you think the dream sequences in the film should

be shot with kerosene lamps? There's a strange misty quality about this light.'

'Marvellous idea. Why don't you suggest that to Deboo?'

'Me? Suggest it to Deboo! You forget I am the petty errand-boy on the set.'

'Oh, come on, you seem to have taken his remark badly. It was just tension. It can happen to any of us. But does Deboo need all the dream sequences in the scenario? The King, the barber, Miss Walters, the whole world seems to be dreaming all the time in this script . . . '

'That's just the point. Dreams were so central to that whole epoch.'

'Modern times have killed dreams, haven't they?' I remarked, looking at Awaara's eyebrows which were beginning to sweat. 'Do you dream a lot, Awaara?'

'You mean, me?' Taken aback by a personal question.

'Yes, you.'

'A bit. Like everyone else.'

'Well, I dream a lot.' Then looking into Awaara's eyes, I asked, 'Do you believe in dreams?'

'Thinking about the barber's bubbling clairvoyant dreams, are you?' Awaara asked, chortling.

'Not really. I think dreams can often predict reality.'

'But then, what is a dream and what is reality in the first place? The line is quite thin, isn't it?' philosophised Awaara. 'Do you know Robert Desnos?'

'The French poet?'

'Yes.'

'What about him?'

'Remember that beautiful poem, "I have dreamt of you so much that you have lost your reality" . . . '

'Oh so you know Desnos! My favourite poet.' I recited the next line from the same poem, '"I have dreamt of you so much it may already be too late for me to reawaken" . . . '

Awaara recited again:

'"I have dreamt of you so much,
walked and talked so much

43

slept so much with your phantom presence" . . . '
Now my turn:
'"that all I can do now
and perhaps all I can do ever
is remain forever a phantom among phantoms" . . . '
His turn:
'"a shadow a hundred times more shadowy
than that shifting moving now
moving forever,
stepping lightly across the sundial of your life."'
Awaara finished reciting, looking dreamily away into the
distance.

'Gosh! You know it all by heart.'

'Just a few lines. I've translated Desnos into Urdu.'

'You speak French then?'

'No. I translated him from an English translation. In fact, I've
translated quite a few of them – Apollinaire, Breton, Soupault,
Aragon, Eluard . . . ' Awaara suddenly stopped, embarrassed.
'Pardon my French. You must have found my pronunciation
atrocious.'

'Better than mine in Urdu, at any rate,' I added. 'So
you're a poet.'

'An amateur translator I guess. You can't live off literature
in this country.'

'But I thought India had a lot of poets and writers.'

'Yes, and a lot of starvation too.' Awaara laughed. 'No,
seriously, you can't live off poetry here. Surest road to starvation.'

'What do you live off then?'

'Odd jobs. Like this one. At times a film extra. That's
how I got my name.'

'What do you mean?'

'I played a short role in a film called *Awaara*. A one-word
role.' He laughed self-deridingly.

'What was the word?'

'Awaara. Someone asks me in the film what's your name,
I answer Awaara. That became my name.'

'Which means?'

'Vagabond,' He mused. 'Vagabond I was, and a vagabond I have remained.'

I touched his arm, and asked, 'What was the best thing about Desnos, Awaara?'

'His poetry obviously.'

'Another guess.'

'His eyes. I believe his eyes drove girls mad . . . '

'And has no one ever told you that you have Desnos' eyes?'

I stroked his neck, and twisted my finger through a lock of his curly hair, tugging at it. Awaara was trembling, when Deboo barged in on us again, snapping loudly, 'You'll have enough time for your surrealist poetry later, Awaara. For the moment, Valerie's to concentrate on her role.' Awaara stood stunned. Deboo rushed for the camera, and I floated slowly back to my entry, unrhythmed by a Desnosian metaphor.

After the shot was over, the unit sat down to discuss the outdoor shooting programme in Lucknow. I quietly slipped away and walked back to the makeup room. The brief exchange of metaphors with Awaara had cast a strange spell on my mind. I felt as though a child within me had suddenly woken up. Deep inside my womb, I could hear and feel someone alive and kicking and pulsating. I changed my clothes, and while I was struggling to get the makeup off my face, Deboo barged straight into the room:

'Ready to leave?'

'Where to?'

'Cocktail.'

'Oh yes. Sorry, with all this heat and muggy weather it had slipped my mind completely.'

'Shall we leave then?'

'I think I need to do some work on my dialogues,' I replied, sounding serious.

'Come off it, Val, you look more worried about your lines than your *réalisateur*.' He enjoyed using French words.

'Because Monsieur le Réalisateur speaks Urdu and his *actrice* does not,' I said lightly. 'Seriously, there's virtually no time before we leave for Lucknow, and if we're going to be

45

shooting two shifts a day, I had better get some more work done, Deboo. I think I need to put in a lot more work.' I leafed through the script in my hand, and asked, 'Do I have to go?'

'You never have to go anywhere.' He sounded annoyed. 'But it's as you wish. If you feel you have to work, you have to. There's not much choice in the matter, is there? So you want me to stay on and work with you.'

'Good heavens, no!' I exclaimed with unconscious aggressivity. Then, more diplomatically, 'How could I be that inconsiderate? It's kind of you to offer, Deboo, but don't ruin your evening for me. I'll work with the dialogue assistant.'

'You mean Awaara?' he said.

'That's his name, isn't it? It's so difficult to pronounce.'

'But I'm afraid he's already left.'

'That's a shame!' I said flatly, concealing my disappointment. 'My mistake. I should have thought of that before. I guess I'll just have to work on my own.'

'I could ask someone else, if you like.'

'No, don't bother. I'll work on the book tonight.' Checking my diary, I said, 'I have Awaara down here for Thursday morning. Does that still stand?'

'Yes, if that's what was arranged, no reason why he shouldn't show up.'

I returned to my room at the guest house that evening drunk on Awaara's words and smells. The pigeon symphony in the air-conditioning was once again reaching a crescendo, and over the cooing I could hear Lingappa say to me, 'Good luck, Madam. Pigeons bring good luck . . .'

FOUR

MOTHER LOVED KATHAK.

She was convinced that no dance on this earth could reveal the beauty of the feminine body as Kathak did. When she first arrived in Lucknow with her husband, Alan Whearty, and discovered this native dance, she was so enthralled by it, that she left the house for days on end, chasing its enchantments in the dancing houses of the city. Luckily for her, unlike the other English residents of Lucknow, her husband was himself a Kathak-lover, giving her full freedom to pursue her passions. But happy days turned out to be brief; her husband died. A year later, she met another Kathak-lover, George Hopkins Walters, an ex-half-pay officer in the British regiment of the Dragoons, and after a short period of courtship, she married him. But marriage and an unexpected promotion in the army awakened in her new husband a different sense of morality, and he began to disapprove of his wife's visits to the dancing houses. The day that I was born, my father became astonishingly possessive, and put an abrupt end to all contact between my mother and Kathak. Since her love for dance now seemed crushed for good, she invested her passion in me, and I was initiated into Kathak at a young age by a private tutor called Buksh Mian. Not very long after, my father died. With his death returned my mother's passion for Kathak, and she fell in love with the dancing instructor at home. When the British officers around her raised disapproving eyebrows, she stowed me and her lover into a carriage, and we moved from Lucknow to Cawnpore.

I grew up to be a talented Kathak dancer, known particularly for my western, yet exotic features and the fluency with which I could speak English and native languages. If, at times, the fact that I was English stood against me, it helped me too, for there was many a Nawab who preferred a European body to that of a native dancer. But being able to dance gracefully was only one half of the craft which my mother had wanted me to master in learning Kathak, the other being how best to make use of this art to win the Nawabs and the Rajas who, after all, possessed the wealth and power of the country. When I turned sixteen, Buksh Mian and my mother introduced me to the world of the Nawabs, and soon after, the Nawab of Ittawa sent a feeler to Buksh Mian, showing his interest in marrying me. The Nawab was generous and wealthy, but a lot older than I was. I turned down the proposal. My mother, however, insisted that I reconsider my decision, saying, 'Take stock of things, Ann, this Nawab is not necessarily the end of things, he could quite likely be just the first rung of the ladder.' Leaving the final decision to the stars and planets, my mother sent for a Hindu astrologer. The wise old man looked at my horoscope and then read my hand. Astonished, he exclaimed, 'Good God! This is a Queen's hand.' My mother was overwhelmed, convinced that the Nawab of Ittawa's wealth was already inscribed on my palm. I found it difficult to share my mother's avaricious happiness — money and land could not, after all, satisfy the fancies of a sixteen-year-old. When the astrologer left, there was much excitement in the house, and the family sat up late after dinner, discussing the Nawab's huge estate and its likely inheritors. I got up and went to bed, leaving the others to their candle-lit gossip.

A vigorous rattling of the door chain woke me up. It was dark and misty, and from the stars I could tell there was still time before dawn. The man at the door called out, 'Buksh Mian! Buksh Mian!' The voice sounded familiar. I heard Buksh Mian lighting the oil lamp by his bedside. 'Who's there this late at night?' my mother asked. Buksh Mian looked up at the sky and cleared his throat, 'It's soon going to be dawn,' he said. Walking towards the door, he asked out loud, 'Who is it?' 'Adabarzai, Bhaijaan,' the person answered. 'It's me, Rashid.' Buksh Mian unchained the door, and his coachman walked in, muffled in a dark blanket.

The two men whispered to each other, and then walked back towards the main door. 'Get some breakfast ready. We'll be back soon,' Buksh Mian said. My mother hurriedly put some order in the house, dusting the cushions, and straightening out the wrinkles on the sheets in the drawing room. Buksh Mian and Rashid returned, less conspiratorial than before, followed by a third person, a eunuch. Without waiting to take his seat, the eunuch said to my mother, in a rather gay and boisterous manner considering the early hour, 'Mubarak ho. Congratulations, Begum Sahiba!' My mother was confused. The eunuch burst out giggling, clapping his hands with glee, repeating, 'Congratulations, Begum Sahiba! Congratulations! Thank Allah Mian for his kindness to you and your daughter!' The eunuch abruptly stopped giggling, and announced, with a flowing, majestic gesture:

'The Asylum and Refuge of the Universe, the Ruler of the Age, the King of Awadh, Nasiruddin Haider has desired your daughter's hand, Begum Sahiba. His humble servant has been sent to convey the King's message.'

'Meaning what?' my mother interjected. 'You mean, you mean the Nawab Sahib of Ittawa, don't you?'

'No,' shrieked the eunuch, insulted. 'I mean the King of this land. The King of Awadh! The King has desired your daughter's hand, Begum Sahiba.'

'The King! You mean the King! The King wants to marry my daughter?' My mother's voice was choked with emotion.

'Royal wedlocks are not decided by mortals, Begum Sahiba. They are the direct orders of Allah himself.'

Tears welled in my mother's eyes, her voice trembled. She found the news hard to believe.

'The King wants to marry her, is that it?' Mother asked again.

'Yes, the Ruler of the Land, the supreme patron of Kathak, has cast his eyes on Ann Walters.'

'But does he want to marry her?'

'Aha! Aha!' the eunuch teased playfully. 'But only on one condition.'

My mother paled, muttering: 'Huzoor?'

'She must leave immediately. She must be in Lucknow by Friday.' The eunuch turned theatrical once again. Stretching his arm out heavenwards, as though making a royal announcement. 'This Friday, the Kingdom of Awadh shall be graced by a new queen.' Then opening his palm out before my mother, the eunuch winked and said, 'Bakshish, bakshish. What will you give a poor eunuch for bringing good news.'

Buksh Mian gave him a pair of silver anklets, and the eunuch left, promising to return later in the forenoon. We sat stunned for some while. Speechless, paralysed, as though a death had been announced. Every now and then, my mother burst out crying hysterically, 'But what do I have? Nothing, nothing. I have nothing to give in our daughter's trousseau. What can a poor girl offer the King of this land!' Buksh Mian tried to comfort her, 'We certainly can't produce a throne of gold, but let us give what we can.' Since it was common knowledge that the King returned three times the gold that was offered to him, Buksh Mian got up to rush to the goldsmith's to buy two gold mohars. My mother, becoming suddenly active, emptied her whole jewellery case into my trunk – necklaces, rings, earstuds, stones, all that she possessed. Overtaken by the sheer pace of events, I left my mother to her jewels and clothes, and climbed up to the terrace.

It was a cold, wintery morning. A grey haze hung over the city, and in patches the sun shone weepingly, lighting up childhood memories. Watching the smoke spiralling above familiar rooftops, I felt nostalgic, overcome by that peculiar sentiment that one feels on leaving a childhood city. I sat in a corner, resting my back against a chimney-stack, staring out into the vast expanse of the city before me. Stray, sad images danced before my eyes – my dead father, childhood friends, the rooftops where I had played hide and seek. Then gradually, images gave way to thoughts of what the future might hold for me. I was happy that the King desired me, but I wondered if all the opulence of a King was worth giving up the simple warmth of a family. Remembering stories of court intrigues and pages of history soaked in blood, I was filled with apprehension, feeling unprepared to meet the challenge of a life that was opening before me. But then, I would soon be his queen, and that thought itself was enough to build the resolve of an ambitious girl. My mother suddenly came up, bursting on my reveries. 'The whole world has turned upside down, and here you are staring up into the sky! Quick, get ready. The eunuch will be here any moment.' Sensing my pensive mood, she took me aside and whispered, 'Courage, Ann. Feeble women get nowhere. Don't let the King overwhelm you. Even Kings become fakirs before the body of a woman. Like dancing, love is an art.'

The eunuch arrived with his coachman, and we left for Lucknow. Passing the British Commandant's residence in the Cantonment, the last construction of Cawnpore, we entered complete wilderness. The sight of a long and winding track leading nowhere filled me with fear, and I started to sob. Burying my tears under a shawl was of little use, for Mumtaz-the-eunuch leaned his head against the netted window, and asked, 'Beti, is that you sobbing there?' He peeped in, and remarked, giggling, 'Look at her! She's crying! You must be only woman on earth who cried because the King desired her.' When he found that his words of solace couldn't hold back my tears, he was more consoling, 'You can't be that thankless to God, Beti. He has bestowed on you the fate he reserves for his favourites. Thank him like a true believer.' Then again, rounding his eyes, and with a firmer voice, 'Stop being silly! Do you realise who desires you? The Asylum and Refuge of the World! Have you seen him? More handsome than your King of England! Oh! You couldn't imagine a better man. Generous as God! Lover of dance, poetry, animal-fights, cock-shows. More intelligent than any of his ancestors.' Mumtaz then winked at me, with typical feminine complicity, whispering, 'You're lucky, Beti. He's as virile as a bull.'

51

At the beginning, Mumtaz's unnaturally confiding and loquacious manner made me suspicious of him. It was common knowledge that eunuchs were more loyal to the Kings than mares to their masters, and story-telling and gossip sessions were mere means for them of spying into the minds of harem-inmates. So I let Mumtaz do most of the talking, answering his questions with due care and caution. It was difficult though, not to lend an ear to his irresistible tales about the court of Awadh. Dissolving one story into the other, Mumtaz could talk for hours on end about the harem, the court-intrigues, cock-fights, royal hunts, astronomy, anything. He had just finished recounting the story of a corrupt Prime Minister who ended up on the gallows, when the coachman suddenly stopped, and turned towards Mumtaz, 'What do we do now?' 'Why? What's happened?' asked Mumtaz. 'Can't go ahead. Too much slush. Rear wheels won't take it.'

I looked out of the rear window — the sun had already set, and the sky had turned ink-blue. The coachman and the eunuch got down, testing the ground, and then walked away. Mumtaz returned. 'Nothing to worry,' he said reassuringly. 'We'll take the jungle track until it meets the old road.' The coachman turned into the jungle, and Mumtaz started another story, this time about the King and his passion for thick jungles.

'He-he-hehe-heehee, he-he-hehe-heehee,' a shrill, neighing sound pierced the jungle quiet. The coachman slowed down. The eunuch cut his story short, and said giggling, 'Huh! A wild animal. Oh! Wouldn't the King love to be here with his Joe Manton?' 'Hihi-hihi-hihihi.' The sound became more staccato, woodpeckerish, and seemed to be nearing. The coachman halted, and the eunuch, hearing something charge through the thick jungle, paled with fear, 'What now?' he croaked. 'He-he-hehe-heehee, he-he-hehe-heehee, kuk-kuk-kukkuk-kukkuk-kukkuk, la-la-lula-lula.' We were still trying to decipher the sound when four men running on high stilts, shot out of the forest. 'Thugs,' muttered the coachman. 'What? Thugs! Allah!' sighed the eunuch, losing his balance and falling off the coach.

I was petrified. Very recently my mother had told me that the thugs were a living nightmare for journeymen in Awadh.

Merciless, born and brought up in the culture of blood, they were notorious highway robbers. Shown the slightest resistance, they strangled or hung their victims on the spot. Their bloodthirsty deeds were so much part of the sinister mythology of the land that often mothers would scold their infants, 'Quick, drink that glass of milk, or a thug will come and catch you.' The thugs had ruled the Awadh highways for many years, and neither the local Kings nor the British had been able to get rid of them. The greatest handicap in apprehending the thugs was obviously their art of running on stilts, which they had perfected to a point that not even trained horsemen could outrun them. Of late, since the British administration's drive against them, the thugs had become more cunning and more vicious to their victims, especially if they were white. The only ray of hope for me in this situation was that the thugs never attacked women and the poor.

'Move. Move, you haramzade,' thundered a thug at the coachman. The coach advanced, jolting. The thugs jumped off their stilts and surrounded us on all sides. Their chief laughed triumphantly, mocking the coachman pleading at his feet:

'How many nooses will we need?'

'Poo, poupou, poor man. I'm a poor man, Huzoor.'

'Of course I know you're a poor man. But how many rich men are you carrying?'

'Na, na, na . . . '

'Stop this nonsense,' The thug snapped. 'Tell me who's hiding in there?'

Suddenly the eunuch, still lying on the ground, burst out wailing like a dog. Crawling up to the chief, he threw himself at his feet. 'Mercy, mercy, My Lord.' The thug pushed his face up with his foot, and jeered:

'Ah ha! Is that a eunuch I see there?' Then laughing lazily, he picked the eunuch up by his neck, as though lifting a cat. Suddenly enraged, he thundered:

'Who's in there?'

'A lady, My Lord.'

'And whose daughter have you stolen now?' Eunuchs wer
notorious for kidnapping and castrating children.

'No one's, no one's, My Lord,' implored the eunuch, clutch
ing the thug's feet. 'Innocent, poor eunuch, My Lord.'

'Poor, yes, but not as innocent as you sound.' The thug
menaced again, 'Quick. Out with it. Whose daughter have yo
kidnapped?'

'No one's, My Lord. I am but a poor palace guard.'

'Ah ha! Ah ha! A palace guard did you say?' Pleasantl
surprised, the Chief probed further, 'Which palace?'

'King of Awadh's, My Lord.'

'So, you are a royal eunuch! Not bad, not bad at all. An
you say you're poor,' scoffed the thug. 'Don't come across suc
dignitaries that frequently, do we? Who's this woman?'

'Someone for the King, My Lord.'

'You're the escort, are you?'

'Yes, My Lord.'

'Where are the jewels then? The King's gifts for his ne
Begum.'

'He didn't send any, My Lord.'

'Nonsense! The King always sends jewels for his women.'

'Yes he does, but this time he didn't, My Lord.'

'Liar. Out with the jewels, or you know what awaits you.'

'But I have none, My Lord.'

'Liar!' thundered the Chief, kicking Mumtaz hard in hi
face.

Through the large gash on his lip, blood gushed, staining hi
clothes. The thug kicked him again in the face, and stamping o
his neck, he threatened, 'Out, out with the jewels, or you will b
hanged right here and now.'

Mumtaz searched in his pocket, pulled out the silver anklet
Buksh Mian had given him, and handed them to the Chief. Th
thug kicked his hand, sending the anklets flying into the air
and cursed:

'Bastard! You think you can please me with flakes o
silver. Where's the gold! Out with it.'

Mumtaz pleaded, blood spattering from his mouth as h

54

poke, 'In the name of Allah, My Lord, I swear I have nothing
on me.'

'Incorrigible liar,' ranted the Chief, poking a stump into
Mumtaz's ribs. 'Typical eunuch. He'd give his life but not his
gold.' Turning towards one of his men, he ordered, 'Take him
away. He doesn't deserve to live. Hang him instantly.'

Two men promptly took Mumtaz by his legs and dragged
him away towards a tree from which hung a hangman's noose.
Shrunk to a quarter of his size, Mumtaz resembled a lamb before
the butcher. He struggled, he howled, he implored and swore
by the name of his god that he was innocent and poor.

'Begum Sahiba, Begum Sahiba,' cried Mumtaz, the jungle
reverberating with his agony. Unmoved, cold as a sword edge,
the hangmen positioned the noose, and dropped it over Mumtaz's
head, jerking it a couple of times to make him stand up straight.

'Shall I pull the cord, Chief?' asked the hangman.

'Mercy! For God's sake, mercy!' I screamed, with all my might.

The Chief turned towards me lazily, 'Yes, lady. Do you
have something to say?'

'Just one thing, Huzoor. You are about to hang a poor
and innocent man.'

'Let him not fool you, lady. A King's eunuch is never
poor. Eunuchs have emptied the King's coffers.'

'But not this one, Huzoor. He is poor.'

The Chief began to reflect, as though reconsidering his
decision. Finding him in a mood to listen to me, I tried to
appeal to his sense of justice. 'I thought the thugs were known
for their compassion towards the weak, Huzoor.'

'Indeed they are. Our goddess commands us: treat a poor
man as thy brother and a woman as thy mother.'

'Then will you not believe a woman's word of honour?
This man is innocent and poor.'

'No eunuch at the palace is poor, lady. He can deceive
you, but not us.' The Chief laughed in disbelief, and added,
'It's simple. He hands over his jewels, and I return him his
life.'

'But if he doesn't have any?'

'He loses his life.'

'If on his behalf I give you the jewels I am carrying, will you spare him?'

'Your wish.'

I pulled out the box of jewels my mother had given me, and handed it over to the Chief through the window. He smiled, accepting the box with a gracious bow, and gestured to the hangmen to release the eunuch. 'Now clear out of here,' the Chief roared. 'And tell the King there wouldn't be any thugs on his roads, if there weren't any famines in his kingdom.'

The coachman quit the forest and returned to the main road. Stars were beginning to shine, though their glow was far from enough to permit a carefree night-ride. Mumtaz and the coachman, both badly shaken, debated for a while whether they should light an oil-lamp. Since it would only end up attracting more attention, they decided against it, and proceeded slowly further. Jackals and wild dogs wailed in the forest, and the pounding echoes of horse-hooves added to our sense of fear. On the outskirts of Nawabgunj, we were fortunately joined by another coach which was heading in the same direction. We followed it right up to our night-halt.

It was only when we had reached the inn, that it dawned on me what I had inflicted on my mother. In giving away her jewels, all that she had possessed in her life, I felt I had cheated her more badly than a thief could. A horrible feeling of guilt began to gnaw me and I was haunted by a dreadful vision of my mother. Haggard, ruined, wearing a dazed look, like a corpse half-alive − I saw her sitting on the footsteps of our house. This image then slowly melted into a sinking feeling: just below my throat. I felt a deep hollow, and each time I tried looking inwards, it sucked me into a dark, sinister well. Unable to get rid of this frightful sentiment, I began to sob.

The inn-keeper, a Kathak-lover, recognised me instantly, and hearing me sob in a corner, asked his wife to attend to me. The eunuch started recounting to him our misadventure, whilst his wife led me up to the zenana, the female section of the inn.

The inn-keeper's wife was kind-hearted, and sharing my sense of loss and guilt, took my hand in hers, 'Don't be upset, Beti! The ways of Allah are indeed strange and unfathomable. Who knows, The King may well give you ten times the jewels you have lost for saving his eunuch's life.' Then, touching me on my shoulder, she said with a mischievous smile, 'Saving a eunuch's life has at least won you his loyalty. They say winning a royal eunuch's loyalty is worth more than winning the King's.'

The next morning, Mumtaz-the-eunuch, who had been subdued since the event with the thugs, woke me early to inform me that a court horseman had arrived at the inn to escort us on the rest of our journey. 'Does the King know we were attacked?' I asked, surprised. 'I don't think he does. The horseman has been sent to make sure we arrive by Friday.' Noticing that I hadn't quite understood what this information was meant to imply, he rubbed the point in, 'It means the King is impatient to meet you.' Disappointed to see that he had again failed to raise my spirits, the eunuch moved back towards the door, muttering, 'It would be better if we left by sunrise.'

We started off early, escorted by the guard from the royal cavalry, his fluttering red and yellow Awadh flag attracting many a curious eye. The eunuch, I noticed, had changed his position, sitting at the back of my enclosed cabin, instead, as was the case until now, in front. Once out of Nawabgunj, we were back on the lonely track meandering its way through the jungle. The sun had risen, melting the sheets of winter mist floating on the rice fields. Turning towards the sun, Mumtaz bowed and whispered, as though talking to the sun. 'May you rise on a day which brings happiness to the lady who has saved my life.' Mumtaz looked so unlike his usual self – quiet, pensive, praying. Suddenly, I heard him sobbing. 'Is that you, Mumtaz?' I asked. He answered with a tear-choked voice, 'How can I thank you, Beti? You've saved my life. How can a poor man ever redeem such a debt!' Saying that, Mumtaz went back to his thoughtful posture, his chin resting on his half-bent knee, looking away into the horizon. After a long silence, he giggled, more like himself, saying, 'I know how I can thank you.' Then bursting

57

into a giggling fit, 'Yes, yes, I know. I know. Now listen to my story.'

One day, King Nasiruddin Haider, wandering about the banquet hall in the palace, came across a panther-skin hanging on the wall. Looking at it, he flared up. 'Horrible! What a disgrace to the palace! This is not a panther, looks more like a scabious monkey!' He promptly summoned the Royal Hunter, and fired him for hanging something on the wall that was so unbefitting of royal taste. After some hesitation, the Hunter disclosed that the panther in question was shot by the King's father himself, and it was on his orders that it was put up on the wall of the banquet hall. The King laughed. 'Oh! No wonder. My father couldn't tell a lion from a jackal!' The Hunter, in any case, was scolded for his undiscerning taste, and the King ordered a panther hunt, so that the palace walls could be adorned with a panther that the King had shot himself.

The King left for the hunt next day, accompanied, as usual, by an entourage of ministers, nobles, harem inmates, dancing girls, musicians, beaters, eunuchs, palace guards, counting in all one thousand heads on carts and carriages. But there weren't only men and women in the hunting party – knowing the King's unpredictable urge for animal fights, the Royal Hunter had been thoughtful enough to carry along some wild animals from the zoo. Around sunset, spotting a beautiful calm lake teeming with ducks, the King exclaimed, 'Ah! Ah! Ah ducks! I want to take a shot at them.' The Royal Hunter got the King's Joe Manton ready. The King walked stealthily up to the edge of the lake and fired. A flock of ducks flew up in the air, fluttering and quacking. The King burst out laughing. 'Good God! Think I got more than a dozen there.' As the beaters waded through water in search of the dead ducks, the King swanked before his women, boasting of his marksmanship. The Chief Hunter came up to the King, fawning, and said, 'I think the ducks love playing hide and seek with their King, Your Majesty.' The King was puzzled. 'Why? What happened?' 'Nothing, Your Majesty,' the Hunter said hesitantly, 'Would Your Majesty like to take another shot?'

'No,' answered the King, firmly. 'A good marksman never takes a second shot at the same game. How many did I bag?' 'The beaters couldn't find any, Your Majesty,' the Hunter whispered into the King's ear. 'Nonsense,' the King riposted. 'Gibberish! I saw five fall with my own eyes.' 'Yes, yes, Your Majesty. Even I did,' the Hunter vouched, stammering and stumbling. 'I'm sure they must have drowned.' 'Drowned?' the King frowned, turning towards his women. 'Whoever saw a dead bird drown! Who on earth made him Chief Hunter!' The King heaped a million curses on the Hunter's head, threatening, 'Watch out. I can forget the ducks, but if you don't find my panther, I'll put the same bullet through your neck.'

The hunting party reached the thick jungles at the foothills of the Himalayas, where tigers, cheetahs and panthers stalked. Scarcely had they pitched there when the Chief Hunter announced to the King that a lovely panther had been spotted near the camp. Excited, the King slipped into his hunting gear, and climbed up the tall machan. 'Your Majesty, Your Majesty,' murmured the Hunter into the King's ear, pointing to a tree. 'There, there.' 'Where? Where?' 'Behind the peepal tree, there, lying down.' The King fired. He missed it. The panther didn't move. Another shot, another miss. The panther still didn't move. Another shot. He hit the panther between the eyes. 'Hurrah! Hurrah!' the King shouted, jubilant, his voice echoing through the thicket, 'Got it, got it.' Then turning to the Hunter, he said in a light vein, 'Now don't come and tell me your beaters couldn't find the dead panther!'

The King returned to the camp with his trophy, triumphant, patting and slapping his men on the back. After the festivities, the King retired to his tent, and the Chief Hunter said to a confidant, 'Do you know how the King got his panther?' 'A fluke, was it?' The Hunter smiled, winking, 'Yes, but do you know which panther it was?' Puzzled, his friend asked, 'What do you mean which panther? Any one. I guess.' 'No, no, you fool,' laughed the Hunter, 'it was from the zoo.' 'From the royal zoo! You mean one of the two we use for the rhino and panther fights?' 'That's it. I thought why not drug one and push him right under the King's nose, before he asks for my head for not getting a panther!'

Dawn had just broken over the jungle, when the King summoned his Prime Minister, 'What's this I hear, Amir Khan?' he asked. 'Are people dying because of some famine?' The Prime Minister rubbed his hands. 'So I hear, Your Majesty. It seems it hasn't rained here for the last three years. A lot of livestock has perished. Buffalos, cows, bullocks, goats, pigs . . . ' 'Forget pigs, you pig,' fumed the King, 'What about human beings? How many have died in these parts?' 'Fifty thousand,' replied the Prime Minister, producing a figure as readily as the hunter had produced the panther. 'Allah! That's half of Lucknow!' sighed the King. 'Cities are perishing in my empire, and you bring me here for panther hunts! Atrocious! Unforgivable!' Moved by the condition of his subjects, the King ordered a surprise visit to the poor.

Riding through a village, he spotted a poor man sitting outside a hut, and halted. Indeed, the King couldn't have stopped at a more famine-devastated home than Lachchu's. A low-caste, Hindu peasant, he had lost all his land to the money-lender. Lachchu recounted the heart-rending story of his life. Before the famine, he had a family of six. Weak and undernourished, his wife had died of typhoid. Then the typhoid struck his son. To save his life, Lachchu pawned his patch of land with the money-lender, and when he couldn't pay off the loan, the land was confiscated. His son died of high fever, and a year later, two of his daughters died of starvation. Left with only one daughter, Lachchu accepted to become his money-lender's slave, working round the clock for a bowl of rice a day. He thus managed to bring up his daughter, even finding her a husband. Holding the King's feet, Lachchu said, 'Now she is two months pregnant but her husband is starving.' The King was moved to tears. Seeing the King so overcome, Lachchu called out to his daughter. 'Chakri. Eh, Chakri, come and touch the King's feet. Come, offer him some water.' Lachchu's daughter came out of the hut, dressed in rags, a bowl of water in her trembling hand. The King wiped his tears, and looking into her almond eyes, he uttered, 'An angel!

What an angel! Where have you been hiding all these days, my lovely angel?' Then turning jerkily to the Prime Minister by his side, the King commanded, 'Let this lovely fairy lend grace to the King's harem. Make arrangements for her departure.'

The guards picked up the young girl and delivered her to the King at the hunting camp. The King took his new paramour for a long walk into the jungle, promising her a million gifts and unimaginable fortunes. Late at night, when the full moon shone like silver and the guards were asleep and deep-dreaming, the young girl's husband stole into the King's tent. Discovering the King making love to his wife, he roared in anger. 'How dare you, bastard? Tyrant! I'll kill you!' Terrified, the King screamed for his guards. The husband was hacked to pieces, and later, the girl became mad.

'But do you know what happened to the King?' Mumtaz-the-eunuch asked me. 'He became impotent.'

'What? Impotent!'

'Yes.' The eunuch whistled and clapped his hands in glee. 'Ever since, the King has been impotent.'

'Allah!' I asked again. 'He's impotent, is he?'

'Not just impotent, he can't, he can't . . . ' Mumtaz turned his back towards me, as though embarrassed. 'Yes, he can't . . . '

'Can't what?'

'Can't, can't-can't, can't-can't,' wiggling his thumb. 'You know what I mean? He can't come.'

'Oh, I see.' My heart skipped a beat.

'But don't let that get you down,' Mumtaz hastened to add, 'because there's a cure for his problems.'

'For impotence? A cure? Stop pulling my leg. This is not a topic to joke about.'

'I am dead serious, Beti. I swear to God. I wouldn't have told you this had you not saved my life.' Becoming thoughtful, he said, 'But promise me you won't tell this to anyone so long as I am living.'

'Promise.'

'Remember two things when you are with the King. If

you do it well, you'll become his favourite Begum. And, who knows, your offspring may be the next King!'

'Get to the point, Mumtaz,' I said impatiently.

'Two things. One: Never make love to him lying down.'

'Lying down? How else . . . '

'You know what I mean. Never lying under him. Always be on top. The second thing: Never wear red when you are with the King.'

'Why not?'

'Don't ask.'

'But why not, Mumtaz?'

'Because since that attack on him in the tent, the King is petrified of red – the colour of blood.'

'And why never lying under him?'

'Because it reminds him of the mad, spouting eyes of the young girl who was under him when her husband attacked.'

'But how do you know this, Mumtaz?'

'Never ask a eunuch for his key to the vault of secrets.'

'But you have to tell me. You owe it to me.' I persisted. 'Who told you this?'

'Afzal Mahal. One of the King's earlier consorts. She's dead now.'

'And what happened to her?'

Seeing us approach the palace, the eunuch winked, and murmured. 'Shsh! No more of this now. Just remember the two things. And then, may God be with you!'

The coach turned into the palace driveway, making its way through the tall archway canopied by overhanging branches of mango trees. When I caught the first glimpse of the spires and minarets of the palace, towering majestically above the rustling of the mango leaves, something within me began to sing, and my heart beat faster. The coach came to a halt under the portico. Two female attendants opened the coach door, bowing in the typical Awadh style. Before they could show me in, a smartly-dressed curly-haired English gentleman rushed out of a room in the verandah. 'Welcome, welcome, Miss Walters,' he greeted from a distance. 'His Majesty has been waiting for you all day.' Doffing his felt hat in the good old English manner, he shook hands with me, introducing himself.

'My name is Samuel de Russet. They call me Sarfaraz Khan here.'

'Who hasn't heard of you in these parts, Mr de Russet?' I said, flatteringly.

'Good things, I hope,' said Khan-the-barber, with an officious smile. Showing me into his office, he added, 'Sorry for rushing you after a long and tiring journey, but the King wants to see you instantly, Miss Walters. I'm sure you too must be impatient to offer him your greetings.'

'Right away? With all this dust and sweat?'

'Oh! Don't worry about that. Dust and sweat are of little importance to His Majesty. He's a sportsman you know — one of the finest hunters in this land.' The barber lit a cigar. 'Come, let me show you to his private castle.'

Noticing the tunic I was wearing was red, I asked Khan, 'If you don't mind, may I change into a fresh set of clothes?' 'By all means,' said the barber, then adding hesitantly, 'Being English, I'm sure you won't mind changing in one of these rooms. It'll save time.' The eunuch brought my clothes in, and I changed into a new costume — a light blue tunic with transparent sleeves over white, silk-frilled pyjamas. As the barber escorted me to the King's castle, he peered at my face curiously, and remarked, 'You don't fancy cosmetics, I see. No reds and pinks on your face.' I answered with a coy smile. Khan opened a heavy ivory door and, stepping aside, motioned to me. 'Through here to your right. His Majesty is expecting you.'

Pulse racing, I opened the door to the King's chamber, and saw reclining on a long easy chair — a person with fine features, and long frizzy hair from the sides of which dropped two curly side-whiskers. He was slim, fair, elegantly dressed like a European gentleman in a three-piece suit. What was indeed startling about the man was the thick black band he wore over his eyes. Puzzled, I stood still, wondering if I had walked into the wrong chamber. He let forth a burst of crackling laughter and spoke in English. 'I know, I know, my eye-band has confused you.' He laughed again. I greeted him in English. 'Wah! Wah!' he exclaimed. 'Wah! Such a treat to listen to a genuine English accent! Good, good, now I know where to improve my English.' The King motioned to me, 'Come on, don't be scared of me. Approach the King.' I walked up and boldly sat on one of the arms of his chair, and the King began to feel my body with his hands — he had a soft touch. 'Wah! Wah! Wah!' he uttered repeatedly. 'What an honour to the race of women is your body, young lady!'

Slowly, his caressing, fondling hands reached my lips, and stroking them, he whispered, 'Your lips are even more intoxicating than your accent.'

'But won't His Majesty like to look at them?' I asked.

'No,' replied the King firmly. 'But do you know why? Because I distrust my eyes.'

'Would His Majesty never look at me then?' I couldn't fathom the King's strange behaviour.

'Being an artist, you would agree that reality is so banal before imagination. The idea of a woman is so much more beautiful than she herself.'

'But would Your . . . '

'Yes, yes, yes,' the King cut me short. 'Don't worry — I will look at you. But not before you have passed the test.'

'A test, Your Majesty?' As I was getting more and more confused, my mother's words rang in my ears — Be bold, Ann. A King is but a fakir before the body of a woman.

The King sat up in his chair, and said:

'Now, if you can answer these questions correctly, you will pass my test, and be my first consort. What is love?'

'Passion, Your Majesty,' I replied with whatever came to my mind.

'And what is passion?'

'Madness of heart, Your Majesty.'

'Madness of heart — I see. What is sacrifice then?'

'To forego my pleasure for that of my lord, Your Majesty.'

'Good, good,' muttered the King. 'What is pleasure then?'

'The dance of senses.'

'And what are senses?'

I decided to be bolder, and kissed him on his lips. 'Um!' sighed the King. Encouraged, I began untying his eye-band. 'No, no, no,' the King resisted playfully. 'Don't you see. I like it that way. Just let my eye-band be, and you can begin with your English lesson.' The King smiled mischievously, asking, 'Now where would you like to teach me – on the bed or the floor?' 'On the floor, My Lord,' I answered, playing my next card fearlessly.

I undressed the King – he wasn't just a King, he was also wickedly beautiful. Bearing in mind what Mumtaz-the-eunuch and my mother had told me, I lay on top of him and began my first lesson in the grammar of love. The King quivered, shook, trembled and rippled below me. When the King had spent his passion, he dug his nails deep into my waist and sighed, 'My manhood, you've returned my stolen manhood.' I felt relieved, half my battle for Awadh was already won. He removed his eye-band and gazed dreamily into my eyes, 'Ah! You're more beautiful than my dreams.' I retied the band on his eyes, and said coquettishly. 'Now do you want another English lesson, My Lord? But this time in the royal bath . . . '

FIVE

LINGAPPA KNOCKED

at the door. I shut the book, and asked him to enter. 'Madam, article. Article, Madam,' he said, smiling black-and-white, and vigorously waving a magazine at me. 'Look! Look!' he said, excited as a child. 'Article on you. Yes, on you, Madam.' When he heard me say rather dismissively that I had stopped reading such stuff many years ago, his bright shining face shrank, now resembling a sulky burnt toast, and his eyes looked perplexed. Then trying to coax me, he opened the magazine out before me. 'But your photo, Madam. Madam, big photo of you.' I recalled the photograph – a still from an old American film, *Love in the Green Room*. Finding the title amusing, 'Sex Goddess Casts Spell on Bombay', I took the magazine from Lingappa, and started reading it:

'She came to India to shoot *Shamebegum* (*Twilight of a Begum*), the fascinating, rags-to-riches romance of a nineteenth-century Nawab with a poor English dancer, but left behind an even more gripping scenario of love between herself and her dialogue assistant. She came to Bombay to fall in love with Nasiruddin Haider, the fifth Nawab of Awadh, but ended up in the arms of her half-employed, poetry-spouting, Francophile assistant. Abandoning a life of glamour, she came to India, wearing the saffron costume of a sanyasin, but no sooner had a short-circuit plunged the set into darkness than she charmed the pants off the

66

nearest available man. Who is the famous actress in question?

'You've guessed it – Mademoiselle Valerie Scott, playing Miss Walters in Deboo Ansari's new venture, *Shamebegum*. Paris-based, of French and English parentage, Miss Scott is a genuine, bilingual actress, described in Paris as an English sex-bomb who can whisper soft, loving things in Shakespearean English, and in London as a French sex-bomb who can murmur in your ear (not yours, if you please) in a typical Parisian accent: "*Je t'aime.*"

'It all started a week ago with an electric short-circuit at the Filmwala Studios. (Ironically, while most love-affairs trigger off with an electric spark, this one seems to have done so with a short-circuit.) The black-out at the set might have caused anxiety to the film director, but for some others, it was a blessing in disguise. When the lights suddenly came on, unannounced, where was Miss Scott? Ha! Ha! Yum! Yum! Mouch! Mouch! – practising Urdu dialogues with her dialogue assistant, not through lip-reading, instead through lip-licking. Quite sensible to think of it – why waste time listening to a dialogue when you can have it straight from the horse's mouth, all its flavour and nuance intact.

'After the shoot was over, Miss Scott and her assistant headed for the lovely hills of Mahabaleshwar. Apparently, the small-time hill-town couldn't come up to Mademoiselle's refined alpine taste, so the love-birds drove back to a five-star hotel in Bombay. She checked in alone first, asking her assistant to join her later. The teenagerish strategy back-fired, for when the poor assistant turned up at the hotel – shabbily, nay poetically dressed, sozzled, beer froth still bubbling at the edge of his mouth – the door-attendant refused to let him in. The young man argued back – alas, only to be roughed up and handed over to the cops for drunken behaviour. Without any sign of her lover, Miss Scott then came down to figure out what had happened to him. As she was pacing up and down the lobby in her torn-to-order F.U. minier than mini shorts, a petrodollar businessman suddenly developed a night-itch: "Wah! Wah! How many US dollars for your company, Madam?"

'But Bombay has not just been a bed of thorns for the Anglo-French actress. Miss Scott has now found a more hospitable host in another five-star hotel of the Bombay suburbia, and that's where a celebrated actress and an uncelebrated poet are rehearsing the difficult dialogue of a nineteenth-century Anglo-Indian romance.

'Love is blind, indeed it is, but should some glow still remain in Miss Scott's lover's eyes, he might like to read the writing on the wall. A visiting European journalist in town would have us believe that Valerie Scott, with two abortions and one miscarriage to her credit, has left each of her ex-lovers with serious psychic problems while, of course, keeping a fair share of the latter for herself. At Cannes last year, the young actress survived a suicide attempt, though that only seems to have whetted her appetite. Interestingly, while she was recovering from the mental shock of the Cannes experience, she sent her treating psychotherapist, allegedly her last love-victim, reeling to his own psychiatric ward with depressive schizophrenia.

'Halt! Halt Valerie! Thy name is nymph! When Ansari begins shooting in Lucknow on 15th March, an Awadh soothsayer might like to warn Miss Scott's naïve, desi assistant – *Beware the Ides of March! Beware the Ides of March . . .* '

JOY PANGAWALA

I put the magazine away, feeling as though I was back in Cannes – the same revengeful sensationalism, the same trick of passing off white lies as unquestionable truths. Yes, I knew, as a friend once said, that one must distinguish the wheat from the chaff, the good from the bad papers. But nothing could ever distract me from my belief that behind the most painstaking piece of journalism, there is always a bug and a rat – a bug of being compelled to furnish immediate, seemingly authentic answers, and a rat of megalomania which screams, 'I am the ruler of this world, and the plague is my law.' I was furious with the article but in some ways it was also amusing to see how the vampires of the western media I had wanted to flee by coming

68

to Bombay, had only reappeared before my eyes, now in their Indian incarnation.

What disturbed me about the article was not so much its wild-horse imagination and puerile insinuations, but the heartlessness with which it could dig open, and distort, a buried past. I picked up the magazine, wanting to reread the article, when Deboo called. Before I could utter a word, he burst forth:

'Have you seen this article in *Starlust*, Val? I couldn't believe my eyes. Vicious, isn't it? What a bastard!'

'A real bastard! If I could lay my hands on the man, I swear I'd wring his neck.'

'Incredible sadist!' he fumed. 'Digging up personal things. Journalists here get away with murder. In the West, he would have had a million-dollar suit on his hands.'

'That's what you think, Deboo! They go scot-free everywhere.'

'Any idea who it can be?' he asked.

'Who else? The European journalist he mentions. It must be one of those Cannes rascals!'

'False lead. How could he know all these details about Bombay?'

'Which details? Oh the rubbish about hotels, hill-stations and drunken orgies!' I said, laughing. 'It doesn't take much imagination to concoct such adolescent gibberish. Do you know who it is?'

'The one who's written this? Not a clue. A ghost, a complete ghost. No one has ever known who he is, where he lives, where he gets his facts from? Complete mystery.'

'And the editor, do you know him?'

'Yes, I do. Though I try and keep my distance from such people. Why? Did you want me to talk to him?'

'Why not? Give him a piece of your mind. The least he can do is to check his facts before publishing such rubbish.'

'Yes, I could talk to him. But if I were you, I'd just drop the matter where it is. Why bother with such stories of rag journalism? *Starlust* is known for such cheap scandals.

Scandals die their own death, and sooner than you think, Val.'

'So you think I should just forget it.'

'That's it. Just switch off and get busy with your film.'
Then Deboo gently asked, 'But would you allow me to give
you some advice? Shall I say elder-brotherly advice?'

'Most welcome.'

'Just stay clear of all those petty people on the set.'

'Like who?'

'Anyone. It seems awful saying things against one's own
unit, but at times there's no choice. Seriously, don't give any
chances to assistants, junior artists, technicians and what have
you . . . '

'You mean Awaara?'

'Not just him, anyone. You see, this is not Hollywood.
Cultural signs and symbols matter in every context. To you it
means nothing being friends with an errand-boy but the world
can make a mountain out of a molehill. When in Rome, do as
Romans do. Seriously . . . '

'But what have I done, Deboo?'

'Nothing. That's just the point. When you do nothing,
people make a novel out of it. Why play into people's hands?
Just don't mingle with these petty fellows on the set. For
instance, I must confess that after reading the article this
morning, I suspected Awaara.'

'You mean he had it planted?'

'Why not? These half-assistants and half-actors are always
looking for cheap publicity. They say — if I can get some
mileage out of her, why not? Where's the harm?'

'But he's not the sort.'

'You are naïve, darling. The ways of the world are more
devious than you think.'

'And on top of that I'm supposed to be meeting Awaara
this evening. Someone will obviously see in it another fabulous
orgy.'

'That's it. You've got the point now. So just stay clear.
Don't get into situations people can exploit. For instance, why
call Awaara at home when you can work with him on the set?'

'Difficult world, your Bombay, isn't it?'

'Now don't get too worked up about it. In any case, we're off to Lucknow tomorrow.'

Love is the first martyr on the battle-fields of doubt. Talking to Deboo was reassuring, but he'd poisoned my head with a horrible stench of doubt. The first victim was obviously Awaara. All my Awaara-fantasies burst like a bubble, and a peculiar hopelessness began to overcome me, the feeling of a sentimental betrayal. If the past years had destroyed almost every form of trust in human beings, I still had some faith in poets. For some reason, I had always felt that such people were themselves too tortured and wounded to be dishonest. They could be possessive, jealous, nagging, wild, violent, murderous, anything, but rarely dishonest. Awaara's suspected involvement in this affair smashed this last conviction, making me a complete sceptic in the land of a million believers. I lay back on my bed and reviewed, in slow motion, image by image, my every moment with Awaara, dissecting time and word with the precision of a surgeon. When I thought of his avowed nostalgia for the world of dreams, and his passion for William Blake, Desnos, Rimbaud and Baudelaire, the purest landmarks of our literature, I wondered just how hypocritical the world could get but, as Deboo said, the world's more crooked than we think . . .

Suspicion about Awaara really grew wings in the evening when he failed to show up for our rendezvous. As the minutes ticked by and there was still no sign of him, it was frightening to see how Awaara's face began to disfigure before my eyes — cold white marble eyes, huge pouting lips, a brussel-sprout cancerous lump on one cheek, a vomit-yellow liquid dripping from his ears. Awaara's face was turning into another hallucination, when I got up to call Deboo:

'Awaara hasn't turned up for the appointment.'

'I told you, I told you,' shouted Deboo, triumphantly. 'So it is him. Bastard!'

'I find it hard to believe.'

'World's shrewder than you think, Val.'

'Perhaps.'

'Who else then? Why should he not turn up?'

'Could have been held up somewhere.'

'That's what they all say, couldn't get to a phone-box, lost the number, phone lines were down.' Deboo laughed, and added. 'Not just a rascal, a moron at that. Not too intelligent of him to miss the appointment, was it?'

'Yes, lends himself to suspicion. As the French say, *une histoire sordide*. Anyway, let's drop it.'

'Yes, it'll die its own death. So what are you doing in the evening?'

'I'll stay in and pack up for tomorrow, I guess.' Adding, 'And marvel at the devious and dark back-alleys of your city, Deboo.'

'Stop it! Cheer up! See you tomorrow at the airport.'

I drew the curtain and opened the window. A full moon shone in the sky, and a cone of silver light wallowed on the waves of the Arabian Sea. On the path along the beach, three fisherwomen were threading their way home, laughing, indifferent to the wind bloating their saris into balloons. I envied their laughter, and being able to hear them clearly and not understand them, how I wished I could speak their language. I looked at them long, until their saris dissolved into the dark, leaving behind rings of laughter and a narrow grey path resembling a piece of asphalt frozen in time. I poured myself a whisky, switched off the room lights and put on Keith Jarret, a trusted companion for such moments of love and doubt.

My head was full of the Köln concert when Lingappa frantically pounded at the door. 'Madam, Madam.' Unnerved, I opened the door. He was standing in a state of semi-paralysis – head bent, eyes looking upwards, lips downwards. The only sign of life on his face was his mildly twitching nostrils. 'Hani, Hani,' he muttered. 'What? Who?' He tried again. 'Come to see you, Hani. Come to see you.' 'Who?' Blinking his eyes together, he pointed repeatedly towards the drawing room, and whispered. 'Star, film star, Rani. Come to see you.'

I figured out at once that the cause of Lingappa's momentary

facial paralysis was a surprise visit from Rani, the Indian super-
star. With her lovely rainbow eyes, long arching eyelashes, dark
blueing lips, and features that nature seldom offers to one single
human being, Rani was not just one of the most beautiful women
I had ever seen, she even sounded rather too human for one of the
greatest film stars this land had seen. I had first met her on the
second day after my arrival, at the producer's party. I remember
her taking me into a quiet corner, and asking me, 'So how's it
going, now?' I couldn't quite fathom what she meant by that,
but nevertheless answered diplomatically, 'Great. Marvellous.'
She slanted her eyes, as though dissatisfied with my answer.
'No. I meant the Cannes thing. Did you know we have similar
pasts? Identical − you attempted suicide at Cannes. I at Venice.
You survived. So did I. You were fed up with the cinema. So
was I. You got back to work. So did I. So you see . . . ' That
short conversation made us instant friends − death brings human
beings together better than life can. Rani left that party half-way
and, parting, she said, 'Don't be surprised if I knock at your door
unannounced one night, Val. I am a night-bird, and feel more
at ease in the company of bats and owls.'

Rani breezed into the room, brushing past Lingappa's dream-
come-true smile.

'Gosh!' she exclaimed, blowing the smoke away with her
hand. 'What have you been up to, Valerie? Seems as though
the room's on fire?'

'At least it's not my lungs, I hope,' I replied, opening
the windows. 'You don't smoke I presume.'

'Huh! Smoke, drink, pot, hash. I revel in vice. Pity I
don't have the time to gamble,' she said. 'So why don't you
be an angel, and pour me some whisky. To wash down a hard
day's fatigue, shall we say.'

Rani exuded warmth the very instant she walked into
the room. Shockingly unassuming, informal, free. Like a girl
back from school, she tossed her hand-bag on the carpet, flung
her shoes off into the air, and sat on the bed, leaning against
the backrest. 'Oh my toes!' she grumbled, putting her feet up.

'Shootings are the hardest on them. I fear my big toe will just drop off one day like a loose cork in a bottle.' I served her a drink — a large one. Rani gulped it down in one shot, and said, *'Encore, Madame*. If that doesn't shock your view of the coy Indian woman too much.' I served her another. Inspecting her glass measuringly, she remarked, 'Now why is this drink smaller than the first, my fair Lady? Scared of being landed with a drunk, are you?' 'Hope all's well with you, Rani,' I enquired, with concern. 'Couldn't,' Rani said gulping, 'couldn't be better. Someone just said I'm on the list for another Best Actress Award this year. Will be this country's first hat-trick. Oh ho! Stop treating me like my grandmother. I enjoy my drink.' Rani knocked off another, as though to shock me, and passing me her glass, said, 'My principle is simple. When you're a guest, demand hospitality.'

The light from the table-lamp cut Rani's face in two. Noticing her eyes glitter, I remarked:

'You have gorgeous eyelashes, Rani.'

'False ones,' she chuckled.

'And beautiful hair!'

'Wig.'

'Exquisite features.'

'Ask my plastic surgeon.'

'All fake, is it?'

'Faker the face, more genuine the star.' Rani laughed drunkenly. 'But tell me, how is life treating you in Bombay?'

'Bad.'

'Why?'

'Haven't you seen it?'

'What?'

I showed her the article and she started reading, an unlit cigarette in her hand. Half-way through she giggled and asked:

'Who's this chap?'

'My dialogue assistant.'

'So he exists. Is he handsome?'

'Oh! As a God.'

'Lucky you!' Rani said, licking her lips. 'Handsome, poet,

adventurous, Francophile – sounds splendid. So what are you brooding about?'

'Come on, be serious, and read on.'

She tapped me gently on my shoulder and asked, a mischievous glint in her eyes, 'And all this business about the hotels? Is he fun?'

'Haven't been that far, Rani.' I answered. 'Go on, read on.'

She finished the article. 'Splendidly erotic. Didn't know such people existed in Bombay. Trust you to take the best in town.'

I tried to put some order into her swirling head. 'Would you shut up now and listen to me. I find this article revolting.'

'Article, yes, but not the man. How did you get hold of this magazine in the first place?'

'Why? The man at the guest house showed it to me.'

'Oh! He should have kept it for himself, just the kind of people it's meant for. *Stardust* is the most lurid that any film magazine could get, and by no means a reflection of our journalism. I am surprised you read such rubbish.'

'Well, not much you can do if someone slips it under your nose.'

'Bad nose that can't smell the rat!' Then, as though suddenly sober, Rani advised, 'Just don't bother with these idiots!'

'Do you know the editor of this magazine?'

'Yes, I do.'

'Can we find out who's behind this?'

'Pointless. Just forget it.'

'Deboo feels it is this assistant who's behind it. For cheap publicity.'

'Ah ha! That gives the story an interesting turn. Could well be. And Deboo's got a good nose for such things. I see, now I know what you mean. It's awful to be backstabbed by someone you've liked.'

'Exactly.'

'Are you in love?'

'Well, I was, I guess.' I lit a cigarette. 'Before Deboo said it could be my assistant.'

'But can you be in love?'

'Why not?'

'I don't think stars can love.'

'Why not?'

'How can they love when they've lost the capacity even to communicate. Let alone communicate. They can't even understand themselves. They live in a perpetual void. No, no star can love.'

'Depends who you are talking about?'

'That's just the point. A star can't love in spite of his or her wish. Being a star means to deny yourself.'

'You mean you can't love any more.'

'Not just me. Nor you, for that matter. Infatuations, passions, sensual relationships — that's not love, not real love at any rate.'

'Now stop philosophising a minute, and listen to me. I want you to find out who's behind this article.'

'A real masochist, aren't you? What if I confirmed it was your assistant.'

'Well at least I'd know. Go on. Call up one of your million fans and see if you can track him down.'

'What's the time?' muttered Rani to herself, looking at her watch.

She picked up the phone and I went out to try and get some dinner ready before the cooks called it a day. To my utter surprise, I found that Rani's presence had electrified the whole guest house. The entire squad of servants, dressed up as though for a marriage ceremony, was wide awake, dusting furniture, mopping floors, arranging flowers. John, the long-haired, side-whiskered, slightly junky son of the caretaker, who I had always taken to be the local variant of a sixties' hippy, seemed to have suddenly slipped a generation, now wearing a navy blue summer suit, with a dark green shirt and a flashy purple neck-tie. Lingappa, in his traditional white dhoti and kurta, was obviously playing the master of ceremonies, commanding operations with a sense of self-conscious authority. When I told him that Rani would dine at the guest house, he laughed. 'Of course! How can I let her go without eating at my house! I will make her eat. I will make her eat.' Then he beckoned me to follow him up to the front terrace overlooking the main road. I looked down: a crowd of two hundred people was hustling and bustling at the main gate, waiting to catch a glimpse of Rani.

'Neighbours, neighbours,' whispered Lingappa. 'Rani very popular. Very sexy. People madly crazy for her, Madam.'

I returned to the room. Rani announced:

'Good news first. It's not your assistant.'

'It's not him.' I was relieved, though slightly embarrassed to show emotion. 'I knew that! I knew that!'

'Stop getting hysterical and tell me now, who do you think it is?'

'The European journalist.'

'Which European journalist?'

'Remember the article quotes a visiting European pressman.'

'No, not him. It's someone else – an Indian. Guess.'

'Give up.' I was in no mood for games. I asked again, impatiently, 'Tell me, who is it?'

'Deboo.'

'Who? Deboo! You mean my director.'

'Yes.' Rani laughed incredulously. 'Unbelievable. A director doing it to his own actress.'

'Are you sure your source is correct, Rani?'

'Absolutely. Besides the story fits in. A real Pandora's box.'

'Another court intrigue à la Awadh, is it?'

'Nearly, but Deboo is at the root of it all. Now listen carefully, it's slightly complicated. Deboo had the story planted through Madhu, his daughter. Madhu is going around with Rahul, the *Starlust* magazine editor, whose wife killed herself a few months ago. His wife was a writer, who used to hang around with the Bombay Poets Guild, an organisation run by Awaara and a few others. A few weeks ago the *Starlust* editor had a tiff with Awaara and his friends over his wife's suicide. So when the editor got his chance, he put the story through.'

'Gosh! So the editor carried the story because it was anti-Awaara, and Deboo had it pushed in because it was anti-Valerie. Am I right?'

'That's it.'

'But why should Deboo do it? What has he against me?'

'Obvious. He's interested in you and you're interested in Awaara. So in the good old tradition of love, he was just being vindictive.'

'How does that help him?'

'Ask Deboo,' said Rani, blowing out a ring of smoke. 'Fits of jealousy rarely help, but we all have them. I can quite see how Deboo must feel. Let's look at the story through his eyes. He turned the whole world over to get you to act in this film because he had a crush on you. He fought with his producer who found you too expensive. He delayed the project to suit your dates. Finally, when you did accept the film and came out to shoot, you chose to fall into the arms of one of his umpteen assistants — Deboo must have hit the roof! So erupted the volcano of jealousy.'

The next day I reached the airport to catch my flight to Lucknow. Someone from the unit came up to me and handed me an envelope. I opened it, it was from Awaara.

Dear Valerie,

When I met you the other day, I didn't know that my first day on the set was also to be my last. After the shoot, I was informed that the film unit no longer needed my services. Which explains why I didn't show up for our appointment yesterday.

I must admit that the decision to drop me has come as a big shock, but such facts of life rarely announce their arrival. So I am back to poetry, back to Baudelaire, back to that drunken boat, floating on the waves of surprise . . .

An old dream stands shattered. All my life I had dreamed of Miss Walters' book becoming a film. And now that it has, it seems strange to see everyone involved in it, except the man who brought Miss Walters' autobiography to life. But that is life.

I was looking forward to working with you in Lucknow. I would have loved to have shown you my city — the city of ruins, the city of distant childhood memories, as distant as the face of the beautiful woman that inspired Robert Desnos to write: I have dreamt of you so much, that you have lost your reality.

It was wonderful meeting you. Do you know who wrote these lines:

> I have found
> the secret of loving you
> for the first time for ever.

Awaara

I folded the letter, my hands trembling. The flight was boarding. Spotting a phone-box in the departure lounge, I called Rani and read Awaara's letter out to her. My voice choked with emotion. Rani too was moved. 'Didn't expect Deboo to stoop quite so low. Leave it to me now, Valerie, and don't worry. Awaara will join the unit in Lucknow by tomorrow latest.'

The plane was airborne when a passenger in the next seat said to his friend. 'Have you seen the latest *Starlust* which speaks of this English actress taking her assistant for a ride . . . '

NOTE IN MISS WALTERS' DIARY:

Important: Given the personal nature of my observations in the following pages, no part of this section may be published, copied or read out in public for a period of fifty years after my death. Ann Walters.

SIX

ONE DAY

the King and his entourage were on their way to the Dilkhusha
Palace to watch a wild animal fight. The cavalcade was half-way
through the town, when a tall, dark, monstrously muscular man
jumped from the terrace of a house and landed right in front of
the King's carriage. Alerted, the bodyguards positioned their
lances to attack the trespasser, but the King raised his hand and
restrained them. The wild, half-naked man greeted the King,
and began to sing. His squeaking, creaking voice, which had
nothing of a melody in it, was soon accompanied by a slow,
grappling movement of his limbs, as though he were struggling
to wade out of a swamp. His languid movements became faster
and faster, until he broke into a demented fit of dancing, kicking
stones and pebbles in all directions and raising clouds of dust.
The nautch girls in the entourage endured the man's singing
and dancing for a while, but when his song started resembling
the nocturnal wailing of a dog, they began to giggle and laugh
in their sleeves. He continued dancing for a good while. Then
exhausted and gasping for breath, he collapsed before the King's
carriage with a thud. The entire entourage burst into a chorus
of mocking laughter. Just then, the King got up and asked the
tired dancer, 'By what name shall the King of Awadh address
this great artist?' 'Peeru,' mumbled he. The King offered him
a bagful of gold coins, and announced to the great bewilder-
ment of his entourage, 'Never before has Awadh heard such an

exquisite song, nor has it seen such a dance. Peeru will be the Chief Musician at the Court of Awadh.'

Peeru became the Chief Musician, winning titles and riches from the King, but his rise to this powerful position was for ever a mystery to the great music masters of Awadh. That Lucknow was a natural, gravitational centre for the poets, musicians and dancers of the country was common knowledge. Lucknow was even renowned for having discovered hidden talents which, in any other state, might have perished without seeing the light of day. But when it came to the unmelodious Peeru, nobody could unravel how Nasiruddin Haider's ears could transform 'the wailing of a dog into the song of a nightingale'. The King though, was impervious to what the others said of Peeru. He was so captivated by the unrhythmic, off-beat, and unconventional quality of Peeru's singing and dancing that for months he hummed and sang his songs, offering a taste of this unhearable art to whoever visited the royal palace. The King's obsession with unconventional music reached its climax the day he told me what his next musical obsession was — the sound of the height of my passion!

When he first confided to me his new, sonorous obsession, I laughed it off, taking it to be yet another eccentricity of a man who might go down in history as its greatest eccentric ever. But, ostensibly, the King was more serious about his obsession than I had imagined. A couple of days after he first disclosed this to me, I saw the King sitting in a chair, his hands tightly pressed against his ears, as though in great pain. 'What's the matter?' I enquired. 'Quiet, don't disturb me,' he protested, and then added, 'echoes, echoes, thousands of them.' 'What echoes?' I asked, slightly anxious. 'Echoes! Of the sound of your love sighs. Beautiful! Magnificent! It's like a raga!' Then looking imploringly into my eyes, he urged me to repeat the sound, and when I refused to take part in his infantile pranks, he mumbled and grumbled and went up to the terrace overlooking the river. There again, he set about reproducing the sound of his echoes, interrupting himself every now and then. 'Oh no! — too much base, too throaty.' Then again, 'Too much treble. Too shrill.'

Disheartened with his experiments, he lamented, 'Impossible. Just can't get it. It's too primordial that sound, too unreal.' He tried again and again, until he gave up, moaning before me, 'Why can't I have that sound of yours, Ann? Why couldn't I be a beautiful English girl like you?'

Convinced that the mystery of the ungraspable sound lay in the fact of being a woman, the King's obsession now became compounded with another — that of becoming a woman. So he gradually started dressing like a woman. To begin with, he adorned himself in the costume of a male Kathak dancer, which was only a shade different from that of a female dancer. But he soon found it too half-hearted an attempt to get into the being of a woman, which, after all, was the secret behind the magical sound. Deciding to be more daring and brazen about his motives, the King now tried a complete vestimentary transformation, and once a week, started dressing in silk tunics, frilled pyjamas, transparent dupatta, and even my underclothes which were still an English novelty in India. Once the King felt at home in his feminine attire, and had acquired the gestures and mannerisms that went with it, he resumed his initial experiment to reproduce the carnal sound — but, alas, in vain. After a while, it dawned on him that the cause of his artistic failure was the grain of his voice, too untrained to capture the sound of a sensual spirit. So he decided to repeat the same experiment with an exotic wind-instrument that a visiting musician from America had offered His Majesty.

The change produced magical results, for when the King played out his composition to me, I was amused to hear the King reproduce sounds quite similar to those of feminine passion. The King was overjoyed. He promptly summoned Peeru, the Chief Musician, and offered him a rendering of his latest musical feat. The disputed music master relished it. The King thus immortalised his music by giving it a name — Raga 'Ah! Ah!'

For a few days, the King enjoyed playing his sensual raga on the banks of the Gomti. But soon, like all great masters of music, he got tired of his own composition, saying, 'My music is good, but too artificial. What I want is your sound, the sound of the primordial scream, played over and over and over again.' The King sat reflecting for a while, humming bits and pieces of his favourite raga, and then called Khan, and enquired:

'Do you know anything about the English industrial revolution, Khan?'

'I know more about the French revolution, Your Majesty.'

'Oh! That terrible butchery!' the King snarled. 'No, I am asking about the English industrial revolution.'

'I know a little, Your Majesty.'

'I hear the English have invented a number of machines.'

'Indeed, Your Majesty. The latest is the steam-locomotive. It can haul ten carriages along metallic lines at one time. The first line between Stockton and Darlington was completed a week before your humble servant left the shores of England. There was great excitement in London about that, Your Majesty.'

'But do you know if the English have invented something that can memorise sounds, and reproduce them?'

'A sound-reproduction machine?' Khan scratched his head. 'Not to my knowledge, Your Majesty. The finest echo of human sound I ever heard was in the terrace chambers, Your Majesty. They can produce sixty-nine echoes of each human sound, Your Majesty.'

'Wah! Wah!' exulted the King, his eyes lighting up as though with a long-awaited answer. 'What a store-house of ideas is this Khan! Wah! Wah!' Then in a more matter-of-fact tone, he said, 'Issue orders, Khan, that my sleeping chamber be shifted to the terrace chambers. But not the whole paraphernalia — if they stack it like a fodder-house, there'll be no room for echoes. Just a bed and bedding. That will suffice.'

'And what about His Majesty's well-being?' Khan murmured, as fear of being poisoned rose once again to the King's head.

'Indeed, indeed,' uttered the King, contemplatively. 'Have my water bucket placed by the bed. I'll go down to the well to draw my water.'

'And the personal guards, Your Majesty?'

'Throw everyone out of the palace. I don't want anyone to disturb us. Just the guards at the gates, and that's it. Everyone else out – the fewer the people, the fewer the risks.' The King reflected, and then added, 'On second thoughts, I wouldn't mind having my Joe Manton by my side. And in case of an emergency, only Mumtaz-the-eunuch or yourself will have access to the King.'

'I will see to it that the Prime Minister takes care of all urgent matters, Your Majesty.'

'Good. And see to it he doesn't sign in the King's name!'

The King and Khan-the-barber laughed, as if sharing a private joke, then Khan asked, 'When would the King like to move upstairs, Your Majesty?'

'Tomorrow. After the Friday prayers.'

'Your orders,' said Khan bowing, and he left the room.

The King took a long puff at his hukka, and sighed dreamily. 'Ah! The terrace chambers! That's the place for your echoes, Ann. That's where your passion will bathe my soul!'

The one person the King wished to meet before leaving for his one-week séjour in the terrace echo-chambers, was Majoon Mian. Short, stocky, guava-faced, deaf and dumb, Majoon Mian always wore a tiny silver bell around his neck. It was this bell, and its rhythmic ringing against his wind-pipe that was rumoured to give Majoon Mian his boundless mystic-alchemic powers. In fact, if the Kings and Nawabs of Awadh could manage to satisfy the appetite of the umpteen Begums in their harems, it was largely due to the speechless, silver-haired genius of this man, and the gift of endless love that he could bestow on his believers. But, ironically, despite his fame, none of the Kings of Awadh had ever conferred on Majoon Mian a title. 'Why so?' I once asked the King. 'He doesn't need one. His name itself is a title.' Literally translated, Majoon Mian meant Mr Aphrodisiac.

Majoon Mian arrived, trotting, as usual, to the sound of the silver bell. He greeted the King and sat down on the floor. The King, communicating effortlessly through a private sign-language, started explaining to the aphrodisiac wizard what he desired. Majoon Mian observed the King attentively,

85

nodding and bub-bub-bubbing and um-um-umming, till wit
a final snort, he seemed to declare that he had got the King
point. Majoon Mian picked up a piece of paper, and starte
calculating something on it. Then, getting up, he showed th
paper to the King which was, in all likelihood, his prescriptior
The paper was divided into two columns – one red, and th
other green. Between the two columns were marked Majoo
Mian's mathematical codes – $1/7 = 1$ $2/7 = 2$ $3/7 =$
$7/3/4$ $3/4 \times 2/1 \times 7 = 4$ $1/2$ 1 . . . 3. 'Good heavens! Th
is incomprehensible!' I exclaimed to the King. 'Don't worry. It
not meant for you,' the King said teasingly. 'I've been readin
this handwriting since I was fourteen.' The King's aphrodisia
expert then gave him one red and a set of seven green sachets
the mathematical calculations ostensibly explaining how to mi
the different-coloured sachets to obtain the best results. The Kin
motioned his hand to say that he had understood the prescriptio
and then gave Majoon Mian ten gold mohars. He bowed and left
Dangling the coloured sachets before my eyes, the King winked
'That'll keep me going through a whole week of English lessons
Come, let's have some champagne before savouring your echoes.

Since all the attendants had been ordered out of the palace
the King himself carried a bottle of champagne and two cryst2
glasses up to the terrace. The moon shone in the sky and a filn
of light fluttered on the waves of the Gomti river. On the fa
bank a group of Hindu devotees were celebrating a religiou
festival, floating a string of oil-lamps on the mildly quiverin
surface of the river. Watching hundreds of lamps twinkling i
the river like stars, the King remarked romantically, 'Look, th
whole world seems to be celebrating our love. May this wee
give Awadh the successor to its throne.'

It was beginning to get cold on the terrace when the Kin
poured himself his last glass of champagne and then, carefull
reading Majoon Mian's instructions, he mixed the ingredients c
the two sachets in exact proportions and swallowed them wit
his drink. We moved towards the echo chambers. Once inside
the King tested his new abode, whispering, 'Ann, Ann,' and
indeed, my name reverberated for a considerable length of time

he echo chambers appearing like a mirror of sounds. The King took me by my waist and looking drunkenly into my eyes said, 'The mixture is starting to work, Ann.'

Majoon Mian's aphrodisiac might have had an immediate effect on the King, but not without causing anxiety. The King's turgescence I noticed was quite unlike before, becoming stranger and stranger by the second. First it swelled up along the stem, becoming hard, like a crooked root. Then the stem started to droop, becoming more and more limp. But the top bud began to stiffen, until it looked like a bloated mushroom, oscillating nervously on a fragile stem. Slowly, the turgescence flattened out, appearing more symmetrical and human, but I observed to my utter astonishment that the King's manhood was now beginning to change colour. Its brown became darker and darker, then in a flash, it started paling, stabilising for a while at light orange. Then again, the colour changed — the orange deepened into red, red into scarlet. When the King's manhood had exhausted all the colours of the spectrum, and had assumed the mythological proportions of those in the Khajurao temples, I asked him with affection, 'Are you feeling alright, My Lord?' The King didn't answer. I asked again. He still didn't answer. Since he loved having his chest caressed, I tried to do that, but he shrugged me off and arose from bed.

He went and sat quietly in one corner of the room. Then, slowly, he sat up straight, crossing his legs like a musician, and began to hum. The soft humming broke into a full-throated rendering of his raga 'Ah! Ah!' his voice echoing hallucinatingly from the walls of the terrace chambers. Leaving the King to his familiar pranks, I decided to call it a day, and slipped under my muslin sheet.

Suddenly, I heard the King and a woman whispering to each other. Startled, I turned over to see what the King was up to — he was talking to himself, playing, alternatively, the roles of a man and a woman, caressing and fondling his own body. I was still trying to fathom how Majoon Mian's aphrodisiacs, instead of giving a greater sexual appetite, had transformed the King into a hermaphrodite, when the King cried out, 'Thirsty,

thirsty, the King is thirsty.' I offered to go and draw water from his personal well but the King declined, saying that this was the only thing in the world which he could not entrust to anyone, not even me. He picked up his bucket, and went pottering down the steps. Tired of his endless eccentricities, I fell asleep.

'Ann, Ann.' The King jostled me awake in the middle of the night. 'Ann, the moon has got stuck in the mango tree.'

'Which moon?' I asked sleepily.

'Moon, the moon. It's stuck in the mango tree.'

I sat up in bed. Wiping the sweat from the King's forehead, I asked, 'Are you feeling alright, My Lord?'

'Perfect. I am fine, but it's the moon that's unwell. It has fallen.'

'Fallen? From where?'

'From the sky. And it's stuck in the mango tree.'

'You must have seen a shooting star, My Lord.'

'You're not trying to teach the planetary system to an astronomer, are you?' the King rebuked. 'I saw it with my own eyes.'

'What?'

'The moon falling.'

'How?'

'I had gone down to draw water from the well. I was sitting and drinking water on the steps, when I looked up at the moon. Just then, it dropped like an apple from the sky, and got stuck in the mango tree. It's there, right there, perched between the two top branches.' The King became thoughtful and then said, 'It's a bad omen, I think.'

I caressed the King, trying to calm down his excited imagination. His manhood, I noticed, was now a leaden aubergine blue. The moment I touched him, he shrieked. 'Leave me alone. I think it's a bad omen.'

'What, My Lord?'

'The moon falling.' Then turning his head jerkily, he asked. 'Did you hear that?'

'What?'

The King rushed to pick up his Joe Manton, and loading it with the swiftness of a hunter, he charged down the steps towards the garden. I took the oil torch and followed him. Scared of becoming the object of his wild imagination, I decided to stop short of the garden, and look out from the banquet-hall window. Under the sprawling radiance of the full moon, I saw the King crawling, worming his way through to the mango tree. Then taking an aim at something, he fired once, twice, three times, and shouted, 'Hurrah! Hurrah! Got you.' Fearing that the King might harm himself, I rushed out into the garden:

'What happened, My Lord?'

'Nothing! I finished him!' he bragged. 'You see. There was this man hiding behind the cliff on the moon. He was trying to kill me. Huh! So I pulled out my Joe Manton and finished him. Huh!'

The King took me by my hand and walked up to the mango tree. Pointing to the bullet-ridden body of a moon-yellow grapefruit which had branched out into a mango tree, he said, 'See that man there, lying dead on the moon. I've finished them both – him and the moon. Too bad for the universe and the lunar festivals of this earth. Come, let's go up.'

It was still dark and the King's delirious imagination had finally given way to slumber, when Mumtaz-the-eunuch called out from the banquet hall below, 'Begum Sahiba, Begum Sahiba.' Alarmed by his untimely visit, I enquired, 'What is it, Mumtaz?' Holding a torch in his hand, he motioned with his hand, calling me downstairs. When I reached the hall, I was surprised to find Khan-the-barber waiting for me in the side room. Seeing me walk towards him, he came up to me:

'I have a message for the King from the Resident.'

'But this is no time for the Resident to send messengers to the palace.'

'It's an emergency. The Resident came personally to the Prime Minister's palace to convey the message.'

'What is it?'

'Some of the Governor-General's men have been lynched by a mob.'

89

'So what does the King have to do with some Englishmen killed in Calcutta.'

'It wasn't in Calcutta, Madam. He was touring the famine-stricken areas of our state. In a village, his party was attacked by a mob.'

'So what does he want now?'

'General John Melon, the Commander-in-Chief, has been despatched with a message from the Governor-General. He is expected any time in the afternoon.'

'Today?'

'Yes, this afternoon. That's why I am bringing this news to the King's notice immediately.'

'Very thoughtful of you, Khan Sahib,' I said, sensing the urgency of the matter. 'But the King is fast asleep.'

'I think we should start preparing for the General's reception,' suggested Khan.

'I agree.'

I asked Mumtaz to send immediately for Majoon Mian, and went up to inform the King. Sleep, I saw, had had no effect on the King's turgescence which was still aubergine-blue, and of the same size. 'My Lord, My Lord,' I whispered, touching him gently on his cheek. The King awoke with a start, and sat up in the bed.

'What is it?' he asked, irritated.

'How are you feeling now?'

'Better.' He sounded in better control of his senses. 'Why are you up so early?'

'There's an urgent message from the Resident.'

'What?'

'Some members of the Governor-General's party have been lynched by a famished mob.'

'Huh! Idiot!' the King blurted out. 'Who on earth asked him to go before hungry people!'

'A General carrying his message is expected in Lucknow this afternoon.'

'Today?'

'Yes, in a few hours.'

'Too bad for the Governor-General then! I can't meet his messenger.'

'He might consider this a sign of disrespect to his authority, My Lord.'

'Can't help it,' asserted the King. Then pointing to his turgescence, he added, 'What could be more disrespectful than receiving the Governor-General's messenger in such a state! I won't even be able to get into a pair of pantaloons. No. I can't see him.'

The King pondered for a while, as though sensing the dilemma before him and then, getting up, he walked slowly towards his water bucket. He splashed some water on his face, and blinked his eyes. Then, in a flash, he plunged his head into the water bucket, and lifting it with his head, tipped it over his body. 'That's better,' he remarked, drenched and shivering. 'Now I am clearer. Send Khan immediately to the Resident to say that the King of Awadh cannot receive the General because the astrologer doesn't consider it an auspicious day for royal hearings.' After some reflection, he said again, 'But just in case we have to meet the wretched General, send for Majoon Mian.'

The deaf and dumb Majoon Mian arrived at the crack of dawn like a physician summoned in emergency. Learning about the King's abnormal turgescence and nocturnal behaviour, he was puzzled and asked for the prescription and the sachets he had given. Barely had he felt the sachets when, rounding his eyes in horror, he immediately scribbled on a piece of paper: 'Good Heavens! His Majesty has mixed up the red and the green sachets. Instead of adding a pinch of the red to the green, His Majesty has added the green to the red! My God!' Since the sign-language between the King and his aphrodisiac wizard was clearly not enough to conduct a sensitive conversation, the King wrote back: 'So what does that mean?' Majoon Mian wrote again: 'His Majesty has taken a week's dose at one go.' The King motioned his hand angrily, writing again: 'So what does that imply? What can be done to set it right?' Majoon Mian reflected, and then inscribed in big bold letters: 'Sixteen hot and cold baths in quick succession should be able to subside it by sunrise the day after tomorrow.' When it was explained to Majoon Mian that His Majesty had to receive a General in a few hours, he belched repeatedly, and wrote: 'Then there is only one remedy. Honey, mixed with tamarind and geroo, should be poured over it to cool down the swelling.' Majoon Mian opened his cloth bag and pulling out a bottle of herb and honey mixture called Shehdechandani, scrawled unsurely: 'Normally, my prescription gives the best results when a honey bath is given under moonlight. But I imagine His Majesty has to attend to urgent work before the moon is out tonight.' The King nodded. Majoon Mian added: 'In that case, let's try it without moonlight.' After some more reflection, the aphrodisiac genius considered it wise to caution the King: 'But there's one problem with this remedy. Honey and tamarind can bring the physical swelling down, but they cannot cool the mind. So in some cases, His Majesty might still feel a sporadic, uncontrollable sexual urge.' The King waved his hand to say he could handle that.

Majoon Mian left, and Khan-the-barber returned from the Resident's Court to announce that tempers in the English camp were indeed high and that the Resident was not willing to accept any pretext to postpone the General's visit. 'Did you tell them that the King couldn't go against his astrologer's advice?' asked the King, hiding his turgid manhood behind an outsize baggy gown. 'I did, Your Majesty,' replied Khan 'but the Resident laughed it off, saying that affairs of state in this century are run by administrators, not their astrologers.' Khan had, however, of his own accord, managed to have the official discussions put down for after dinner, which meant that the King and his staff would now have some extra time to calm down the overheated English minds. Asking Khan to start preparations for the General's visit, the King whispered to me, 'I think the Governor-General is up to mischief again. He hasn't forgotten Mrs Rackets.'

The present Governor-General's anger might have been precipitated by the murderous attack on his party. Its real cause though, was something else, something more private and less known. It had to do with Mordaunt Rackets, the previous

Resident of Lucknow, now dismissed from his services.

Mordaunt Rackets, whose turnip-bald head was crowned by one of Khan-the-barber's wigs, had left the capital of Awadh amid high drama, in which there were four dramatis personae — the Rackets, the King, and the Governor-General. The Rackets seem to have been an extremely happy and family-minded, if practical, couple. After a few months' stay in Lucknow, the lady told her husband that she did not fancy his bald charms any more. The Resident accepted his fate with the resignation of a cold rationalist devoting himself now to his office, while Mrs Rackets moved about freely, in search of appetising young men of culture, until one day she found a willing suitor in King Nasiruddin Haider. She was obviously quite impressed with the harvest of her own charm, but her husband was so thrilled at the idea of the King sharing his spouse's bed, that he began to water the plant of his wife's adultery. By and by, Mrs Rackets started spending nights with the King, returning home each morning with bagfuls of rubies, emeralds, sapphires and gold. While Mrs Rackets dedicated herself to her task with the zeal of an overworked breadwinner, her husband, apparently less scrupulous in his confessions than his wife, was busy charming the saris off the Hindu maids in the kitchen. The showdown for the Rackets came on the day a pregnant maid and her husband arrived at their home, and threatened the Resident with murder. The news of the deeds and misdeeds of Mr and Mrs Rackets reached Calcutta. The Governor-General threw a fit of anger. What infuriated him though, was not the Resident's unworthy demeanour towards his personal maids, but the association between Mrs Rackets, one of his own ex-mistresses and confidantes, and the King. The Resident and his wife were both immediately summoned to Calcutta. Mrs Rackets, who by now had a fortune of £75,000 in her pocket, pleaded before the King, 'The Governor-General is after my blood, Your Majesty. Help me and my husband flee to England.' The King answered with an English proverb he had recently learned: 'A friend in need is a friend indeed.' His men promptly whisked the Rackets off to

Pondicherry, putting them on a boat to Marseilles. The Rackets disappeared, but the Governor-General sat in Calcutta, licking his wounds, and swore to take his revenge on the King.

The first step towards this revenge was the posting of Mr U.F.O. Dow, one of the Governor-General's trusted lieutenants, as the new Resident of Lucknow. Sent on the express mission of catching King Nasiruddin Haider on the wrong foot, the Resident's temperament was ideally suited to the task. Unlike his fun-loving predecessor, Dow loved to remain within the bounds of his Residence; he seldom spoke, and when he did, it was always business. The most remarkable aspect of the middle-aged Resident though, was his enormous, broad-jawed, army-bootlike face, which didn't have a chin to it. U.F.O., as the Resident was popularly called, concealed his chinlessness with a long, conical French beard, but since there was no firm base to support it, the beard was constantly changing shape, depending on which way the wind blew. The changing outlines of his beard gave his countenance as many different shapes, thus lending the new Resident an eerie and perpetually shifty look, a physiognomical quality that well matched his espionage mission.

The Resident arrived that evening for dinner, accompanied by General John Melon and their respective spouses. The King discovered to his dismay that the Resident's nightmarish facial mutations found a perfect complement in the General's funereal laughter and his particularly cutting, squint-eyed gaze. Mauled by the previous night's overdose, the King was at the beginning a little shaky but, thanks to Majoon Mian's honey treatment, he soon recovered his nerve, and became his old frolicsome self. He showed his guests round the palace before bringing them into the dining room. Dinner started. The General was the first to make a tongue in cheek remark.

'What a fabulous treat, Your Majesty!' he commented on the vast variety of delicacies on the table. 'I only wish the poor peasants of Awadh could eat as well.'

'What a noble thought, General Melon!' said the King, adding in a more stoic vein, 'But if you read history closely, you'll notice that a poor man can never eat what he feeds the nobility. It would be interesting to know if the King of England eats a Welsh coalminer's stew.'

The General, discerning the King's subtle remark, cleared his throat and stepped up his offensive. 'I am told that in the last year's famine over 50,000 peasants died in Awadh.'

'So I hear,' said the King, maintaining his stoic posture. 'Questions of life and death, General Melon, are decided by the Almighty. What can a poor King do when God himself has summoned someone to heaven?'

'But a King can help his subjects, Your Majesty.'

'He can but try. For instance, has the British administration in Bengal been able to help the poor man? I am told five lakh peasants died in the Bengal famine. Ten times more than in Awadh!'

'So, in your opinion, Your Majesty, a King can do nothing for his subjects.'

'He can only try.'

'You will be pleased to know, Your Majesty, that to help the poor the King of England has enacted new Corn Laws.'

'Con laws? What are con laws?'

'It's to decrease the burden on . . . '

'Yes, yes,' interrupted the King. 'But we have enough time to discuss such things in the meeting later. Let us not bore the gracious ladies with these dos and don'ts of state administration. Surely there are other subjects of conversation to deepen the bond of friendship between the Indians and the British.'

The General's better half welcomed the King's comment with an enthusiastic smile. It was then that the King asked, provocatively:

'Tell me, General, what do you know about aphrodisiacs? Do you have them in Europe?'

The General's widening squint was still trying to cope with what his prudish ears had just heard, when his wife replied with a chuckle:

'I have read about them in my Greek studies course at Oxford.'

'Marvellous!' exclaimed the King, his eyes scintillating with curiosity. 'Would Lady Melon be kind enough to enlighten us on this subject?'

Lady Melon promptly put her fork and knife on her plate and said in an excited, yet scholarly, manner, 'The word aphrodisiac comes from Aphrodite, the Greek Goddess of love and beauty. Euripedes, the Greek thinker, said of Aphrodite — I can quote for you, Your Majesty — "the Goddess represents human passion, overwhelming in intensity and destructiveness, and yet it is also she who from the streams of Cephissus blows fragrant breezes over Attica, and who sends the loves that are seated by the throne of wisdom."'

'How poetic indeed!' The King cheered, pouring her some more Bordeaux. 'What an ode to the Goddess of beauty!'

'And you know what Aeschylus said of her, Your Majesty?' said Lady Melon, suddenly roused to share a common interest with the King, reeling off the rest of her Greek literature lesson. 'He said Aphrodite was the part cause of love between heaven and earth, the universal power of procreation.'

'Of recreation! How profound!'

'No, of procreation, Your Majesty — the universal power of procreation. But the finest description is in a poem of Lucretius, Your Majesty. He calls her the sole ruler of the world without whom nothing can win to the shores of light, or of joy.'

'Oh! Delightful! What a learned lady of letters you are, Lady Melon!'

The General's wife was about to break off into another quotation when the General intervened, authoritatively: 'The Governor-General was not pleased about the Rackets affair, Your Majesty.'

'Which Rackets?'

'Mordaunt Rackets — our previous Resident.'

'Oh! What a charming wife he had! Why did the Governor-General have to dismiss him? I had such a good friend in his wife. But we'll talk about that later.' The King again turned to Lady Melon and said:

'Now that I know your taste in poetry and arts, permit me

to ask you, lady, do you think an Indian woman can produce the same sound as an English one?'

'Why not?' answered Lady Melon with a polite smile. 'The sound of laughter, Your Majesty, is as pleasing anywhere on this planet. To distort Shakespeare – laughter by any other name would ring as sweet!'

'Laughter perhaps, yes,' the King said, contemplating. 'But not love's sighs.'

'I beg your pardon, Your Majesty,' muttered Lady Melon unsurely, leaning towards the King.

'Love's sighs I said,' the King repeated aloud in her ear. 'You know what I mean – what the Greeks call a female orgasmos.'

The General gaped at the King, flabbergasted, his squint resembling a pair of open hedge-clippers. 'Come on, join in, General, don't tell me you haven't thought about such elementary questions of human philosophy,' remarked the King and then, turning towards Lady Melon again, he urged, 'You must obviously have something to add to this subject. Come, let us hear more of your radiant Greek mind.'

Lady Melon, whose effervescent chuckling and academic exuberance had suddenly sunk into her flushed cheeks, answered the King's persistence with a spraying apologetic sneeze, 'Forgi, forgiv, forgive me, Your Maj . . .'

'Take your time, take your time, Lady Melon,' said the King comfortingly. 'Answers to such questions are not easy.' When the General's wife had let off the last of her seven consecutive sneezes, the King whispered to her, in a spirit of scholarly complicity, 'But don't you think the sound of an English lady's passion is magical? So spellbinding! So matchless! I just can't find words to describe it. With your permission, Lady Melon, I would like you to hear what might be called an ode to Aphrodite . . .'

The King shut his eyes, took Lady Melon's hand in his, and burst into a vocal rendering of his raga 'Ah! Ah!', reproducing the entire galaxy of sounds of a female passion. The virtuosity of his recital was reaching its climax when the General, getting up in a fury, snatched back his wife's hand and commanded,

'English delegation — leave.' Parting, the General half-turned towards the King, and threatened, 'Your Majesty will pay for this misdemeanour.' The King continued singing, raising his hand to say goodbye.

SEVEN

NOTHING

has ever intrigued me more than the coincidence by which
people come to meet each other in life. For years, two human
beings lead independent non-convergent lives, like tracks on the
opposite hills of a valley. Then something happens, they come
face to face. They hold each other's hands, become one pair of
lips, one pair of eyes: their lives get completely transformed, as
though they were reborn in the same life. What makes these
unions happen? What geometry of circumstance brings these
lines to meet at a point where time freezes, where love is born,
as is light? Is there an inner logic behind these encounters? Does
one make them happen? Or, is it destiny which decides one fine
day to write love on walls where suicides were written before,
which makes wild beautiful meadows dance on landscapes that
have never seen a bird? Freud attributed this coincidence to an
unconscious necessity; the surrealists called it objective chance.
But, to me, it is magic, pure magic. The same by which a lens
chooses two beams from an entire sea of sunlight, and makes
them meet at a point where paper turns to ash.

This magical coincidence which brings human beings together has forever puzzled me. I have often told myself to let magic be
magic, and drop the ugly habit of looking for reason in things
of mystical order but, again, how can I forget that each of the
four seminal encounters of my life have been nothing but a stark
proof of this magic? The first boy I met, Marco, in the middle of

the May '68 fever, was actually a passer-by who had, by chance, offered me shelter from rain under his umbrella. Then Costa – I met him just as strangely, he had come to return my passport he had found lying on a road called rue des Milles Rencontres. Alain came into my life next. I met him at the Roissy airport, literally between two flights: he had come to pick up a parcel I was carrying from his mother in New York. And now Awaara – someone I had actually seen in a dream before we met! I can but lie back on the waves of the Mediterranean, and marvel at this magic that makes life, life and love, love . . .

Awaara arrived in Lucknow, as Rani had promised me on the phone in Bombay. I don't know what pressures she applied to whom, but it was quite amazing to witness the jittery promptness with which Awaara had been reinstated in the unit. More amazing though, was the conspiratorial discretion with which the entire operation had been carried out. When Awaara arrived at the hotel in Lucknow one evening, it was obvious from Deboo's behaviour, sitting beside me at the dining table, that he didn't have a clue why his producer had suddenly decided to reinclude Awaara. Seeing Awaara enter the room, Deboo croaked in my ear, 'Here comes the rascal from Bombay!' Awaara walked up to us, first greeted the producer, then Deboo who pretended not to have heard him. I got up to shake hands with him. The sweaty warmth in his hand and the wicked smile on his face betrayed that he knew the story behind his return. The moment he left us, Deboo put on his big-brotherly posture, 'Now don't you mix up with these petty fellows on the set again, Val. You know what it can lead to.' I responded with an ambiguous silence and when he repeated his warning, fishing for an answer, I commented calmly, 'Press articles will come and go, Deboo. I can't change my life for the fear of some stupid article, can I?' 'I agree. I agree,' he concurred, fumblingly. 'True. Press shouldn't be allowed to govern our lives. But what I was meaning was that it pays to be careful.' 'Frankly, I couldn't give a damn,' I retorted, a shade aggressively. 'I've decided to live life as it comes. Be natural and accept my lot with a stoic smile.'

'I agree. I agree,' agreed Deboo disagreeingly, then pretending to relish the Mughlai cuisine of Lucknow.

Deboo obviously didn't yet realise that the *Starlust* article he had master-minded, had only ended up back-firing on him, bringing Awaara and me closer together. In a way, the slanderous story in the press was even a blessing in disguise, another *coup de hasard*. Besides showing Deboo as the 'bad man' in the story, it gave Awaara and me our first adventure, an event to share, and something by which we could measure each other's human quality. The press incident I noticed also had another positive effect on Awaara, it made him bolder, more natural. Since his arrival from Bombay, he was no longer his old, hesitant self. He behaved more freely, sharing not just poetry, but even jokes and personal remarks with an air of casual abandon.

Deboo discovered our growing friendship one evening on the set when I asked Awaara to help me out with an insect that had flown into my eye. Seeing Awaara lean over my face in a way that forced our bodies to touch, Deboo bantered, 'That's a rather intimate way of removing mosquitoes, Awaara.' His real reaction to this incident became clearer at the unit meeting. He made a surprise announcement that Awaara was to be sent out on a special mission to Chunar, a nearby town on the banks of the Ganges, where an important scene had to be shot later. As director, Deboo was not obliged to give explanations for assigning an outstation job to Awaara, but his guilt made him say to me sheepishly, 'Sorry for stealing your assistant, Val. He's the best man we have for the Chunar shots. And don't worry about your dialogues. I'll lend you a hand.'

Awaara left for Chunar. But as luck would have it, the unit's generator broke down on the heels of his departure and the shooting was called off for three days. I promptly went up to Deboo and said, 'I hear Benares is just a few hours' run from here, Deboo.' 'Why?' he asked, frowning, 'You're not planning a pilgrimage to the holy city.' 'Why not?' I replied, laughing. 'I now have a couple of days free, I'd like to make the best of them. Do you mind?' He consulted his schedule. 'Well, I suppose you can go. So long as you don't join one of those hippies who've turned Benares into their second home.' I packed my bags and hopped into my car. The chauffeur turned towards me, 'Benares, Madam?' 'No,' I answered, 'Chunar,' giving him Awaara's address – PWD Inspection Bungalow, Chunar Fort.

It was dusty and overcast, quite unlike the usual glassy transparence I had come to associate with the Lucknow weather. Strong drafts of wind made the roadside eucalyptus and mango trees flap and flutter, strewing thousands of golden and green leaves on our path. At times, the wind pushed the branches so low over the road that they came dangerously close to touching the passengers sitting on the bus-tops. The storm subsided after a while, and it began to rain, making driving difficult and slightly risky on a narrow country road. Slightly alarmed at seeing everyone drive in the middle of the road, often missing each other by a hairline, I asked the chauffeur:

'How far is Chunar from here?'

'Very far.'

'How many kilometres, do you think?'

'Kilometres!' he said, laughing bumpily. 'We still count in miles here.'

'So how many miles would it be then?'

'Many miles,' he replied, reflectingly. 'Many, many miles.'

The chauffeur turned more philosophical, adding, 'But aren't distances so deceptive in life, Madam? What matters really is time.'

Paying homage to his philosophical sense, I then asked, 'How many hours would it take to Chunar then?'

'Difficult question – two, three, four, five, six, seven, maybe a whole day. One can't really predict such things in life.'

Finding his answers a little evasive, I probed him further: 'Why is that? You fear that our car might break down, is that it?'

'No, no, no, my car is in perfect shape. It depends on a bridge break-down, Madam,' said the chauffeur, looking at the dark clouds. 'There is a plank bridge on a river on the way, you see. When it rains, it just starts floating on water like a lotus flower. So questions of distance and time then really become absurd and meaningless. That's why, as a principle in life I never like to commit myself in terms of distance and time. But tell me, Madam, you don't suffer from asthma, I hope?'

'No,' I replied, puzzled by his awkward question. 'But why do you ask me that?'

'Because I do, Madam,' uttered the chauffeur, over the distinctly audible sound of wheezing. 'Chunar is a bad town, Madam.'

'Bad? But I was told that it is a very pretty town on the banks of the Ganges.'

'No!' he protested aloud. 'Very bad town. Very bogus town for asthmatics, Madam. It almost killed me one night.'

His unusually vociferous protest against Chunar, accompanied by a peculiar polyphonic fit of contemptuous laughter, turned his wheezing into a full-scale attack of asthma, and he began gasping for breath. Anxious, I asked:

'Do you have any medicine for it?'

'I hate doctors,' he snapped. 'Nothing like a natural cure. But don't worry, Madam. I know how to set it right.'

The chauffeur then proceeded to produce an assortment of indecipherable sounds. He grunted, neighed, purred, snorted, hiccuped, gargled drily, thumped his chest, patted his back, blew his nose, poked his ears, and then firing one final belch that shrieked across the windscreen like a shooting-star, he proclaimed, 'That's better, much better.'

He took a long breath in to test if his therapy had produced the desired effect. Finding his breathing still not up to the mark, he added, 'It's better, but not completely normal. It will pass. I shouldn't think about it. Do you mind if I put some music on, Madam? It'll help me not to think about my asthma.'

The chauffeur fiddled around with a few wires in the glove compartment and a crackling voice burst forth from a dust-laden box which resembled more a plumber's tool box than a tape-recorder. Slowly, the song began to make more sense, and I figured out that it was a woman singing without any musical accompaniment. Just as I was suspecting that it sounded more like a recording of a woman singing under the shower, the chauffeur giggled, 'My wife, my wife, that's my wife singing in the bathroom. Now listen to the next one.' The female voice gave way to an infant's and the speakers began to screech under the strain of a particularly high-pitched voice, 'Ca-ca, coo-coo, pa-pa, ma-ma, pi-pi, ma-ta, pi-ta, ra-ma, pa-pa, ma-ma, phoo-phee, pa-ppu, kutta, billi, jai-ma-ta.' The chauffeur turned on the volume, as though to listen to his favourite bit, and then burst out applauding. 'Good show! Good show! Wonderful boy!' Then looking at me through the rear-view mirror, 'My son! My son! That's my son learning to speak, Madam. I always carry his recording on outstation trips.'

The chauffeur's asthma might have found an ideal distraction in his child's experiments with human speech, but for me it had become a source of near claustrophobia when I picked up my script to find myself an antidote to the tape-recorder. In the appendix to the script, I came across some interesting information on the shooting locations that I had been looking for. The section on Chunar described it as a small quarry town near Lucknow. The magnificent palaces, forts and mansions of Lucknow and Benares, it said, were built with the red stone from the Chunar quarries. The town was also supposed to have a famous old fort on the banks of the Ganges. A hand-written note at the end of the script said: 'PS: The Chunar fort is an ideal location for the "balloon scene". Permission will have to be obtained from the government since the fort is now a Police encampment', which was, I learnt later, the pretext on which Deboo had packed Awaara off from Lucknow.

By the time I finished reading the script, I noticed to my horror that the infant's voice had not only managed to sedate his father's bronchii, but also his mind. His hands on the steering, the chauffeur was sound asleep, his elliptical snoring punctuating the monotonous gurgle of the engine. 'Ram, Ram,' I cried out, shaking him nervously.

'We're reaching, we're reaching Chunar, Madam,' he answered reassuringly, giving proof of rare Khan-the-barberlike clairvoyance. Blinking himself fully awake, he added, 'There, you can see the Chunar fort on the horizon.'

The brownish red fort in the distance was perched on the summit of a hillock along whose slopes grew wild green grass. It looked magnificent. For a moment, it didn't resemble a fort at all — more like an enormous, ruby-studded band that the beautiful hill wore as a crown. What was indeed so striking about the Chunar fort was that, unlike so many other works of architecture, its beauty didn't wane on coming closer. It increased all the more. Its umbrella-like Muslim chakris, its spacious colonial verandahs and a white Hindu temple hanging by its northern cliff, exuded history through each crack on their surface, blending epochs of history as easily as a Persian tapestry does colours.

We turned into the fort, driving up a narrow weatherworn track, and reached the bungalow situated on top of a cliff. The chauffeur got out and made enquiries about Awaara's room. A youngish-looking man, the caretaker I presumed, fussily cross-questioned the chauffeur a couple of times, but when he caught a glimpse of me, his eyes lit up, 'Ah! Shooting! Madam has come for the film shooting!'

He promptly ushered me to Awaara's apartment. I knocked at the half-open door. 'Come in,' roared Awaara, with the authority of a Nasiruddin Haider. I walked in and saw him, his back to the door, reading André Breton's *Nadja* on his bed. Oblivious, he continued reading.

'Aha! Relishing the unpredictable charms of Nadja, are you?' I said. 'I thought you were meant to be working in Chunar.' Startled, Awaara leapt off the bed.

'Good gracious! What are you doing here?'

'How could I let you savour the charm of this fabulous fort all alone, Awaara?' I said, drawing a chair.

'Well, the fort is not so bad, but have you seen the Ganges?' Awaara slipped a sweat shirt on, and led me up the stairwell. 'Quick, quick, you have to see this.'

As I looked down from the hill, I was spellbound by the sight before me — it was like a glimpse of paradise. Glasslike, silken, twinkling, wallowing somnambulistically, as though afloat on a dream, slipping coquettishly past the demented geometry of her cliffs, the Ganges in real life appeared far more beautiful than the million odes sung in her praise. It wasn't just the physical beauty of the view that created the stunning effect: it was its purity, its foetal-being, its healing glow. Awaara and I stood on the terrace, speechless, contemplating the vast blue expanse of water, the wheeling birds overhead, the dance of the dolphins, the wind that whistled above the chanting of funeral dirges. 'Hey, look!' exclaimed Awaara, pointing to a floating island on which sat huddled hundreds of cranes. Just as we were looking at them, a boatman passed by the island, accidently slapping his oar on the water, and the birds flew off up into the air — all together, like a burst of laughter, leaving behind a naked, breastlike piece of earth surrounded by rings of emerald water. 'Shall we go down to the river?' I suggested. Awaara picked up the book he was reading, and led me down a steep serpentine hill-track.

The sun was setting, spreading an orangish veil over the Ganges. The cacophony of the homebound birds was building up to a crescendo, and after a holy dip, the pilgrims were getting ready to leave. We walked along the bank, until we reached a cliff that jutted out into the river, blocking our path. We waded our way across the water to the other side. The sun was now behind us, the Ganges looked bluer, more nightly, and deserted — there was not a soul in sight. We had been walking some while when we noticed two men sitting around a camp fire, preparing dinner. A little further away, a young man sat by an anchored boat, holding a book close to his eyes, ostensibly trying to read in the fading light. Hearing our footsteps, he looked up and smiled at us. We exchanged a few words, and he invited us to join him. We learnt that Nishant, the young man, was an Indian from Paris, rowing his way down the river. Intrigued by his lonesome journey, Awaara asked him:

'How long have you been on the river?'

'Three months.'

'And how much longer will it take you to reach the sea?'

'Can't say. Another three months perhaps.'

'May I ask if there is a special reason behind this journey?' enquired Awaara, a shade indiscreetly.

'Must there always be a reason to everything in life?' Nishant reflected, chewing a matchstick.

Awaara laughed, as though embarrassed by his own question. 'Oh! The wretched rationality that looks for meaning in voids!'

Nishant offered us a drink, and we hopped across to his boat. He took out a bottle of gin from a cloth bag. Rinsing the glasses in the river water, he looked up at me, saying perkily, 'Well, I'm not quite sure, Madam, if the holy waters of the Ganges will take very kindly to your alien constitution. So I'm afraid you might have to have it neat.'

'Well, to think of it,' I retorted, 'some gin and Indian tonic water from the holy river might even do my soul some good.' He topped the glasses up to the brim. I picked up my glass, but when Awaara stretched forward to pick up his, he was pleasantly surprised to notice a book on the bottom of the boat:

'Ah! What a coincidence! You too are reading *Nadja*.'

'Why?' asked Nishant, suddenly distracted. 'Are you reading it too?'

Awaara pulled out his copy of *Nadja* from his pocket, and handed it to Nishant. 'That's some coincidence. You too are reading *Nadja*! Incredible.'

'Yes. Quite *Nadja*like,' commented Nishant lazily, looking more and more distracted. 'Anyway, what do you think of the book?'

'Marvellous. An ode to coincidence in life.' Awaara then asked:

'Do you think Nadja really existed? Or was she a creation of Breton's imagination?'

'She existed. Of course she did,' Nishant asserted.

'But there's nothing to prove she did.'

'Well, I know that she did,' Nishant reaffirmed irritatedly, as though resenting Awaara's scepticism. Then he laughed jeeringly. 'Proof, proof, yes, if the empiricist world wants proofs, my eyes are the proof of her existence.'

Nishant's laughter, which had an eerie edge to it, doused the discussion on Nadja, and a heavy silence descended on us, punctuated by the chinking of gin glasses and the rhythmic lapping of waves against the boat. Gulping his drink down in one shot, Nishant turned to Awaara:

'Didn't you want to know why I am going down the Ganges?'

'Yes.'

'Would you believe me if I said it is because of Nadja?'

'Because of Nadja? What do you mean?'

'Because I met a woman who was half-Nadja,' Nishant said mysteriously.

'Half-Nadja?' mumbled Awaara.

'Yes. I met a woman called Jaya who was half-herself and half-Nadja.'

'A reincarnation? Did you meet her on the Ganges?'

'No, in Paris. For just one night.'

'How was she half-Nadja?'

'Because she lived two lives – her own and that of Nadja. And she switched from one to the other by changing the hand on which she wore a copper ring. If she wore it on her left hand, she behaved and talked like Nadja. If she wore it on the other, like Jaya.'

'Is this woman still alive?' asked Awaara.

'Can't say. As I said, I knew her for just one night. At dawn she disappeared, as mysteriously as Nadja, without leaving a trace. She was beautiful. My journey down the Ganges is in homage of that meeting.'

The meeting with Nishant seemed to have raked the fire of our own madness. As Awaara and I started slowly trudging back to the bungalow, words dissolved, and a silence enveloped us – a peculiar silence, full of meanings and unwritten poems, like that of a pregnant mother listening to her own womb. Birds chirped in the nests, water lapped on the shore and yet, nothing seemed to perturb the ethereal song of silence within us. From the gait of staggering feet and twilight glances, I could make out that the sun was once again rising over the planet of unknown desires. Half-way through our climb up the hill, I asked for

Awaara's hand. It was moist as my own, secreting desire. He looked at me, and I at him, he looked again, and I again – we were caught in a whirlpool of glances.

Back at the bungalow, Awaara opened a bottle of whisky. We drank many a wordless peg, watching smoke embrace candlelight, hearing the sound of our own crumbling defences. Then Awaara asked, 'Do you like graveyards?' 'Graveyards!' I said. 'Who doesn't like graveyards, Awaara? – those mirages the dead leave behind for the living. To tell you the truth, I am looking for a grave in . . . '

'Then come with me,' said Awaara excitedly, cutting me short. 'Come. I'll show you the grave you're looking for.'

Moonlight paved the way, the sky was strewn with stars. Coming out through the wicket gate at the back of the fort, we took a narrow jungle path that led into a mango orchard. As we entered the orchard, night seemed darker, making it difficult to avoid running into the spiky bushes bordering the path. From the distancing sound of the Ganges it seemed we were moving further and further away from the river. In the nearby fields, frogs croaked and dogs barked. The path ended with the orchard. We jumped over the barbed-wire fencing. Now two new paths appeared, leading in different directions. Awaara stood puzzled before them for a moment, debating which of the two would lead to the promised land of the dead. He lit a match and when that didn't help, he turned left, as though following the glow of his instincts. The path ended before an oval gate. Pushing it open, Awaara said, 'Come, let me show the most beautiful graveyard of this world.'

We sat down on a stone platform. There was an abandoned air about the graveyard, and the first thing that struck me about it was that there were no smells. For a while, I tried to figure out what Awaara had meant by calling it the most beautiful graveyard he had seen, and when I found nothing extraordinary about it, I remarked:

'It's beautiful, but like many others.'

'No,' countered Awaara, a little drunkenly. 'No, it's unique. And do you know why?'

'Because of its broken crosses?'

'No. Another guess.'

'Its epitaphs.'

'No.'

'Its history.'

'No.'

'What else then?'

'Two things — a mysterious grave, and its blond flames.'

'Blond flames? What kind of blond flames?' I asked.

'You'll see.' Awaara disappeared behind sheets of darkness. I began to suspect he had had a little too much to drink.

He struck a match and placed it gently at the bottom of a tall dry plant. The fire caught on slowly, its feeble flames hopping from one stalk to another. As the flames reached the centre, the fire started hissing and crackling. Within seconds, it erupted, setting the whole plant on fire. Tongues of flame leapt out towards the sky, dancing bacchicly in the wind. For a moment, Awaara stood dazzled before the glow and then, in a flash, he picked up a burning stalk and set fire to the next plant. As that caught fire, blowing waves of colour on the moss-grown graves, Awaara set fire to another, then to another, yet another, until the whole graveyard looked ablaze, washed in crimson light, enveloped by fluttering flames on all sides. I was still sitting, watching blotches of light dance on Awaara's face when he called me with an urgent motion of his hand and pointed to a grave on which the epitaph read:

Ann Walters
1811–1859

Born at night
Extinguished at night
I leave to rejoin the night of times

It was an astonishingly neglected tomb. It resembled more a debris of stones and sand than the tomb of the first lady of a

Kingdom. The top part of it, made of ordinary stones, was in ruins. The edges of the base platform had so badly crumbled that ants had found in it a home. Had it not been in a graveyard, it might have been difficult to identify Miss Walters' tomb as a tomb at all. Recalling suddenly that Miss Walters had spent her last days in Lucknow, I asked Awaara:

'But how is it that she was buried here in Chunar, Awaara?'

'That's precisely the mystery.'

'What? That she was buried in Chunar?'

'No, that she has two graves. One in Lucknow, and another here. Nobody knows how or why. That's why I called it a mysterious grave.'

'Are you sure this one doesn't belong to another Ann Walters?'

'They have the same dates, same tombstones, same epitaphs,' said Awaara. 'She had a sad end, you know. It seems her mother wasn't too pleased with the idea of her being buried in the royal cemetery. So they exhumed her and reburied her here. But this is not a proven theory. One among many others.'

'Sad all the same,' I remarked. 'Reading her autobiography one would never imagine such an end.'

'Yes, but as Mark Twain said, wrinkles are there where smiles have been.'

There was something very touching about Miss Walters' tomb. Its blackish stones and weeping moss gave the impression of an unhappy life. I lit a match and reread her epitaph aloud to myself. Awaara must have noticed some emotion in my voice for he put his arm around my shoulder and said consolingly:

'An actress shouldn't get too involved with her role.' Pulling me away from the grave, he added distractedly, 'So you see, I was right to bring you to the grave you were looking for.'

'Oh no!' I hastened to correct Awaara. 'You mean the grave I spoke of before? No, no. I wasn't meaning this one.'

'Then which one?' Awaara asked, surprised.

'That's another story. That grave will probably never be found.'

III

'You're being quite mysterious now. Which grave are you talking about?'

Lighting a cigarette, I asked unaskingly, 'Bibi Humra. Do you know Bibi Humra?'

'Which Bibi Humra?'

'She was a nautch girl.'

'Where? When?'

'In the 1820s. In Lucknow.'

'But who was she? How do you know of her?'

'From Charles Rousseau's diaries?'

'And Rousseau, who is he?'

'The man who bought a baby boy from Bibi Humra.'

'Which boy?'

'The child with whom my family tree ends.'

Awaara reflected for a while, as though trying to put the loose ends of a story together, and then said:

'So if I get you right, she sold a child to a Frenchman in India who went back to Europe and founded your family.'

'Yes. So say Rousseau's documents.'

'What else do they say of Bibi Humra?'

'Nothing. That he bought the child from a destitute dancing girl.' Taking a puff at my cigarette, I remarked playfully, 'So you see how I came to shoot this film in India.'

'In search of your roots?'

'Not really — you know I am not the kind who'll come looking for exotic roots. Because I have always felt a special bond with this country.'

Awaara took my hand, and pressed it as though moved. Then together we sat down on a grave near the cemetery gate. It was cold and wet and mossy. We listened to the sound of the dying fire, watched the flames change colour. When all that was left of the fire was the glow of deep red embers, encircling the time-beaten graveyard, Awaara whispered close to my lips, 'A gift to you, my love — a necklace of ruby embers.' I kissed him, as he lay on his back, holding me by the waist and gently pulling me on top of him. The rubies twinkled in the graveyard, the flames wallowed on the ground, the dead smiled in their graves

— Awaara was beautiful. He was pure-profane, pungent-sweet, man-woman, he was the unity of paradoxes, that moment of incomprehension that is love.

At dawn, Awaara placed a bouquet of wild flowers and leaves on Miss Walters' grave. As I got up from the grave on which we had spent our first night together, I read its epitaph —

Virginia Smith
1742–1832

Spent her life in
service of the Catholic
Church. She died a virgin.

AMEN

EIGHT

'HELP! HELP!'

screamed the King beside me. I got up, and lit the oil-lamp. The King, I noticed, was trembling like an aspen leaf, soaked with perspiration. Strangely, he was still asleep. 'Help! Help!' he cried out again. 'What's worrying you, My Lord?' I asked him, touching his forehead. 'Don't disturb me. Let me sleep,' he protested, shrugging my hand off, and turning over to the other side. The King was still trembling, slowly folding up into the foetal position. 'Shoot! Help! Shoot him down!' – this time the King sprang out of bed, looking around as though for someone, and then came back and sat on the edge of the bed.

'What's the matter, My Lord?'

'I had this terrible dream, you know,' he mumbled childlike.

'I thought as much. Don't worry, My Lord, it's only a nightmare. Nightmares dissolve in the first ray of light.'

'Oh no! But this one was about to kill me with its whips of light.'

'Its whips of light? What kind of light?'

'Oh! It was, it was . . . ' the King whispered, mortified. 'It was . . . ' He produced another cry of horror, and hid his head between his knees. I stood helplessly by his side, not knowing what to do at that late hour. Then the King said in a pain-choked voice, 'Call Khan. He might know what's happening in there – Oh! It's gruesome.'

Khan-the-barber, the legendary clairvoyant of Awadh,

arrived immediately like a doctor about to attend an emergency. Guessing what he had been summoned for at this early hour of the morning, Khan came well-prepared, duly accompanied by his English dream-attendant who carried on him the thick register containing a night-by-night record of his master's dreams. Khan's presence reassured the King, who now looked in better control of himself. The King sat down in his rocking-chair, and the barber gave him a glass of grapefruit juice and a banana, urging, 'First have something to eat, Your Majesty. It's not good to recount dreams on an empty stomach. It can give duodenal ulcers.' The King ate obediently.

Khan pulled up a chair for himself and then asked the King, 'Would His Majesty now be kind enough to relate to his humble servant what he saw and felt during this dream?'

The King sat up and began to concentrate, his hands on his temples, but Khan cautioned, 'But careful, Your Majesty, dreams are like petals. Too much pressure on them can often distort their form and meaning. Just relax, and let it emerge naturally from the mind.'

The King lay back, putting his feet up on the chair, and started recounting his dream. As he spoke, Khan's dream-attendant was frantically turning the pages of his register back and forth, ostensibly trying to find a reference to the nightmare in question. 'It was a peculiar monster I saw, Khan,' said the King. 'A kind I have never seen or heard of before. His body was a hotch-potch mixture of odds and ends of human beings. Animals, birds, plants, things. His face was white — blinding white, made of parched, limestone earth. He had flapping ears, those of an elephant, and for his nose, he wore a pointed, native shoe. His hair was made of greenish brown cacti. And when I looked at him closely, I saw he had a kangaroo's arms, and a horse's legs. His body was wrapped in sheep-skin — yes. I remember someone telling me in the dream that this monster had descended from some forlorn, snowbound planet, and that he seldom drank and ate, and when he did, it was only tea and opium. At first, I was a little surprised to see that he had no eyes, nor a mouth. Gradually, his eyes emerged, like two rings becoming larger and larger, and once they took their full shape, I placed them instantly – they were bullock-cart wheels. But his mouth remained a mystery – he either had none, or had many. I think he used one of the cracks on his parched face as his mouth. Now we come to the second part, Khan.

The King's voice started to quaver, and his body to tremble. Khan quickly got up and gave him another glass of juice, urging, 'Please continue, Your Majesty. I have never heard such an intrepid description of a nightmare before. Did you know, Your Majesty, that the King of England swoons when asked to recount his dreams?'

Being one up on the King of England emboldened the King of Awadh, who continued, 'Then came the worst moment of this night, Khan. The monster said something, which I couldn't quite fathom, but I noticed that the moment he uttered the first word, his cart-wheel eyes began to shine and revolve. It was a terrifying sight! I turned my face away, but he whispered from the back in his needle-fine voice. "Child, child, where is your child?" I looked back. Now the monster had suddenly grown a long, thin beard and from it, leapt out hundreds of whips – yes, whips of lightning! I tried to run away from his beard, but the monster lashed me with his lightning-whip. I knelt before him, and asked, "Who are you? What do you want from me?" "Child, child," he answered. '"Where is your child?" Oh! It is horrifying.'

'That's more than enough for my purpose, Your Majesty,' stated Khan, taking the register from his assistant. 'Now please allow me some time to consult my records.'

The King looked more composed, having got the nightmare out of his system. I took him up to the terrace garden for some fresh air, while Khan plunged himself into his dream records. We had barely done one round of the terrace, debating whether it was Majun Mian's aphrodisiacs that were causing the nightmares, when Khan came bouncing up to us, and exclaimed with an air of self-importance:

'It's nothing, Your Majesty. Nothing to worry about.'

'Nothing?' said the King, feebly. 'It nearly took my life.'

'I beg your pardon, Your Majesty. I meant to say there
no cause for alarm.'

'So what do you think it is, Khan?'

'In the opinion of your humble servant, Your Majesty,
his dream has two explanations to it. As for the first, I
m absolutely positive. For the second, I can only offer a
ypothesis.'

'Let's start with the first.'

'I have found a word-for-word reference in my record-book
the terrifying monster which appeared before His Majesty.
Many a people . . . '

'What did you say?' the King interjected. 'A word-for-word
eference? You mean you also have had the same dream, Khan?'

'No, Your Majesty. My book doesn't only have a record
f my dreams. It has notes on all the major dreams and myths
hat I've come across in my life.'

'Anyway, go ahead with your explanation.'

'This dream, Your Majesty, is called the Koompaany-badur.
With your permission, I would like to read to you the extract on
his dream which many a people in Awadh have suffered from.'
Khan placed his register on the terrace parapet, and started rea-
ing with a scholarly tone. "This terrifying demon is a figment of
he people's imagination. Ironically, the word itself Koompaany-
adur is a local distortion of the Anglo-Indian word, Company
Bahadur, which is just another name for the Honourable East
ndia Company. The country people, who had never seen the
Company but only heard of it, were so puzzled and terrified
y its invincible might that they started hallucinating about
t. Thus Company Bahadur, the English company, transformed
nto the terrifying myth of the Koompanny-badur. This myth,
he village elders say, emerged in India about fifty years ago —
ust when the British were fighting their first colonial battles!
o the Koompaany-badur is nothing but a native's hallucinatory
ision of the might of the British company, and its evil intentions
owards the natives."'

The King laughed, as though at himself. 'But how could
he King have been frightened such a banal myth?'

'Oh no! Who says Your Majesty was frightened! Had h
really been frightened, he wouldn't talk about the dream s
freely,' remarked Khan, injecting into the King his daily do
of flattery. Khan reflected, and then added:

'But there is one mystery in His Majesty's dream.'

'What?'

'The beard. Your Majesty — according to my record
the Koompanny-badur did not have a beard.'

'So you mean the King did not dream of the Koompann
badur.'

'Indeed he did, but His Majesty's flair for adventu
seems to have added a beard to it.'

'And now?' mumbled the King, relapsing into a sta
of anxiety.

'But there is no cause for worry, Your Majesty. Yo
humble servant has an explanation for it.'

'What?'

'In my opinion, the beard in the dream was the Resident
beard.'

'The Resident's? Which Resident?'

'U.F.O. Dow. Your Majesty — the present British Reside
of Lucknow.'

The King shut his eyes, as though trying to compare th
beard in his dream with that of the Resident, and then patte
Khan on his back, 'Shabash! Shabash Khan! That's it. Yes,
am positive the beard in my dream was this wretched U.F.C
Dow's beard. So the explanation to this dream is, in fact, qui
simple — I dreamt of the Koompanny-badur plus the Resident
beard.'

'Yes, Your Majesty.'

'Huh!' the King said, thinking loud. 'A petty Resident
beard frightened me!'

'It wasn't fright, Your Majesty. Just a little surprise. W
all know that our brave King revels in surprise and adventure.

'He does, indeed he does — since childhood days, in fact
the King said, chortling. 'But what a genius you are, Kha
How do you know so much about dreams?'

'With Your Majesty's blessing, I have always been fascinated, our Majesty, by a new science that was being spoken of when I ft London. It's called psychology, the mental science. It comes om the Greek word, psyche, which means a butterfly.'

'Ah! A butterfly!' reveried the King. 'A butterfly! The ght of colour on wings!'

Khan was still showering petals of admiration on his aster's art of spontaneous creation, when the King once again rned pale and pensive, and asked: 'But, Khan, why did the mon say to me — "Child, child, where is your child?" What you make of that?'

Khan couldn't answer that question, but the next day's ent proved that the King had momentarily acquired from s barber his remarkable quality of clairvoyance. An English rseman from the British Residency arrived in the morning ith a letter from the Resident addressed directly to the King. nlike the usual, endlessly long missives of the British admin- tration, this letter was brief, to the point — like a threat. We ad it together.

His Majesty King Nasiruddin Haider of Awadh

His Majesty has already been appraised of the grave discontent caused to the Court of Directors of the East India Company by the deteriorating administration of the Awadh territories. The British delegation, led by General John Melon, special emissary of His Excellency the Governor-General, imparted to His Majesty the genuine sentiment of the British administration at a meeting held at His Majesty's palace on the 6th October 1834 instant.

His Excellency the Governor-General has now ord- ered me to seek an immediate appointment with Your Majesty with a view to obtain full and final information on the question of succession to the throne of Awadh. His Majesty is aware that considerable confusion has been caused by the conflicting claims of two different pretenders to the throne, both of whom claim to be His Majesty's gracious progeny. Since the King of Awadh has himself not been able to furnish a consistent and credible response on this issue, I have been asked to seek His Majesty's clarifications, and despatch the same to the Home Office without any loss of time.

In light of the dire urgency of the matter, it is with your permission, Your Majesty, that I propose to parley with you at 11.00 a.m. today.

I remain your humble well-wisher.

The Residency	Sd/- U.F.O. Dow
Lucknow	The Resident

'That was a clairvoyant dream about the Resident, My Lord,' I remarked on reading the letter. The King didn't react to my statement. Crumpling the letter in his fist, he went and sat in his mahogany chair, looking anxious. He read the letter several times over, getting more and more worried with each reading. The succession problem I knew was the King's real bone of contention with the British. Of late, we had received information that the British, for obvious reasons, were backing Nasir-ud-daulah, the King's eighty-year-old, half-paralysed uncle, as the successor to the throne. I noticed the King was beginning to perspire. Wiping his face with my sleeve, I asked him with affection:

'What's come over you, My Lord? Are you worried about not having a child?'

'Which child?'

'Your child. A prince.'

'I have those two bastards, don't I?' snarled the King, 'But that's not what is worrying me — I can handle the Company officials on the succession issue. It's something else.'

'What else then? Your uncle?'

'That doddering old fool! He won't even be able to climb on to the throne. No — something else.'

'Your anxiety is the cause of my concern, My Lord,' I pleaded. 'What's worrying you?'

'I'm surprised at your lack of common sense, Ann,' he snapped. 'What drives me mad is the Resident's beard! Yes, that awful cobweb on his face that he calls a beard. Oh! I'm terrified of it. Worms, bats, cockroaches, snakes – God knows what all breeds in that stinking bush. His beard moves with the slightest breeze, it changes shape, colour – my God, it's a devil's nest. Oh! This monster is not a Resident of the British Government, he is the Resident Ghost of Hell posted in Lucknow.'

Khan-the-barber, the resident psychologist at the court, as he fancied to be called of late, was once again summoned for advice. The King placed his cards before him, and Khan set about thinking. Given the rather delicate nature of relations with the British Government, Khan cautioned that it would be untactful to cancel the proposed meeting with the Resident. But, in the same breath, he strongly advised against a face-to-face confrontation with the Resident. The barber suggested that the King meet the Resident across a thick, opaque black screen on the opposite sides of which would be seated the two conversing parties. The King accepted Khan's proposal half-heartedly, fearing that the over-inquisitive Resident might be tempted to peep round the other side. To which Khan provided another answer – the screen should be guarded by two armed men, posted at each end. The King agreed with the overall strategy, and a royal horseman was dispatched to the Residency with a note saying: 'The King would be delighted to meet the Resident at 11.00 am.'

The Resident arrived at the palace, his long beard looking particularly ferocious on a wind-swept morning. The protocol officer showed him and his assistant into the gardenlike Kashmere lounge, renowned for its turquoise-rimmed, indoor fountains that could keep the room cool and pleasant even on a sweltering afternoon. The French butler served the British guests some champagne, and they sat comfortably in their seats by a wide, black screen, flanked by two statuesque guards. They waited for quite a while, but when the Resident found no sign of the King, he asked one of the screen-guards:

'Has someone informed . . . '

'No, no,' replied the guard, interrupting him. 'No English, no speaking English.'

'Oof! How shocking indeed!' cursed the Resident. 'We've been here for over half a century, and these natives still can't speak a word of English.' The guard smiled back, incapable of distinguishing insult from compliment.

At the end of his tether, the Resident whispered into his assistant's ear:

'How ill-mannered of the King to keep us waiting here in this room!'

'Indeed. He seems to think that the Resident has nothing but his endless pranks to attend to. How utterly disrespectful of him!'

'Well, if all goes well, his days are numbered.'

'Won't that be a great day when our flag will fly from the palace mast.'

'That day is not too far, I assure you. I won't give this demented man more than two years if he doesn't mind his deeds.'

Intercepting the butler who had come in to check if the champagne glasses were doing well, the Resident's assistant asked:

'Where is His Majesty? Has he been informed of the Resident's arrival?'

'Hullo there!' croaked the King from behind the screen. 'The King is here. Oh! He is here.'

The Resident leapt out of his seat, baffled by the King's divine transparence. He stood perplexed for a minute, looking around him for his host, but when the King refused to show he enquired with a laugh as curious as his beard: 'But where are you, Your Majesty?'

'Here, behind the screen.' answered the King, in a plain businesslike tone. 'I've been waiting for you to start the meeting. Let's get on with it, because I'd like to finish it as soon as possible. I'm in the middle of Shabegham.'

'Shabegham? — I beg your indulgence, Your Majesty. What's Shabegham?'

'How strange,' the King said, 'the British have been in Lucknow for nearly half a century, and they still don't know

122

what Shabegham is. It is a two-day mourning period for the death of a beloved.'

Suspecting that the King had overheard his conversation with his assistant, the Resident coughed nervously, mumbling:

'I'm sorry to hear of your bereavement, Your Majesty.'

'Don't worry about my loves, Mr Dow,' snubbed the King with unexpected aggression. 'Let's get on with the meeting.'

'But where is it going to be held?' the Resident stuttered.

'What do you mean, where? – right here! Hasn't Khan informed you about our customary prescriptions? Normally, the King shouldn't be conducting any official business during this period. Since you seemed to have some urgent work, my Customs and Rites Advisor allowed me to see you on condition that we do not meet face to face. So I'm afraid we must abide by his advice. Let us get on with the meeting.'

The King's unusual aggressivity annoyed the Resident, who snatched the voluminous file out of his assistant's hand, flipped through it, and said:

'I have been asked by the Governor-General to seek clarification on the question of succession to the throne of Awadh, Your Majesty.'

'So I hear. What do you have to ask of the King of Awadh?'

'Let me first recapitulate briefly, Your Majesty, the factors surrounding the issue of succession.' The Resident began reading from his file: 'Your Majesty was married in 1818 to Ruquayya Sultan Begum, his Chief Consort, who was the daughter of Mirza Sulaiman Shikoh, and the grand-daughter of the Mughal Emperor, Shah Alam. Known for her kindness, religious beliefs and refined culture, His Majesty's Chief Consort, according to the information in our possession, is said to have preferred a life of solitude to that of rampant profligacy at the Palace. She did not have any issue with the King.'

'You might like to take it down for your records,' the King riposted, 'that the Chief Consort was frigid, and that the King had better things to do than water lifeless plants. Go on with the rest.'

The Resident resumed his reading. 'His Majesty then married Sukh Chain alias Sharf-un-nisa Afzal Mahal who, according to information available in the Residency records, is said to have been the daughter of a . . . '

'Pardon me for interrupting you again, Mr Dow. What is it that you are reading?'

'The recapitulative notes, Your Majesty.'

'Sounds more like my obituary,' remarked the King scoffingly. 'I thought you were here for a discussion.'

'Which will follow the reading of the recapitulative notes, Your Majesty.'

'What are you trying to recapitulate for me — my wives and children? Well, the King is not that old and senile yet to need reminding of his life. You should have done your homework before disturbing the King in a moment of grief and mourning.'

'How would you like me to proceed with the meeting then, Your Majesty?' retaliated the Resident, helplessly trying to reassert his authority.

'In as brief a manner as possible. And if you must read these boring notes, then I allow you to read one line per wife — no more! Go ahead.'

'The marriage with Afzal Mahal is said to have led to the disputed birth of Munna Jan, one of the two pretenders to the throne. Then His Majesty married Dulari alias Malika Zamani alias Sarfaraz Mahal who, according to the records of the Lucknow Residency, is alleged to have given birth to Kaiwan Jah. In 1827, the King of Awadh betrothed an English woman, Miss Ann Walters, renamed Muquadara Aulia after her marriage. His Majesty does not have an issue from her.' Slapping the file shut, the Resident looked up at the screen, and said, 'That's it.'

'Ah! Finished!' rejoiced the King. 'Congratulations, Mr Resident! I must felicitate you on the infinite romanticism of your Residency's records. Nothing on earth could have murdered love better than the pages you've just read. Anyway, what are the clarifications you wish to seek?'

The Resident put the file on the side-table, pulling out of it an ink-blotched sheet of paper. Then gesturing to his assistant to start taking notes, the Resident opened the discussion:

'There is considerable confusion in the Company's mind, your Majesty, as to the true nature of the birth of Munna Jan and Kaiwan Jah, the two respective pretenders to the throne. I'll take the two cases one by one. Munna Jan is said to have been born in 1822. But the British Government has documentary proof indicating that immediately after the said birth, King Ghaziuddin Haider, Your Majesty's worthy father, denied that Munna Jan was his real grandson. Evidence leads us to believe that Munna Jan was in the womb of a washerwoman when she was first brought into the harem twenty-five days before the delivery.'

'Who said that?' fumed the King.

'The late King, His Majesty's own father.'

'Oh! That bastard!' roared the King. 'And don't your records say that my father was himself the illegitimate child of a palanquin-carrier and a cavalryman, whom a shrewd destiny had hurled to the throne?'

'Indeed they do, Your Majesty.'

'So how can you take a bastard for his word? A bastard sees a bastard in every woman's womb.' The King reflected for a while and then continued, 'But you know why he said that? Because the late King hated his wife, who wanted my son to be my successor. So he concocted evidence to show that Munna Jan was someone else's child.'

'Does His Majesty mean by that that Munna Jan is indeed his son?' probed the Resident, as his assistant scribbled furiously on paper.

'Yes – I hope you are aware that the late King told the truth when confronted with God on his death-bed. He accepted that Munna Jan was his grandson.'

'Indeed he did,' concurred the Resident, checking the sheet of paper in his hand. 'But there, we run into another problem. In 1827, the late King accepted the legitimacy of Munna Jan's birth, but the reigning King – that is, Your Majesty himself –

denied that Munna Jan was his son. The records say that Your Majesty now alleged that Kaiwan Jah, Dulari's son, was his one and only offspring.'

'Yes, I remember telling the Resident that.'

'But we have indisputable evidence to prove that Kaiwan Jah was three years old when he first set foot in the palace, and that he is, in fact, the illegitimate offspring of a relationship between Dulari and an elephant-keeper.'

The King chortled and said, 'Quite right – for once our records concur! Yes, that's why I later communicated to the Governor-General – in 1832, I think – that Kaiwan Jah was not my son.'

'But in 1827 Your Majesty had claimed that he was your son. How did, how did . . . ?'

'How did that happen you mean to ask? Simple – love! I was under emotional pressure. Dulari was blackmailing me. Every other night, she was threatening to kill herself if I didn't declare her son to be my successor. You're a married person, Mr Dow. You know that love has its own compulsions. So to appease Dulari, I declared that Kaiwan Jah was my son. Now I can but laugh at my folly. How could I have ever dreamed of having that scarecrow as my successor! I'm horrified by myself. Have you seen his beard, Mr Dow? At fifteen, he's got a long beard like, like, like that of . . . '

The Resident stroked his own beard and asked, 'So he is not your son?'

'No.'

'And the first one – Munna Jan?'

'Can't say.'

'Did you say, can't say, Your Majesty?'

'Yes, I am not sure. We haven't fully completed the enquiry yet.'

'You must appreciate, Your Majesty, that matters of state cannot be run on conjecture. To avoid any political problems, the Company would like to ensure a smooth and uneventful succession. As of now, the situation is really confusing.'

'So is it for the King.' After a brief silence, the King

remarked to the Resident philosophically, 'Monogamous cultures like yours, Mr Dow, are fundamentally incapable of understanding such situations. Now try and appreciate the King's problem. In 1822 when Munna Jan was born, I had three wives, and twenty-one dancing-girls in the harem. And whatever the Kings might like to think of their Begums, the fidelity of each of these women is fundamentally suspect. One of our poets once wrote — if the courtesans are a misfortune, the Begums are a complete disaster. In such a situation, establishing the identity of a child is like fishing for a needle in an ocean. So how can I be sure if Munna Jan was my son?'

'In which case, Your Majesty,' announced the Resident, 'the answer is simple. The Court of Directors of the Company reserves the right to take a unilateral decision on the matter.'

The Resident's statement outraged the King, who protested:

'The King considers this unwarranted interference in his private affairs.'

'A King's personal affairs are public, Your Majesty,' retorted the Resident.

'Rubbish! This is in breach of the 1802 Friendship Treaty between the British and the State of Awadh.'

'Treaties evolve with history, Your Majesty,' declared the Resident in a tone that clearly overstepped his mission. 'I am constrained to reiterate that the Company shall take a just and impartial, but unilateral, decision on the matter of succession.'

'Thieves! Thugs!' screamed the King, kicking the black screen down and stepping out like a soldier to confront the demonic Resident. 'U.F.O. Dow, you are a thief! You want to usurp the throne of Awadh.'

Frightened by the King's bloodthirsty eyes, the Resident took two steps backwards, and muttered gingerly, 'But I am only speaking in the name of the Company, Your Majesty.'

'No! No! No!' the King shrieked hysterically. 'The Company wants to usurp my throne. You are interfering in my personal affairs.'

'But a King's child is not an ordinary child, Your Majesty,' the Resident tried to reason, 'he is the future King of the land.'

'But it's none of the company's business to find out who the King intends to make his successor. I am answerable to none but God alone.'

'But the East India Company in India *is* God, Your Majesty,' intoned the Resident.

The King stared at the Resident with the helpless vendetta of the vanquished. Then bearing down on him, he plunged his hand into the Resident's beard, and tugged at it — the beard came away as easily as a banana skin! 'Oh! False — it was false, it was a false demon,' the King burst out into a roaring fit of laughter, calling out loud, 'Khan! Khan! Come and see what I have accomplished. I've turned last night's monster into a white mouse. Khan! Quick, Khan!'

The Resident fled from the palace in a towering fury. But his departure also proclaimed an unofficial war on Awadh. Had the Company been strong enough to take over the gigantic state, it would probably have done so right after this incident. But this is not what it wanted, it preferred instead to let a figurehead run the state on its behalf. So it pretended to ignore the beard episode, while subtly mounting pressure on the King. Another 50,000 troops were stationed in Awadh, and its maintenance bill handed over to the royal court. The revenue demand was doubled, and the King was forced to loan to the Company hundreds of thousands of rupees and receive virtually nothing in return. The financial burden on the King was backed by political threats, complaining of his bad administration and profligate life-style. But the strongest issue remained the question of succession. As weeks went by, the British administration excluded the King from any say in the matter of succession, and it became evident that the Company was now playing its cards for installing Nasir-ud-daulah, the King's half-paralysed uncle, on the throne. Nasir-ud-daulah's once-abandoned and bat-infested house was now heavily guarded by English soldiers, and the frequent visits by important Company officials to his residence clearly showed the shape of things to come. One day, the King's disabled uncle, who barely a few days ago had begged at the King's feet for a higher pension, plucked up the courage to taunt him. 'A childless King is like an orphaned child, Nasiruddin.' The King reacted unexpectedly to the statement. Not with anger, but with stoicism. 'We can't change our destiny, can we?'

The King returned to his palace that night, less humiliated than depressed. Without addressing a word to anyone, he went and sat on the terrace, a hukka and a champagne bottle by his side. He was drowning his sorrows, watching the moon childlessly writhe over the waves of the Gomti, when Mumtaz-the-eunuch came up to the King panting, 'Your Majesty! Your Majesty! Begum Sahiba is expecting.'

'Who? What! Expecting! Ann is expecting!' The King turned towards the west, went down on his knees, and wept.

He then came down to my chamber. 'Ann, is it true that you are expecting my heir?' I answered with a smile. Tears welled in the King's eyes. 'I am too poor to return you what you have given me, Ann,' he said with a choked voice, 'but how can I express my devotion? Is there anything I can do to fulfil your desires?'

'Nothing – be a good husband and a good father.'

'Yes, but there must be something . . . '

'Nothing, My Lord.'

'But how do we celebrate this event? We must do something.'

The King asked his advisors for suggestions to celebrate the auspicious event. Some proposed animal fights, others, jugglery shows, but the King dismissed them all as too common. Just when everyone seemed to have run out of ideas, a dwarf unexpectedly arrived at the palace. Fair, frizzy-haired, he had beautiful features, everything except height. The dwarf introduced himself as Charles Bonnet. The King shook his head, as though in disbelief, and asked, 'What did you say your name was?' 'Charles Bonnet.' The King laughed, putting his arm around the dwarf with affection. 'Do you know what Bonnet means in our language?' asked the King with a glint in his eye. 'No. Your Majesty,' replied the Frenchman nervously. 'A dwarf! Yes, a dwarf!' Charles Bonnet burst out laughing at the linguistic coincidence, but hastened to add like a precocious young boy, 'But your humble servant is not just a dwarf, Your Majesty, he is also a mechanical magician!'

Charles Bonnet we were told was a Frenchman from Paris. He was born to Jacobin parents in the midst of the revolutionary fervour. Since his parents were too heavily engaged in the social upheavals of their times, his childhood was spent in solitude. That was perhaps why Charles, when he grew up, developed a passion for making toys. After a while, Bonnet started mechanising his toys, inspired by the latest inventions of the industrial revolution. This blend of toys and mechanics won Bonnet immediate fame in the city, and the 'little mechanical genius' as he came to be titled, was invited by King Charles X for a public demonstration of his skills. Charles Bonnet made quite a fortune from his royal admirers, but when Paris was once again on fire during the 1830 revolution, his dormant Jacobin blood suddenly started boiling, and in the thick of the anti-monarchy riots, he floated in the Parisian skies in an enormous smoke-balloon on which was inscribed in red letters, 'A bas le roi! Down With the King!' The King's brigands reduced his home and workshop to ashes, and threatened him with murder. Bonnet's ephemeral revolutionism evaporated into despair, he picked up the only smoke-balloon that remained and left Paris, much like Khan-the-Barber, for the Orient. He travelled through many a royal court in search of his lost wealth — but without any luck. After many years, Bonnet reached Lucknow and recounted his life story to his cousin, a local French chandelier-dealer. The dwarf had barely finished recounting his tale of adventures and inventions when his cousin lifted him up in his arms, 'What a genius you are, Charles! I bet the King of Awadh can give us bagfuls of gold for your smoke-balloon.' So the two promptly set off to meet the King who, as luck would have it, was still searching for an idea to celebrate the event of my conception. His Majesty was delighted to meet the dwarf, and asked him to prepare for a balloon show on the banks of the Gomti. Patting him on his back, the King gave him a bag of gold taller, broader and heavier than the 'little genius' himself.

On the day of the balloon spectacle, the city of Lucknow

donned a mantle it had never worn before. For miles on end, one could see nothing but colour – on trees, on walls, on people's faces, on their clothes and carriages. Hundreds of thousands of people turned up on the banks of the Gomti to watch the dwarf flying the balloon. The mammoth crowd was beginning to get restless and unruly, when the little genius and his assistant came winding down the river on a light sail-boat. Bonnet unleashed the gigantic balloon, and within seconds, he flew up into the air. On the balloon was marked in big, red letters: Murad, or desire, the name the King had already chosen for our child . . .

NINE

AWAARA LOVED KABABS.

More than he did his William Blake, Baudelaire, Ghalib or
Rimbaud. But kababs, to Awaara, were not food, far from
it. They were what he called a concrete poem, at once real
and unreal, concealing within it the transparent beauty of a
poem-*objet*. For him, the process by which a kabab came into
being revealed, as nothing else could, all the mysterious prin-
ciples of alchemy. Strangely, he claimed to have learnt more
about poetry and epistemology through watching kababs being
made than from the great thinkers of our times. The notions of
good and bad, of beautiful and ugly, of order and disorder, of
revolution and restoration, the magic by which words secreted
pleasure and dreams, our psychic truths, were all hidden, said
Awaara, in the making of a kabab. One evening he had broken
into one of his panegyrical tributes to kababs, when I cut him
short:

'Stop it, Awaara. You and your kababs sound a bit like
the mad King in our film.'

'So you too think this is trash,' he remarked, dead serious,
then adding with a pinch of self-mockery, 'You'll discover the
truth of these words once I am gone – like all great men.'

'But what you're saying is nothing new, Awaara,' I said,
chuckling, though without meaning offence. 'Beauty lies in the
eyes of the beholder. You can find it in a woman's eyes or in a
button-hole – depends on you, doesn't it? Ask the French, they

find alchemy in wine-making, the Germans, in beer-brewing.'

'And the Americans, in McDonald's hamburgers!' jeered Awaara, then adding with a sense of self-resignation, 'All I can say to you, Valerie, is that if you don't understand kababs, you'll never understand the culture of this city. Kabab is the collective unconscious of Lucknow.'

The discussion ended with Awaara hailing a rickshaw, and dragging me off to Munne Mian's, the most famous kabab-shop in town. More than the kababs, what interested me in this riverside tin-roofed foodstand, was the legend behind it. Munne Mian traced his roots back to a Muslim cook called Iqbal Rahim, who set up a small shop on the banks of the river Yamuna in Agra, nearly five centuries ago, roughly around the time when the Mughals arrived in the Indian sub-continent. Empires were being lost and won, battle-cries rent the air in the country, but Rahim was deaf to the sound of history, devoting himself to his kababs, and to the alchemy of odours and spices. He received his first lesson in history the day the Mughal Emperor's royal guards forcibly shut his shop down on the grounds that the Emperor had ordered the construction of a mausoleum on the space where stood the kabab-shop. Rahim was indeed grieved, for he had always felt that the humid riverside air had something to do with the process through which a good kabab came into being. Since he didn't have much of a say in the matter, he quit his premises, as did many other shopkeepers, and the Emperor built on the land the love-monument he had wanted to build. The Taj Mahal.

Rahim moved into the city, now setting up his shop by a lake. Over the years, his gastronomical genius won acclaim, winning the fidelity of many a royal palate, but his reputation really hit the sky when the Mughal Emperor, Akbar the Great, summoned him one day to his Court, and offered him a handsome jagir in recognition of his achievements. Rahim humbly turned down the offer, preferring his modest shop to the lavish style of the Mughal nobility, though, while leaving, he took a promise from the Emperor that his kabab-shop would never again be displaced. Akbar gave him his word of honour, but his successor betrayed the royal promise, forcing Rahim once again to move to another place. The kabab-master who, by then, was in his eighties, was so heart-broken that he abandoned Agra for good, and set up his shop in Delhi – once again on the banks of the Yamuna.

Rahim died, but his descendants continued the family business which became a culinary legend in north India. Several decades later, the Rahim Kabab Shop, which, by then, had become the shrine of carnivorous delights, was ransacked and reduced to ashes by a band of angry Hindu vegetarians. Rahim's successors were thus forced to move again, this time to Lucknow, where the local Vizier offered them a place on the banks of the river Gomti. Since, the famous kabab-shop has stood there, virtually in the same place and shape, for nearly three centuries. If the testimony of Lucknow kabab-gourmets can be believed, Munne Mian, the present owner of the shop, still uses the same pots and pans that his ancestors had come to the city with: his firewood, recipes, spices, everything has resisted the force of change. Twenty-one generations after Rahim, Munne Mian's seems just the same as his ancestor's shop, a kabab-island frozen in time.

But more fascinating than the story of the Rahim family was the way its legend came to be written. Rahim was not just a great kabab-cook, he was also a prolific diarist, maintaining a day-to-day record of his thoughts and their relation to his vocation. This tradition of maintaining a written record of kabab-meditations was assiduously followed by each of his descendants, so much so that when Munne Mian got down to writing his *Kababnama*, the rare treatise on kababs, he was confronted with the gargantuan task of sifting through seventeen-thousand-seven-hundred-and-seventy-seven pages of heterogeneous material, including verses, odes, plays, anecdotes, aphorisms, essays, memoirs, discourses, homilies, commentaries, pamphlets, synonyms and kabab-sermons. Awaara's odes to kababs thus, I was to discover later, were scarcely original, only a tiny reflection of the thought of Munne Mian, whose surrealist treatise immortalised kabab, and made it the kernel of all human philosophy.

We reached the kabab-shop, and joined the jostling crowd

134

around the service counter. Just when I remarked, 'But wouldn't it have been easier for everyone to form a queue?' Awaara wormed his way up to Munne Mian, salaamed him, and came back with two plates of sizzling kababs, surrounded by heaps of onion rings. The kababs were indeed delicious, and matched every bit their legendary reputation. There was a succulent, creamy, and yet non-greasy, quality about them, which made them melt in the mouth even before one had started mashing. We ate by the river, before returning to the hotel.

It must have been fairly late at night, when I discovered that Munne Mian's kababs, as indeed his philosophy, were easier to swallow than to digest, and were now beginning to play havoc with my stomach which was but an ardent adept of the *nouvelle cuisine*. To avoid making a fuss in the middle of the night, I popped a few Gelusils, and decided to sleep my agony off. But the cramps became worse and worse, and I was soon turning and twisting and coiling in pain. Awaara's room didn't have a phone, yet to call Deboo, whose list of flaws included an absolute lack of discretion, would really have been like broadcasting to the world. Then this time at least, Deboo would even have had good reason to get worried: the shooting was already behind schedule, and were he not to catch up with the time lost we were bound to come up against bigger problems with Vikram-the-King whose own programme was so tight that it didn't allow any room for accidents and illnesses. The stomach-ache however became unbearable, and I called Deboo. As expected, he panicked, and began ranting and raving in the corridors, waking up the entire hotel in the process.

Finally, a doctor was called. His clean-shaven head, dull, drugged eyes, high black boots and sinewy physique brought a skinhead to mind. Without greeting me, he began, strangely, by examining my pupils, which I thought one only did to those who were about to breathe their last. Then he felt around my tummy, muttering every now and then to himself some indiscernible exclamations: Vouf! Kya! Kaun! Atcha! Unh-Unh! Ouf-ouf! Oh-ho! Ah! Oups! I couldn't fathom most of what he said, but it was nonetheless reassuring to observe that his unusually

135

effeminate voice and warm touch perfectly neutralised his otherwise terrifying, skinhead appearance. Opening his briefcase, he asked me:

'What did you have for dinner, Madam?'

'Kababs.'

'Good God! Kababs?' he asked with the friendly curiosity of a doctor. 'Seekh kababs or shami?'

'Shami.'

'Ha! Ha! Shami? Good show!' exclaimed the doctor, sounding a shade too garrulous for the late hour. Then he asked, 'How is it that you know so much about the Indian delicacies?'

'India can teach you a lot in two months, Doctor.'

'Quite true, quite true.' The doctor began by re-examining my stomach. 'Intelligent people pick up things quickly, don't they?' he observed. Then feeling just below my liver in small circular movements, he squeaked. 'Good God! The beautiful kababs are sitting here just as fresh as they were on your plate. You should have been careful, Madam. The food here is horrible.'

'Yes, I think it's the kababs that have caused this.'

'Oh! You think? – I am positive. The hotel food here is very bad, you know. They call themselves five-star hotels but, in reality, they are fifth-rate hotels. Vouf! There is so much adulteration in their food. And so much corruption, and so expensive . . . I never eat here. They are . . . '

'But I didn't have kababs at the hotel, Doctor,' I clarified, interrupting what looked like a personal grouse between the doctor and the hotel. 'I went to that wretched Munne Mian's!'

'Munne Mian's? You mean *the* Munne Mian.'

'Yes.' I repeated. '*The* wretched Munne Mian.'

'Why wretched?' the doctor asked reprovingly, suddenly losing his after-hours loquacity. 'Wretched – why wretched?'

'I am sure these cramps are his doing.'

'Impossible,' admonished the doctor. 'Munne Mian? – Never! It's the safest and the cleanest food in town. Are you aware of the history behind the great kabab-shop?'

'Yes, a little.'

'Have you read Munne Mian's great treatise on life — the *Kababnama*?'

'I have heard about it.'

'Well, if you had read it,' said the doctor, with a tinge of condescension, 'you could never in your wildest imagination have insinuated that his kababs caused this stomach upset. Ouf! *Kababnama*? — *Kya jabab hai*? It's my Bible on life.'

'I must admit his kababs were delicious, but . . . '

'Then how can you say they caused this? No, no, no, no, no, it can't be his kababs. Anything but his kababs. Tell me, have you ever suffered from mental illness?'

'I beg your pardon?'

'Mental illness — have you ever suffered from it? Madness or hallucinations? Like most film stars in Bombay.'

I didn't quite see the link between what was obviously a gastric disorder and hallucinations. Finding me reluctant to answer his questions, he asked again, clicking his fingers to draw my attention:

'Hey Madam? Hello! Hello! You haven't answered my question. Have you ever suffered from hallucinations?'

'Yes,' I replied weakly. 'For a short spell.'

'There you are!' The doctor jumped up from his chair, now beginning to stride up and down the room. 'I've found the answer. Your stomach-ache is psychosomatic. It has nothing to do with Munne Mian's kababs. It's your mental problem, plus the hotel food.'

I avoided any more arguing. The doctor gave me three different-coloured pills, and then called Deboo into the room. 'I've given her some pills which will settle her for the moment,' he stated, 'but I think her problem is psychosomatic. In any case, she should avoid the hotel food like the plague. Food here is bad enough for us — for foreigners, it is surely worse. Let her be on a bland diet for at least a couple of weeks. Any problems, please don't hesitate to call me.' The doctor left. That in itself was enough to put me to sleep.

My gastroenteritis expectedly made more news at the break-fast-table in the morning than the day's shooting programme.

The producer was so distraught that he politely banned me from eating at city restaurants and wayside foodstands. Lingappa, the pigeon-worshipping cook at the Bombay guest house, was urgently flown in to Lucknow to attend to my culinary needs. And since the hotel could not provide for private cooking arrangements, I was shifted bag and baggage to a nearby bungalow.

The new set-up looked perfect, more posh and private than the hotel, a little too privileged perhaps if compared with the lot of my other colleagues at the hotel. My bungalow, I was to discover later, was initially an outhouse of 'The Bohemia', a mansion built in the early nineteenth century by an ingenious Frenchman called Claude Marteau. Much like Khan-the-barber, Marteau, who had a pathological knack of shifting loyalties at the right time between the French, the English and the Nawab of Awadh, had amassed stupendous quantities of wealth in India. But Marteau was not just a smooth wheeler-dealer, he was also a man of arts and aristocratic taste. Instead of hoarding his riches away in France, he had preferred to settle in India, setting himself up in Lucknow like a local Nawab. 'The Bohemia', originally his residence, was considered a mini European architectural wonder, known particularly for its sprawling lush-green compound which had six fountains, each adorned with imported statues of Louis XIV, Jean-Jacques Rousseau, Diderot, Louis XVI, Robespierre and Napoleon. Marteau's carefully-picked, eclectic choice of statues was itself a demonstration of his philosophy — 'nothing serves business worse than political loyalty'. But the greatest invention of Marteau's architectural mind was his bathroom at 'The Bohemia', a perfect blend of the European mechanical genius and the insatiable erotic appetite of the local Nawabs. The bathroom had six levels, each heated to a different temperature. The weary bather, who often spent an entire day in this soul-cleansing bathing chamber, went through each level, before reaching the steam-bath at the end. What was erotic about this bathroom though, was not the aquatic steam but the feminine steam, as each of the levels was provided with a different concubine. It was rumoured in Awadh that 'Miss-you' Claude Marteau, as his concubines came to fondly name him after his death, could never, owing to his old age, make full use of the delights that his bathroom was equipped to offer. It was here that the King of Awadh lent Claude Marteau, his close friend, a helping hand . . .

I was reading a book on Claude Marteau at my bungalow, when Lingappa quacked, 'Naga! Naga!' The sound came from the bathroom, once the Frenchman's famed steam-bath, but was indiscernible. 'Naga! Naga! Naga!' he repeated again, loud, now seeming to raise an alarm. I shut the book, got up, and rushed towards the bathroom.

'What's the matter, Linga?' I enquired.

'Naga! Naga!' he quacked again, looking petrified, and pointing his finger repeatedly towards the squatting-type flush-pot in the bathroom. Unable to discern anything unusual about it, I asked again:

'What's the matter, Linga? What is a naga?'

'Wait, Madam. Madam, wait. Look there — look, look, a naga will come.'

As we both peered at the flush, waiting for some unknown action to take place, a snake raised its hood out of the water-hole, viciously flicking its fangs — I leapt backwards. Oblivious of our presence, the snake looked around, left, right, merrily flicking its fangs. Lingappa pulled me out of the bathroom, and went capering out of the house towards the servants' quarters, shouting: 'Naga! Naga! Naga!'

His code sound worked better on the others than it had on me. Within minutes, the watchman, the gardener, the sweeper, the room-boy, the caretaker, the whole bungalow staff came charging into my room, each armed with whatever he could lay his hands on. The multiplicity of batons, swords, rods, shovels and spades had transformed my room into a panic-stricken battle-field, when the caretaker's voice rose above the pandemonium:

'Quiet, you fools! Stop behaving like someone who has never killed a snake.' Turning to Lingappa, 'Now where was the snake?'

'Flush, flush, bathroom flush!' replied Lingappa, showing the others into the bathroom, while choosing for himself a safe place at the entrance.

The snake-killers tiptoed into the bathroom, but the snake was nowhere to be seen. Lingappa who, by then, was so self-conscious of his bare feet that he looked all set to hold them up in his hands, carefully stuck his neck out into the bathroom, inspected the space around him, up, down, left, right, and then indicated in a tortured voice:

'There, there in the flush. The naga came out of the water-hole, and like this — ai-ai-yo!' — he cupped his hand to mime the snake's hood — 'like this, the naga stood. Now it has gone back into the water.'

'Back into the water-hole?' wondered the caretaker, adding with a tinge of disbelief, 'Are you sure? Snakes here like neither water nor slippery surfaces.'

'Sure, sure. I am sure. Madam also saw it,' reaffirmed Lingappa.

'Did it have a spotted hood?'

'Yes. Brown spots, and big like that.'

'Aha! It must have been a cobra then. But in the water-hole?' mused the caretaker, sceptically.

He then took a stiff thick wire, and going round the flush, stirred the water. The cobra raised itself — the caretaker recoiled clumsily, though still clutching the wire. The snake emerged further, holding itself erect, seemingly unperturbed. 'Pull, pull the chain, pull it hard,' spouted the gardener. 'Flush it down.'

The caretaker pulled the chain, water gushed out, but the snake raised its hood even higher, like the fearless Hindu snake-God relishing his bath in the Ganges.

The cobra began to tauten its body. 'Watch out!' the gardener rattled, picking up his shovel. 'Careful, it's about to leap out.'

Everyone retreated two steps backwards. Just then, the cobra sprang another surprise — it dipped back into the water-hole.

'Clever bastard, this one!' swore the caretaker. 'This won't do. We'll have to kill it with petrol. Gasoline fumes can finish a snake off in seconds.'

The caretaker asked Lingappa for a bucket, and stepped out of the house in search of petrol. He didn't have to go too far, since my car was parked right at the doorstep. Its driver, the one who had driven me to Chunar, was sound asleep on the front seat, his feet up on the window and his inclined, salivating mouth staring at the brakes like a spotlight. The caretaker quietly pulled the keys out of the ignition switch, unlocked the gasoline cover and siphoned the petrol out into the bucket. The driver was still asleep, beginning to snore with the stroke of the midday hour.

The caretaker returned to the bathroom, and gently poured a mug of petrol down the pot. The snake didn't react. He poured another. The cobra stirred lazily beneath the water. 'There, there, the petrol is getting the bastard now,' said the caretaker, gnashing his teeth.

He poured another mug. The snake raised its head sluggishly, then collapsed back on the water, its hood floating like a lotus. Gradually, it became more and more inert, until its motionless, overturned head signalled its long-awaited death.

'Finished!' exulted the caretaker. 'Finished. It's dead.'

The caretaker tumbled one last mug triumphantly, this time right on the snake's lifeless head. In a flash, the cobra reared up, alert and fearsome. Seized by panic, the caretaker emptied one, two, three, four, five mugs into the pot. But defying all theories of snakes disliking slippery surfaces, the cobra stretched itself out, and slithered all over the shining white pot, licking with teasing relish every drop of petrol on it.

'Hit, hit, hit it,' exhorted the gardener from the sideline. The caretaker hit the cobra with his rod, smashing the flush in the process. The snake slid back into its aquatic abode.

Just then I heard a voice from the verandah. 'Madam, Madam,' someone screamed, thumping hard at the door. I went out, and found a young, lean and bony gentleman with a

141

briefcase, behind whom stood another man — unshaven, middle-aged, moustachioed, with a large, saffron-coloured bundle slung from his shoulder. Before I could utter a word, the young man stuttered nervously, snivelling:

'Good morning, Madam. My name is Shahid Asafal. Uh! Uh! Yes, yes, I admit it's a difficult name for a foreign ear. It's an Urdu name. It means an "unsung martyr". 'Sniffing around, he added. 'I hear there is a snake in the house.'

'Indeed there is one.'

'Have you killed it?'

'We are trying to.'

'So it's still there! How lucky!' jubilated the young man, clapping his hands. Then he introduced the man behind him. 'He is a snake-charmer, Madam. He can trap the snake for you. Two good deeds in one — you'll get rid of the snake, and he'll get one easily.'

Without quite figuring out the reciprocal arrangement the young man was suggesting, I ushered both of them into the bathroom. The snake-charmer exchanged a few words with the caretaker, then untied his bundle, taking out of it a large piece of cloth, a round cane basket, a half-filled milk bowl, and a peculiar wind-instrument, like a flute bored through a pumpkin shell. He spread the cloth on the floor, and placed the milk-bowl in its centre. Asking everyone, except the young man with him, to move to one side of the bathroom, he began playing a tune on his instrument, moving his torso to the music in rhythmic, round movements. The snake-charmer's assistant stirred the water-hole with a stick, the snake popped its hood out, and within minutes, the music began to cast its spell. The snake-charmer enticed it out of the flush on to the cloth, and then up to the milk-bowl. Once it was fully on the cloth, the charmer's assistant wrapped it in from all sides. The snake was packed into the basket. The brief event looked like magic.

'That was smart, Shahid,' I said to the snake-charmer's assistant. 'Have you been in this job for long?'

'Who? Me? Good heavens, no!' He looked horrified. 'No, Madam, I am not a snake-charmer. I am a double doctor.'

142

'Please forgive me. I didn't mean to . . . '

'No worries, Madam, no worries. I'll tell you more about myself later, but let's first pay the snake-charmer off. One hundred will do.'

I gave the snake-charmer a hundred-rupee note. He left with a smile, but Shahid took a seat on the sofa, placing his briefcase on his lap.

'I am a double doctor, Madam,' he repeated, then asking with an air of wonderment, 'How could you possibly think that I was a snake-charmer? Do I look like one?'

Discreetly skipping his question, I enquired, 'What is a double doctor, Shahid?'

'A double Ph.D., Madam? Someone with two Ph.D.s — like me.'

'I see, so you've done two different theses. That's very impressive indeed. What did you work on?'

'On two very interesting subjects,' he replied, grinning from ear to ear. 'Inter-related, yet independent. The first thesis was on — solid thesis! 800 pages! Full of field work and primary sources! — it was on the snakes and Nawabs of Awadh. That's how, you see, I know all the snake-charmers in town. And the second one was on the kababs and Nawabs of Awadh. Incidentally, have you tasted Munne Mian's kababs, Madam?'

Once again I skipped his question, and remarked, 'Marvellous subjects, I must say. So original. Are you an anthropologist or an ethnographer?'

'A historian really. Or let's say, a social scientist — the umbrella category that takes care of all of us. I tackle subaltern issues but with an interdisciplinary approach to things. It's the latest and the best approach.'

'It might disappoint you to learn that I am a college drop-out,' I said.

'Drop-out?' Shahid shrieked.

'Yes.'

'But how does that matter?' said Shahid, turning his sense of disbelief into a ticklish laughter. 'What matters is that

143

you are a star. Can I ask you for a small favour, Madam?

'Well, if I can be of some help, by all means.'

'Madam, I have just finished a 500-page monograph combining both my theses. It's called *Nawabs, Kababs and Snakes in Awadh: a Contribution towards a Theory of Leisure*. It has come out quite well – readable and less technical than the theses. Panbahar publishers are even willing to publish it.'

'That's not bad for a start.'

'Yes, Madam, but they will publish it only on one condition – if I can get a famous person to write a preface to it. I tried to contact the Chief Minister – he didn't answer. I wrote to the Minister of Sports and Cultural Affairs – he didn't reply either. Then I thought – why not ask a film star? Now who could be a better choice than you?'

'But I know nothing about the subject.'

'I know, I know, Madam, but you are a star – an international one at that. In fact, I discussed it with my publisher last night. He was so thrilled with the idea that he promised to send the manuscript to the printers the minute your preface was ready. And then he'll release the book with your film, which will give us both some free publicity. Madam, please do me this small favour. For you, it's nothing, but for me, it's a question of life and death.'

'But, Shahid, who am I to write on the Nawabs, kababs and snakes of Awadh? I know next to nothing about the subject.'

'That's precisely the point, Madam. The last thing the publisher wants is a scholarly preface. He wants something light-hearted – fast-moving, thrillerlike, full of anecdotes. Please Madam . . . this book can make or break my career. If I can have it published, I'll find a job at the University – otherwise I might just have to live all my life taking commissions from snake-charmers.'

'You mean you took a commission from the snake-charmer? For having got him a snake?'

'Of course, yes, Madam. Money is money. Business is business,' asserted Shahid forcefully. 'Please, Madam.'

'You don't seem to appreciate my position, Shahid. How can I write a preface on a subject I know nothing about?'

'Why not? If the uneducated Ministers and Presidents here can write five prefaces per day — why can't you? Write anything, Madam. You don't even have to read the book. Please, Madam . . .'

The desperate double Ph.D. dumped the manuscript on my lap and left. But he couldn't have come across a more unwilling reader of his subject than me. Between the kababs and the snakes, my fate already seemed well-sealed from all ends: Munne Mian's kababs had killed my appetite for ever, and now with a cobra peering from the flush-pot, I looked all set to acquire a life-long constipation. Let alone read, the mere sight of Shahid's manuscript in the drawing room made me shudder with horror. I asked Lingappa to put the monograph away in the kitchen, lest the highly-charged mythological atmosphere of the bungalow attract snakes to words written in their honour.

Shahid's persistent phone calls for the preface ended up forcing me to brave the inferno of snakes and kababs. I leafed through the manuscript. Most of it was unreadable, replete with endless details that left me cold and indifferent. In fact, the footnotes occupied more space in the book than the text itself. At times, the thin, rectangular strips of prose laid out in tall and bony, vertically-arranged footnotes resembled a 500-page-long river bridge, precariously balanced on shaky pillars. Perhaps the only tolerable section of the book was its last part — called 'the Nawabs, Kababs, and Snakes, a love story' — which was livelier than the rest, and narrated stories about a few kabab and snake-maniac Nawabs. The chapter on a snake-temple near Lucknow was quite captivating, giving gory details of the shrine. If the documentation of our double Ph.D. could be believed, this temple, said to be the earthly abode of Lord Shiva, was home to hundreds of wild snakes: in its compound, snakes hung from trees like tap-roots and crawled on the ground like ants. The snake-temple was also the last hope of infertile women, and it was alleged to have such supernatural powers that none of its female pilgrims had ever returned from it dissatisfied. (One of

Shahid's many hypotheses was that the temple's highly charged fertility-inducing atmosphere could well be due to some invisible sperm haze that Lord Shiva had sprayed around the temple.) I found the chapter quite fascinating, even if it required a double dose of Valium to put me off to sleep.

'So how did you find the book, Madam?' asked Shahid when he came to pick up the preface.

'Interesting – well-researched, carefully structured.'

'I was sure you would enjoy it,' he said self-appreciatingly. 'It's just the book for a foreigner. Nawabs, snakes and good Mughlai food are the three things the Europeans love about India. In fact, to tell you the truth, I wrote it keeping the foreign audience in mind. And did you read the bit on the snake-temple?'

'Oh yes! I meant to ask you – does it really exist?'

'Of course, yes. If you like, we can go there one day. It's barely 147 kilometres from Lucknow.'

'Oh! No, no,' I said, shuddering unconsciously at the thought of that temple, 'I don't think I'll find time for that. But I thought that was the strong point in the book. You could have written a little more on it.'

'I had, in fact, but the publisher slashed it. He didn't want the book to exceed 500 pages, you see. Otherwise, I had recounted this fabulous story of how the temple came into being. Do you know it was a Muslim Nawab who had it built?'

'You mean it is a Muslim shrine?'

'That's the fascinating thing about it, Madam. It is a Hindu shrine, but built by a Muslim Nawab. Do you know why? You see, the Nawab had a wife who, before her marriage, used to be a poor dancing-girl in Lucknow. She was so poor that she had to sell her child to a European. Now, after she married the Nawab and became rich, she wanted her child back, but the European had already left India. She was so disturbed by the fact of having lost her child, that she became mad. In fact, she had another son with the Nawab, but she was still obsessed with getting her first one back. Then, in her madness, she somehow started feeling that only snakes could return her child. She started worshipping snakes. After her death, the Nawab built the temple in her memory and only God knows how, snakes started coming there.'

'Do you know the name of this European?'

'Yes, Charles Rousseau.'

'And the woman.'

'Bibi Humra.'

Bibi Humra?

TEN

THE KING WAS CONVINCED

that the child in my womb was a boy. He was so excited at the thought of having a son, that he could not bear to be separated from him and his mother even for a minute. He spent his days sitting crouched by my side, his ear gently pressed against my stomach, listening to the throbbing bubble of life inside. At night, he slept with his head between my thighs, his ears carefully positioned to eavesdrop on the events of the pre-natal world. The King claimed to hear Murad, the name we had given our child, sing his favourite ragas, and play the sitar with the virtuosity of a maestro. One night, he saw him in Napoleon's costume, exchanging a pleasantry, ironically, with the King of England. Another time, he saw him fight a fierce dual with the British Resident, giving the bearded monster a fatal blow below his belt. 'Oh! What an angel of a boy we will have, Ann!' sighed the King often, 'Quick, quick, push him out quickly.'

The King's heart skipped a beat the day I nearly lost the foetus in the third month of my pregnancy. I thanked God for having averted the miscarriage, but the King put the blame for this near mishap squarely on himself. 'I am sure this was caused by my injudicious prying into the pre-natal world,' he said, remorsefully. 'My childish excitement must have ended up inciting the wrath of the evil spirits.' Taking this event to be a veiled, divine warning, the King vowed to make amends,

d never to try listening into the burping metamorphosis of
e inside my womb.

To avoid any more misadventures of the sort, the King
ked me to move to Murad Mahal, my private palace, where
was to stay until the birth of the child. It was decided that
e would now communicate to each other through letters.
umtaz-the-eunuch was appointed as our personal messenger.

At the palace, I maintained a diary.

* * *

ages from my diary)

an is born with a deep, internal divide that separates his
ul from his body. This is the root of his loneliness.

Since this divide is inherently unbridgeable, he is con-
mned to a life-long loneliness. His body will grow with time,
indeed his soul, but both will grow parallelly, independently
each other — they will never meet, for they are destined not
meet. As a deer looks for musk all his life, so does man. He
arches mothers, fathers, men, women, for a throb of life that
n bridge this divide, but, alas, all this is illusion. He is looking
r something that does not exist, neither in transparence, nor
en as an invisible presence. It is a key that he is asked to lose
fore opening the door of human life.

Do yogis, saints and sadhus overcome this divide? Perhaps.
t in so doing, don't they lose the very palpability of life? Its
nsuality, its heart-beat, the charm of its illusory pleasures.
on't they attain nirvana by living a life that is not life?

If there is anything that can overcome this deep innate
vide, it is motherhood. At least, in its gestation period
hen the child and mother are still existentially one and
e same. The presence of a life within, palpating, breath-
g, watching, listening, touching, feeling, makes the mother
hieve a moment of existential self-sufficiency, of completeness,
 the whole. It is a moment of sublime unity, the bridging of
e body–soul divide not from outside, but from within. That

is why motherhood is also the season of our purest dream
. . .

I dream a lot these days. Last night, I dreamt of a divine
sculptor, but one could only see his hands. He was sitting inside
my womb, beside a candle. Waves of darkness and light floated
on his hands. I asked him: What are you doing? What else? he
replied. Sculpting your child. He was working with light brown
clay, shaping a little doll. When the body of the doll was ready
he opened a small, turquoise box, and took out of it a pair
live, human, light green eyes, and set them into the doll. The
sight of a lifeless doll with real, sparkling eyes, frightened me
The sculptor then gently patted the doll once on its cheek. The
doll suddenly came alive. Clay turned into flesh, and the child
began to cry. I took it in my arms.

The divine hands by now had disappeared.

Oh Motherhood! You are a season of dreamy dreams.

* * *

The King is madly in love with me. Much more than he
ever was before. He writes long letters to me every day
at times, twice a day. He is such a wonderfully wicked man
At times, I wonder if his imagination will ever be understood
by his mundane contemporaries. I received another marvellous
letter from him today. He writes:

> I dreamt of our child again last night. Or was it
> today? — I don't remember. You see, my slumber
> lately has been so full of him that I try and sleep
> for as long as possible — since that is the only way
> of keeping him before my eyes. So I sleep seven times
> a day, in snatches. You might like to ask, why seven?
> Because the court astrologer has told me that seven is
> our auspicious number. Yes. I now recollect. I dreamt
> of him today, in my after-breakfast nap.
>
> Oh Bap-re-bap! He was such a good-looking boy I
> saw in my dream. Fair as a cow, sharp perfect features,

light green eyes, tall, well-built, with long, frizzy hair, yes, with long, black, natural frizzy hair. Poor Khan-the-barber! What will he do when our son takes over the throne!

It was late evening. The three of us, you, me and our son, were sitting out in the garden under a full moon. Murad winked at me, and said cheekily: in your days you couldn't go to the moon, Father. Come, let me have the pleasure of showing you another land. He asked one of his attendants to fetch his lunar-cloak from his chamber. When the blue, satin, whale-shaped cloak arrived, Murad spread it on the lawn, and sat on it, and then asked me to sit beside him. Hold me tight now, father, he said, it gets quite windy up there. The cloak flew off into the air, rising at a slant along two, fine beams of moonlight. At times, it was wet and windy, but not bothersome. When the cloak reached the lunar orbit, it began to circle around it, looking for a place to land. I noticed that the moon was not yellow or silvery, as we had always imagined it to be, but blue – bruise-blue, like the blue of your love-bites. Then we felt a braking sensation, and the cloak descended. Everything around us was blueish – plants, grass, land, mountains. It was a very poetic sight, but I must admit, a little frightening.

How do you find this land, Father? asked Murad. Much to my astonishment, I noticed that as he spoke, with each exhalation of breath, hence with each word, the air in front of his mouth changed colour, describing colourful arches. How do you find it here? Murad enquired again. A little eerie, don't you think so? I replied, observing that my words too had the same effect. The conversation between us thus became an exchange of colours. Strangely, our words had lost their sound, but not their sense; it was probably because now the meaning was hidden in the shapes and colours of the arches. For instance, a short crisp order was usually denoted by a straight, single-colour line, while a poetic couplet was represented by an elliptical rainbow.

We decided to take a stroll. But, my goodness, it was like walking on cotton-wool. We tripped and fell, but hobbled along, until we came across a tall, old man, who was so badly hunch-backed that, from a distance, he resembled a question mark (?). He wore a baggy, blueish white gown, and a round, cloth hat on his head. We greeted each other. His English I noticed was incomprehensible: he had a strong, drawling, nasal accent, which was made worse because he kept nibbling at something. Are you happy here? I asked him. He blew a string of multicoloured bubbles out of his mouth, meaning, Yes, but I miss carrots. There are no carrots here. His remark indeed puzzled me, for I saw that what he was eating was precisely a carrot. But isn't that a carrot in your hand? I asked. Yes, he replied moaning, but it is stale. You don't get fresh ones here. But why did you come here in the first place, old man? I asked him. In search of heathens, he answered, smiling behind a light pink haze.

Come, let's find him some carrots. I said to Murad, and the three of us entered a carrot-farm. The farmer saw us, and came leaping towards us, screaming: Get out, get out of there, go back to your land. Murad and I escaped, but the old man tripped on his gown, and was caught.

What a dream, Ann! Do you know who these fellows in the dream were? The farmer was undoubtedly Bhanu, our palace gardener. And the other fellow who was looking for heathens, was Father Donald Reigen, an American missionary who was found dead a few years ago in a dancing-girl's bed in Lucknow. But what a dream, Ann! Do you think our son will annex the moon to Awadh one day?

I think of you, and our little one . . .

N

It is a full, lunar cycle since the King last wrote to me. His silence has been the cause of my insomnia. I sat up late into the night, watching the moon swim in a pool of water.

* * *

Mumtaz-the-eunuch came to meet me this morning. Has the King sent me a letter? I asked him. No, Begum Sahiba, he replied, taking a seat on the floor. He didn't look his usual effusive self.

You look anxious, Mumtaz.

Palace weather is like that in the mountains, Begum Sahiba, he murmured.

You mean it is as cool and pleasant?

No, Begum Sahiba — as unpredictable. You expect it to rain, the sun begins to shine. You think it will be sunny, clouds overcast the sky. Just like the ambience in the palace.

Why do you say this, Mumtaz? Are the British bothering the King again?

I can't say what exactly is happening, but I suspect something is happening, Begum Sahiba.

I don't understand your riddle, Mumtaz.

Something is rotting in the royal palace, Begum Sahiba. I fear people are conspiring against you.

Who? I enquired, startled. Who is conspiring?

I don't know, but I fear the other Begums are jealous of your child. I am told Dulari is doing everything within her means to have her son accepted by the British as the heir.

Has the King been informed of this?

I doubt it, but our King is naïve, Begum Sahiba. Then, strangely, even Khan-the-barber has been meeting the British Resident behind the King's back. I feel the British are using Khan to introduce another woman into the King's life.

Who? That vicious seductress — Taj Mahal?

No, an English lady – Barbara, the Prime Minister's English wife. She came to visit the King last night.

Is the King being unfaithful to me, Mumtaz?

No, I don't think so, Begum Sahiba. But all I mean to say is that the palace atmosphere is not clean. Stench of intrigue, conspiracy and mischief pervades the air. Every now and then, I find hush-hush meetings in the nooks and corners of the zenana. Something is rotting there, Begum Sahiba. I thought I should bring it to your notice. I didn't want you to be taken unawares by the royal whirlpools of jealousy.

I wrote to the King, hinting at what I had just been told, though I purposely refrained from bringing up the subject of the English woman. Mumtaz took the letter and left, saying, God bless you.

He is a true friend.

* * *

The King answered my letter with due promptness. He wrote:

You seem to be wondering why I haven't written all these days. The answer is simple. I have been busy. Do you know with what?

For seven days, I pretended, to the world and to myself, to be you – yes, a pregnant mother! I dressed in your clothes (stuffed a feather cushion under a loose tunic!), walked, talked and behaved like you. But after barely twenty-four hours, I figured out that pregnancy was indeed very tiring. I felt exhausted, even a bit nauseous. So I went off to sleep, and slept continuously for six days, ceaselessly dreaming of our son. Would you believe it that I dreamt of him once non-stop for seventy-two hours? I wonder how many Kings on this earth have loved their child as much.

Even if I am not by your side to comfort you, don't despair, my love. I am with you each moment in

154

my dreams. Do not be anxious, and have faith in my imagination. My dreams tell me that our child is in the pink of health. I see him grow each hour. I thank God for the lucidity of my dreams. They have enabled me to feel from within the entire experience of pregnancy.

I miss you and the little King of Awadh so much, that I have often felt like breaking my vow, and coming to see you. I yearn for those nights when I used to sleep with my head between your thighs, and listen to the little master sing my favourite ragas.

Since I have never been dishonest with you, I have a confession to make. I have missed sleeping between your thighs so much, that I could not bear to wait any longer for those moments of divine bliss. Since you were away, I asked a young girl called Taj Mahal to substitute for your thighs at night, I swear on God there is nothing more between us than that.

Here is the last couplet I wrote for you:

Since your arrival in my life
Your glances have melted and melted me
Into a lake of spinning pleasures.

God is great.

N

P.S. Oh yes, I forgot to reply to you about the deteriorating palace ambience you mention in your letter. I don't think there is any ground for alarm, but thanks for the information anyway. This British Resident is a real bastard. I am thinking of having him dispatched to heaven a bit too prematurely for his liking!??? So don't be surprised if you hear one day that Mr Resident has been . . . God bless you and the little one.

N

My story-teller hinted today that the King has been having
fun with that witch, Taj Mahal. He went with her and five
other young women to Claude Marteau's famous steam-bath,
the renowned den of royal orgies. She suspected that the King
had spent one whole day there. This could well be another
rumour born in the rather fertile imagination of the palace
gossip-mongers.

The King is whimsical and fickle, but not a liar. He
doesn't need to lie. But, frankly, I am getting a bit weary
of my moody husband's moods.

* * *

Mother came to visit me after a long time today. The other
Begums are jealous of my child, I told her. Take care of yourself
Ann, she said, your child matters to me more than all the Kings
and Begums of this world.

Then she asked me in detail about all that Mumtaz had
said. She even read the King's letters to me. Suspecting foul
play, she took away half my jewels with her.

* * *

Since Mumtaz warned me about the jealousies around me,
I have been constantly anxious. The King's letters no longer
comfort me, and the balmy calm of motherhood has now turned
into a distant dream. My child kicks and moves inside me, but
I do not seem to smile any more. My heart throbs with the
incertitudes of life.

After so many years, I reminisced on the day Mumtaz-the-
eunuch came to fetch me to Lucknow from my mother's house.
Before leaving, I had climbed up to the terrace, and sat against
a chimney-stack, wondering if I preferred the life of a carefree

commoner to that of a queen. I must have been carried away by avarice to have reached the royal palace. If I were asked to choose again, I would probably like to return to the life of an ordinary woman, like my mother. But can we ever rescale the ladder of time? Time, like fate, is an irreversible order. So this palace shall be my prison.

* * *

A bleeding pigeon has been visiting me for many days now. Each morning when I wake up, I see it on my window, fluttering and dripping blood against the first rays of the sun.

It is a strange pigeon. The first day, it was bleeding from its leg. The next day, from its belly. Then from its neck. Then, eyes. This morning I pointed it out to my chamber-maid. Turning her back on the pigeon, she said: You should avoid looking at blood during pregnancy, Begum Sahiba, it is a bad omen.

* * *

Another anxiety-ridden day. After many days, the King wrote to me again:

> I am afraid, deeply afraid. I am surrounded by sinister events and rumours. It's unbearably frightening. Had you not been in the delicate state of pregnancy, I would have loved to share my anxieties with you – especially because they concern you and our child. But let me warn you in advance. I have horrible things to recount.
>
> God is great.
> But I am afraid.
>
> N

The King's letter worried me intensely. I sent Mumtaz back with a short message:

My Lord, you should either fully inform me of your worries, or not at all. Half-news is worse than bad news. Such suspense can be fatal for our child. So I beg of you to share your worries with me. After all, I am your spouse, My Lord. It is my duty to take the weight off your mind. Please write by return of hand.

The King replied:

No, no, how I can share such horrors with you, my love? It can be traumatic for your mental health. If you insist, I will give you one more lead into the mystery. People are asking me to choose between myself and our child. I shall say no more on the subject. Let me not go down in history as a King who wrecked the nerves of his queen during the fragile period of pregnancy.

God is great,
But I am afraid.

N

I sent Mumtaz back with another note:

Anxiety is killing me. Please tell me what has overcome your spirits. Your queen is made of firmer mettle than you think.

* * *

The King responded to my desperate appeal today:

Your persistence has compelled me to share with you the most terrifying experience of my life. In spite of my intrinsic tendency to perceive everything in life with poetic eyes, I shall try and recount the events in as objective a manner as possible. This is what my eyes saw:

I was playing chess with Khan-the-barber on the terrace. He as usual had lost the first three games in a row, but in the fourth one, was putting up a good defence. When I trapped his King once again from all sides, Khan, who otherwise is a good loser, had tears in his eyes. Taking pity on a player of limited mental resources, I said to him: Think carefully, Khan, you still have an opening to save your King. So Khan began to ponder, holding his head between his hands. Leaving him to his studious posture, I got up to ask for a bottle of champagne. On my return, which was after a good fifteen minutes, I was amused to notice Khan in the same position, elbows on the table, head clasped in his hands, staring down at the board. Still haven't moved, Khan, I said teasingly. Don't tell me that I'll have to play for my rival too. Khan didn't respond to my remark.

Tom — remember that Irish opium-addict in the kitchen! — came up with a bottle of champagne, and popped it open. As the champagne started to fizz, I observed that a similar sound was coming from Khan's mouth. Khan, Khan, hey Khan — he didn't answer. He then swung his head back on the chair, his half-open eyes now looking up into the sky. It was obvious he was asleep. The fizzy sound from his mouth then slowly turned into a deep-throated crackling, and three pink bubbles, like small balloons, escaped from his mouth and floated before his eyes. I figured out what was happening, and ordered: Quick, quick, call the dream-attendant. Khan is dreaming.

Ka, ka, ka-ka, ki, ki, ki-ki, King, King — Khan uttered in his dream. He was restless, frantically motioning his hands, as though drowning in water. Yes, yes, I am here, Khan, I am here. I tried to reassure him, without disturbing his clairvoyant dream. Ki, ki, ki-ki, ki-ki-ki, king, se, se, se-se, say, say-say, say-save, save the King, cried Khan, knocking the chess-table over with his foot. I went close to Khan's face, and said: The

King is here, Khan. He is here. He is safe and sound, Khan. What is happening? Khan scratched me in the face, tilted his face to the right, and began wailing like a dog, Noo, noooo, nooooo, noooooo, nooooooo, dooo, dooo, doooo, doooon't, no, dooooon't ki-ki-kee-keel, ki-ki-king, no, don't kill, pe, pee, peee, pee-pee, plee-plee, no, doon't kiill Kiing, plee-please. I panicked and shook Khan awake.

He sat up in his chair, blinked his eyes, and wiped the pink foam off his mouth.

What was it, Khan?

A nightmare. Your Majesty, he answered, shuddering. Oh! I fear it is a sinister portent.

What was it, Khan? Can you recollect it?

Yes, Your Majesty, but I only hope it is not true.

But what is it, Khan? I asked impatiently.

Your Majesty, I saw your own son murdering you.

Which one?

Murad — your son, Your Majesty.

Khan began to cry, praying. I only hope this is not true, Your Majesty. Oh! There was blood all over your face, it was so gruesome.

But do you remember how it happened. Khan?

Yes, Your Majesty. He strangled you. But don't worry, Your Majesty, it may be a false alarm.

What disturbs me, Khan, is that your dreams are never false.

Yes, that is exactly what is worrying me, Your Majesty.

So you can well imagine, my love, how I must take to this clairvoyant revelation. The first consequence of this incident has been that I've stopped dreaming of our son any more.

God is great,
But I am afraid.

N

Begum Sahiba. Begum Sahiba, announced Mumtaz-the-eunuch,
panting. Khan Sahib has run away.

Run away? Where to?

Run away! He has fled the palace!

Where to?

Nobody knows, Begum Sahiba. His house is empty, he
is untraceable. He fled last night.

But how?

Nobody knows, Begum Sahiba. His gatemen are absconding
too. They say two British carriages were seen stationed near his
house last night. I fear his fleeing is part of a larger plot.

Of what kind, Mumtaz?

Can't say, Begum Sahiba. Since your pregnancy, the palace
has become a nest of intrigues. Beware, Begum Sahiba, beware.
I fear Khan is up to mischief. His loyalty has been bought off
by the British, I fear.

But the two persons the British have hated all these years
are Khan and me. What use is he to them?

He is a store-house of secrets, Begum Sahiba. Without
Khan, there will be no King.

So you suspect that he has joined the British, is that it?

Yes, and Dulari too. I fear the King is being marooned
from all sides. That's what the British did with the King's
father.

* * *

The king confirmed Mumtaz's information a few days later.

Khan has vanished. His mysterious disappearance has
been the worst blow to my morale. First I suspected
that he had been abducted. But then, his house, his
cupboards and his safes were absolutely empty. So he
has fled. The Prime Minister has charged him with the

theft of ten lakh pounds. What worries me more is that he has taken along with him the keys to my private well. I have had no water for this whole week. Just champagne and wine. I feel dry inside, like a tandoor.

If things on earth have looked bad, those in heaven are no better. I called in Ram Papita Shudh, the state astrologer, to seek a second opinion on Khan's gruesome dream about our son. The Brahmin may not have Khan's visual insight into the future, but he has surely been known to read the mood of the planets with flawless accuracy. I explained to him the problem. He asked for our respective horoscopes, and then did some serious calculation. He came yesterday with his predictions. Alas! We are all, you, me and Murad, menaced by Satan from the time of your delivery. In fact, he felt that this whole year is bad for us. So I am afraid Khan-the-barber might once again have predicted the sad truth.

Now that Khan-the-barber has vanished, and with him our only access into the unknown, I have asked the Brahmin astrologer to move into the palace. His pious shadow in the house is comforting, though frankly, his noisy midnight rituals and pre-dawn chants — bells ringing all over the palace — have been the main cause of my delirious fits of rage. Do you think I am going mad?

I asked the astrologer if he could suggest something to counter the evil influence of the planets. He advised me to give up meat and alcohol. Giving up meat should be no problem, but without champagne and wine, especially when my well-water is no longer safe, I fear I might die of dehydration. So you appreciate my dilemma . . .

I feel weak. Please do not worry if I don't write as regularly as before.

God is great,
But I am afraid.

N

* * *

Mumtaz-the-eunuch brought some more news from the palace. A General in the King's army who has been asked to conduct an inquiry into Khan's mysterious disappearance approached the King, and confided in his ear:

It has been brought to my notice, Your Majesty, that Khan had illicit relations with Begum Ann Walters. He took to his heels because he was afraid that His Majesty would discover this.

Preposterous! snapped the King. Unthinkable! What kind of an inquiry have you conducted if you don't even know what every street-urchin in Lucknow knows — even Cleopatra could not seduce Khan! He was a sworn virgin!

* * *

Mother came to visit me again. I told her all that had happened since her last visit. Fearing the worst that might befall us, she took away the rest of my jewels, leaving me with a few ruby and diamond necklaces.

* * *

I have a premonition that the King will end up killing my unborn child. He cried out in his letter today:

Horror! Horror! What a blood-curdling dream I have just woken up from, my love! I was surrounded by thugs, armed with spears and lances. Among them, I spotted the Resident, the barber and our child — strangely, all three of them together in the enemy camp. They wanted to slay me. I went down on my knees, and wept and begged them mercy. But they burst out jeering and laughing. As I was still looking at them, their faces suddenly vanished, and all I could see around me now were rings and rings of laughter — laughter laughing laughter, laughter laughing murder, laughter laughing revenge, laughter laughing hammers, laughter pounding my head with stones of laughter. The laugh-rings then slowly transformed into a huge, revolving, flour-grinding stone. Through the hole in the centre, I saw my body go down into the grinding stone. There was a stream of blood on one side, and a thin, tonguelike sheet of flesh on the other.

What misdeeds are we paying for, my love?

God is great,
But I am afraid.

N

* * *

ELEVEN

(pages from my diary)

RAIN WOKE ME

again last night. I got up and sat on the bungalow verandah. It was a beautiful downpour – straight, soothing, like threads of milk in black wine.

As I was sitting, Awaara emerged unexpectedly from the rain, drenched.

'What are you doing loitering around this late into the night?' I asked him. 'Do you realise what time it is?'

'As I said – vagabond I was, and vagabond I have remained,' Awaara said drunkenly. 'But why are you up so late, Valerie?'

'Just felt like watching the rain.'

We sat for a while, our chairs facing the rain. Then lighting a half-wet cigarette, I reflected. 'It was quite a coincidence to find a reference to Bibi Humra in a book on snakes and kababs.'

'Aha! So you were thinking about your roots in India.'

'Oh no! What roots can I look for?'

'Why? Your roots.'

'Trees need roots, sweetheart, not bohemian autumn leaves like me.'

'That's a very despairing thought,' said Awaara, removing his wet shirt. 'Why do you say that? Everyone thinks of his roots some time or other.'

'Not me. You know what my mother once said – don't dig for your roots, you might sink into the earth.'

'Gosh! What a violent thing to say to a daughter.'

'She probably had her reasons for it. Did you know she didn't even know the name of her husband? He flew into her life one night, and the next morning, he flew out of it. A few months later I was born. So, to speak of roots was a bit delicate at home.'

'But that's strange. From the way you speak of Bibi Humra, I thought your family had a well-researched family tree.'

'Indeed it did, but the research ended in my mother's life-time. After she died, I was the only survivor of my family. So I took my rootlessness as freedom, and tried to make the best of it.'

'But doesn't the idea of meeting someone from Bibi Humra's lineage excite you? I find it fascinating to see two families come together after a century and a half.'

'Not me. We relate to time differently in the West, you know. But what I find intriguing is the way a string of coincidences is pushing me towards Bibi Humra — without any effort on my part. Do you think it is destiny?'

Awaara brought two glasses and poured drinks. It was still raining.

* * *

Awaara, whose character I am discovering more and more every day, is a man of seasonal fixations. In summer he was obsessed with kababs: his eyes saw Munne Mian and his kababs everywhere. These days his obsession is the monsoon. Rains have cast a spell on his mind. He gave me one of his writings today. It's called 'Black Rain' and reads like a play:

SCENE I

Storm
Yellow sky — pent-up, bloodshot, like a schoolboy itching for revenge. The sky becomes more and more tense, convulsing

166

into a dusty brown cloud of dust — until its nerves explode, and its sabulous anger slaps the earth.

Wild dust-tops spin above rooftops. Newspapers, Berlin walls, Ceaucescus, perestroikas, leaves, rags, paper bags, a million objects dot the sky.

Window-panes protest, doors slam in anger, skylights commit suicide, trees bow and plead, dogs bark and cats purr, but the wind reigns supreme.

SCENE 2

Thunder
Slow fade out. Grains of dust dissolve one by one. The stage turns light grey. Then, slowly, fluffy balls of deep grey clouds appear on the wings. Wind whistles, rolling the clouds out towards the centre of the stage. Clouds break into a roaring celestial laughter. Lightning protests, scratching the clouds mildly with its lightning-claws. Clouds roar back laughter. Lightning licks its lips, and whips the cloudy pitcher with its electric chain. Clouds protest, roar, shriek, plead, seeing their wounds become large and black. Lightning whips again, and again, and again. The clouds burst, the pitcher explodes. Black-out.

SCENE 3

Rain
Begin with flat dim lights. Sound of rain — on roads, in woods, on tin rooftops.

Torrents and torrents of naked white rain, free, unchained, rolling, dancing, disordered, demented, mad — mad like that jubilant girl who died laughing into the pouring clouds.

The monsoon is not rain, it is the shadow of a dancer raining at her best.

Rain, rain, my beautiful rain. I shall receive you naked to feel you, rain.

'Rain is the shadow beneath the immense straw hat of the young girl of my dreams, the ribbon of which is the rill of rain.'

167

Black-out.

Sunset

During the black-out, rivulets overflow the stage into the audience, wetting those in the front seats. After the first sounds of protest and unease have been heard, lights come on.

Shafts of light slicing through the fretting clouds. Blotches of homeless clouds floating in the sky, gazing down at the earth the way a mother-bird does at her eggs fallen from the nest. Silence, pin-drop silence. Listen to the light weep, the cloud sail and the bird mourn.

The cloud half-uncovers the face of a blushing bride that the audience had thought was the setting sun. She raises her veil and smiles, letting escape from her lavender mouth a lyre-bird that goes and perches on a cloud. Then the bride takes her jilted lover by her hand, and slowly slips under the crimson, love-moist sheet. So begins the night of adulterous pleasures — well before the priest had finished chanting the hymn on marital obligations. Black-out.

SCENE 5

Night

Rain and night are sisters. Just as night dreams at the crossroads of memory and fantasy, rain rains at the same place and time. Nightly rain invokes nostalgia. It freezes clocks, and shows you the raindrops on your retina that have now turned into moss. Rain is green, like a *cadavre*. Black-out.

* * *

Shooting has been quite hectic of late, especially for Vikram and the Resident who have been working night and day to wind up their scenes. Deboo looks a much calmer man now, having caught up with the original shooting schedule.

We saw some of the rushes today at the Smita Patil Memorial theatre. Unbelievable results! Vikram was splendid, so tacitly eccentric and funny, just like the King. There is something uniquely versatile about Indian actors — act, fight, dance, sing, they can do virtually anything under the sun.

But then there is one great difference between acting for the cinema here, and for that in the West. The accent in Europe is on underplaying, on dissolving oneself into the image, while, over here, emphasis is more on drama, on action, on dialogue. But that's the old, endless debate. What is cinema — filmed action or the film itself as action?

Whatever one may say of the differences of perception between the Indian and the western cinema, one thing is quite clear: *Shameawadh* is shaping into a good film. Unless they kill it on the editing table . . .

* * *

After kababs and the monsoon, Awaara's latest obsession has been Bibi Humra. He got up this morning saying:

'Let's try and track down Bibi Humra's descendants.'

'What's the use?'

'It's fascinating to see two families come together after nearly two centuries.'

'Well . . . '

'Don't be a spoil-sport now, Valerie. Let it be just for fun.'

'Okay, but how?'

'We'll consult the Wasiqua records,' said Awaara, and then explained the nature of these records.

Wasiqua in Urdu means pension. A system of royal pensions was created by the Kings and the Nawabs of India for their widows. They deposited large sums of money with the English Company, and asked it to pay out monthly pensions to their Begums after their deaths. Often, these stipends were the Begums' only source of income.

The Wasiqua system at the beginning seems to have functioned quite efficiently, but over time, it became more and more complex, the main problem being the identification of the King's legal heirs. What rendered this difficult was the custom of Muta, temporary marriages. Strictly speaking, the Kings were supposed to have only four wives, the first being the Queen. But, in practice, they had many more, which is what complicated the task of the Wasiqua Office.

Over generations, this played havoc with the pension record books. It had been difficult enough to keep a track of the legal and semi-legal descendants of a King's harem, but when his descendants, in turn, had their own harems, and they, theirs, and they, theirs, turning the virile King's family-tree into a wild tropical forest of trees, bushes, shrubs, and umpteen varieties of wild grass, it became impossible to maintain a who's who of the blue sperm.

The Wasiqua Office in Lucknow maintains a record of this generational confusion, and disburses what is now a pittance to each of the thousands of members of the King's flora and fauna.

We reached the dilapidated red-brick Wasiqua Office in the morning just as it was opening. Awaara's wide array of contacts at the Office surprised me. A salaam here, another there, almost everybody seemed to know him. He walked up to an old family friend and explained to him the purpose of our visit. The gentleman replied in a matter-of-fact but polite manner, 'Come back tomorrow, Awaara. It's going to be quite hectic today. It's the Wasiqua disbursal day.' Awaara didn't insist, and came out of the Office.

'But you must witness the pension scene, Valerie,' said Awaara. 'It's quite a sight. Till now, you've only seen the Nawabs in films and TV soap operas, here you will see another kind.'

We waited on the steps of the Wasiqua Office. Gradually, the Nawabs started to trickle in. The first one had no shoes. The second one's betel-stained pyjamas were tearing at their seams. The third wore an elegant achkan, the traditional long coat, but came in his bathroom slippers. Another, who apparently ran a horse-carriage for a living, discreetly parked his ramshackle carriage a little distance away from the Wasiqua building, and came trotting on a moth-eaten horse.

The Nawabs greeted each other with the flamboyant bow and salaam of the old aristocracy, the very gestures I had been taught for the film, and then queued up to collect their pensions. The first got 10 rupees, the next 5, the one after him, 19 – the total amount of pension for the first five Nawabs still fell short of five English pounds. After collecting their pensions, the Nawabs swaggered out of the building and gathered around a street-hawker sitting in the portico. One by one, they majestically ordered a banana-guava-papaya fruit-salad – all that the pension could buy. They chatted about the good old days that democracy had ended. Then, throwing the banana-leaf bowls away, they salaamed each other again, and left, until the seventh day of the next month would reunite them for the next disbursement.

'But are these real Nawabs?' I asked Awaara, amused.

'Of course, yes – the descendants of great Kings! The world only knows the rich Maharajas and Nawabs. But these ones are equally genuine – in fact, at times, more.'

* * *

I was getting ready to go into the shower, when a voice sang out from the verandah, 'Miss Valerie, Miss Valerie, please.' It was Shahid, the kabab and snake expert, looking unusually scrubbed and clean, his hair swimming in mustard oil. In one hand, he was carrying three plastic briefcases instead of the usual one, and with the other, he was furiously scratching his sparse dry coconut-like beard. 'Good morning, Madam. Very good morning to you,' he wished me, and barged straight into the drawing room, promptly taking a seat on the sofa. It must have been a towel in my hand that made him remark:

'I suppose you were going to the latrine. Go ahead, go ahead, you must never miss on the morning ablutions. Please take your time – finish with the latrine, feel lighter, brush your teeth, have your bath, and then we can have a chat.'

'I am running late, Shahid,' I said, feeling slightly offended. 'Have you again come in connection with the book?'

'No, no, Madam, no problems on that front. I've actually come to return your favour.'

'Return my favour? How?'

'Your preface was a great favour to me – so I thought why not do you one in return,' he said grinning, mildly salivating at the edge of his lips. 'Did you go to the Wasiqua Office the other day looking for information on Bibi Humra?'

'Yes, I did.'

'I knew that! I knew that!' he jubilated, clapping his hands. 'I knew that my book would end up enchanting you. But why did you take the trouble of going to the Wasiqua Office? You should have asked me. I have all the information on the snake temple. Now what do you want to know about it?'

'Nothing – who told you that I wanted information on the snake temple?'

'You didn't? That fellow at the Wasiqua Office said that you had gone there to find out more about Bibi Humra.'

'Yes, about Bibi Humra. But not the snake temple.'

'Oh! One and the same thing! Theirs is an egg-and-hen relationship – if there had been no Bibi Humra, there would be no temple.'

Shahid then looked at his briefcases, muttering to himself, 'Humra, Humra, Humra, Humra – now where did I dump the data on Bibi Humra? In this one I think.' And he plunged his hand into a yellow briefcase on which, strangely, was marked in black bold letters: Disaster Relief Information – a Humanitarian Programme.

He hurriedly scanned dozens of loose papers, mostly in Urdu, but didn't seem to find what he was looking for. Checking his papers a second time, this time more carefully, he looked up at me with dull apologetic eyes:

'No I don't think I have anything on Bibi Humra's ancestors. Before she married the Nawab, she was a poor dancing-girl, you see. Who keeps a track of poor families?'

'But I am interested in her descendants, not her forefathers.'

'Ah!' — Shahid let out a crisp steam-engine shriek — 'You should have said that before. No problem then. I don't even have to consult my data for that, it's all there in my head. In fact, she belonged to a very well-known family of Awadh. It's called the Eklauta Khandan.'

'Called what?'

'Ek-lauta Khandan. That means a family in which each generation has had only one child. You see, Bibi Humra and her husband, Nawab Shahadat Ali Khan, had one son, and so on for six generations. The strange speciality of the snake temple family thus has been that each generation has had only one child until 1960, and always a son.'

'And after 1960?'

'Wait, wait. I'm coming to that. Now in 1960, Nawab Safdar Ali Khan, the descendant of the snake temple family, for the first time had a girl, and not a son. The Nawab was so dismayed at not having a son, that he named his daughter, Tanhai, which means solitude.'

'Is this girl still alive, Shahid?'

'Now wait, wait, let's proceed step by step. You see, this girl, Tanhai, was brought up in a real misogynous atmosphere. Her father was an awful patriarch — he mistreated his Begums, he abused and beat his daughter in public. 'Now, we know' — Shahid pinched a cigarette from my pack, cleared his throat, and continued — 'now we know the end of such stories from Sigmund Freud's analysis of human psychology — Tanhai became mad.'

'Mad!' I uttered, startled.

'Not mad, mad, but half-mad — let's say cracked.'

'Is she in an asylum then?'

'Patience, patience. Madam, you have to be patient to listen to a million-dollar story. When Tanhai joined the anthropology department at college, she went crazy. For some strange reason, she now became obsessed with the idea of building a polyandrous society. Do you know what polyandrous means? It's a category of anthropology — meaning, many men to one woman. You know what I mean,' he winked, 'a society run by nymphomaniacs. With both her parents dead, and no one to check her, Tanhai

173

played havoc with her freedom. She quit college, and set up a polyandrous community which was her way of naming a high-class brothel. She started at home, inviting all kinds of men to her house. In fact, it was even rumoured that she flogged her men. Now the whole thing flared up one day, when a Chief Minister was found half-dead in her community. There was so much hullabaloo that Tanhai was kicked out of Lucknow.'

'So where is she now?' I asked.

'In a jungle. She squats in an old ruin with fifteen other men. She claims to have founded the first utopian polyandrous monarchy on this earth. And she even has offered herself a title – Queen of the Free Women's Utopia of Auratabad.' Asking Lingappa to serve Shahid a drink, I went in to tell Awaara what I had just been told. Expectedly, Awaara was excited, he suggested that I shoot off a letter to Tanhai, seeking an appointment with her. I scribbled a few hasty lines explaining who I was, and requested Shahid to have the letter delivered.

* * *

Shahid dropped into the costume room today, and handed me a detailed sketch of Bibi Humra's family tree.

Snake Temple Family

NAWAB SHAHADAT ALI KHAN
Died 1858

BIBI HUMRA
(note: BH's first son was stolen by a Frenchman, Charles Rousseau)

NAWAB SALAMAT ALI KHAN
1830–1880
(Begum Zehra Bai, Begum Tehmina)

NAWAB MANSUR ALI KHAN
1850–1912
(Begum Zohra, Begum Tuntun, Begum Chameli)

NAWAB ALI YAVAR KHAN

1880–1947
(Begum Rehana, Begum Farida, Begum Shabana)

NAWAB MAHFUZ ALI KHAN
1920–1965
(Hasina Bai, Begum Muqqadara)

NAWAB SAFDAR ALI KHAN
1945–1985
(Begum Shaheen, Begum Roshini, Begum Shah Bano)

TANHAI KHAN
1965–
(Tanhai studied at Oxford Montessori School, Freedom Fighters' Model School, Sacred Heart Convent, and I.T. College, Lucknow.)

Copyright Shahid 'Asafal'

* * *

The love-scene has of late been the bone of contention between the film crew and the Liaison Officer. The LO, as the latter is called, is a representative of the State Censor Board, and his job on the set is to check the shooting of any scenes that might violate the Censor regulations. A couple of days ago, when Vikram and I were shooting the scene in which Miss Walters first makes love to the King, Mr LO stood on top of us like a wrestling referee, keenly supervising the action and the camera angles. For six long hours, he stared at and ogled us lasciviously, and when the scene was at its last shot, he took Deboo aside, and protested. 'Foul play! I've already been lenient enough to permit proper kissing, but this scene is pure pornography.' The producer tried to reason with the LO, arguing that a King admiring his wife's nude body was by no means pornography, but the Censor Officer refused to budge. The verbal tug-of-war ended in the producer insulting the LO in a patently original manner, 'Shut up, you petty, third-rate clerk! You know what you are? – you are a sexually frustrated mosquito! Yes, that's what you are –

a sexually frustrated mosquito! And I will mince you with my fingernails.'

The producer then decided to pull political strings, and contacted the State Chief Minister, who invited us over for a drink at a lakeside bungalow called 'The Lovers' Nest'.

(The Chief Minister, it was common knowledge, was addressed as 'Tiger-Eater Sahib' by his entourage. Apparently, his nickname derived from a daring face-to-face encounter he had had in his youth with a ferocious man-eater in the hills of Kumaon. The Chief Minister, then an adventurous young lad of eighteen, had torn the man-eater to shreds without a semblance of weapon in his hands, and the villagers thus honoured the local hero with a title — the 'Tiger-Eater of Kumaon'.)

In his old age though, very little of the Tiger-Eater seemed to have survived. In fact, when I first saw him, his wiry, hunch-backed, slightly Giacomettian physique made me seriously doubt his fabled tiger-killing capacities; his stalky body under a grossly oversized cap somehow reminded me of a broken pedestal lamp one had put away for repairs. Besides, the brave politician's legendary physiognomy had in the recent past suffered another devastating blow — a massive politico-cardiac attack, from which the Tiger-Eater was still limping back to normality.

The Chief Minister greeted us with the fake warmth of a politician. When a waiter came round to serve drinks, he went up to the Chief Minister holding a tall glass three-quarters filled with whisky in one hand, and a bottle of Pepsi in the other. 'Shall I destroy the colour, Sahib?' asked the waiter. 'Destroy it,' ordered the Minister. For a while, I wondered what that short exchange of words between the master and the slave meant, but the message was decoded the moment the waiter poured a few drops of coke into the whisky, and the dark yellow alcohol turned a gentle Pepsi brown. The Chief Minister gave me a wicked glance, and said 'Who says I am having whisky? This is not whisky — it's plain Pepsi. Oh these public offices are awful! You just need to be seen drinking with an actress once, and the entire press will be talking about the Chief Minister's drunken orgies. Believe you me, the problem in our country is not our poverty, it is our press!'

The Tiger-Eater was the first to down his drink, and sure enough, also the first to soar into the clouds. Eyeing my legs voraciously, he remarked:

'What a smart skirt that is, Madam!'

'You mean what a beautiful pair of legs it shows,' I said spontaneously, putting words in the Chief Minister's mouth. Realising the provocative nature of my remark, I tried to cover up with a more polite statement. 'You like my skirt, and I like your silk shirt.'

'Oh, thank you, it is a designer make,' said Tiger-Eater. 'But more than men, I love women in designer clothes – a slit here, a slit there, they whet an admirer's appetite, you see.' He looked back at my skirt, exclaiming drunkenly. 'A slit in a short skirt is like watching a beautiful valley through a chink in the curtain.'

The Chief Minister must indeed have seen some valley through the slit in my skirt for he then asked me to take a stroll in the lakeside garden. I looked at Deboo and Awaara – they replied with half-amused, half-embarrassed smiles.

'But, but, but,' I stuttered. 'Shouldn't we discuss the censorship question first?'

'Patience, patience,' urged Tiger-Eater, belching out soft whisky and Pepsi fumes. We have enough time to discuss work. If work is worship, relaxation is its reward.' And he led me down a fragrant bougainvillaea alley, at the top of which a sign-board warned, 'Tiger-Eater's Private Grove'.

'How beautiful is the garden in the monsoon!' sighed Tiger-Eater, inhaling fresh air.

'Monsoon is India's best season.'

'Aha! We have similar tastes, I notice. Just look at that patch of green,' said he, pointing to a lush-green thicket, and then added with a strong Wordsworthian overtone, 'so green, so cool, so romantic. Greenery is the music of rain.'

He dwelled on the theme of romanticism for a while, until we turned into a dark alley, and two armed guards popped out of the blue and saluted Tiger-Eater with due ceremony. The Chief Minister jumped backwards, slightly embarrassed by the untimely salutation, and then marched on, pretending not to have noticed the guards. Becoming more businesslike, he said:

'I have seen the Liaison Officer's notings on your shooting. It says your film leaves nothing to imagination.'

'Firstly, this is not true, Sir,' I said, defending our film. 'Secondly, he doesn't seem to understand that this is a historical film. To some extent we have to do justice to reality. What we are showing is only a scratch of what really happened between the King and the Queen.'

'Why? What happened between them?'

'The book speaks so vividly of their erotic relationship. It describes plain and simple oral sex.'

'What sex?' the Chief Minister asked leaning his ear on my mouth.

'Oral sex.'

'Oral? What do you . . . '

'Oral, oral sex — you know what that is. Through the mouth, and . . . '

'Oh! My God! You mean blow job! Gosh! You mean you are doing blow job in the film. To whom?'

'Listen,' I snapped, 'what I meant was that what we are showing is nothing as compared with the reality.'

'But is it true that there are scenes of your — of your fully naked body?'

'Not scenes — just a scene.'

'But one is enough to cause harm!' croaked the Minister. 'You don't murder the same man twice, do you? Once is enough.'

'You surely don't think that an actress commits a murder merely by showing her body?'

'She commits a moral murder — murder of mind.'

'Come off it now, Sir,' I said, chuckling seductively. 'I

thought you loved admiring valleys through chinks in the curtain.'

'Yes. I do, but there is a difference between suggestive and vulgar exposure. Nudity corrupts mind.'

'But do I look vulgar?' I asked, staring invitingly into his eyes.

'No, no, no, no – of course not.' Tiger-eater shuddered, disconcerted. 'You are just perfect.' Recovering his nerve, he continued. 'But tell me, Miss Scott, is it true that you make love to two different actors in the film?'

'Yes. It could have been more had the script demanded it.'

'Excuse me for asking you a personal question – how many different actors have you made love to on screen?'

'Can't say. Ten, fifteen, twenty . . . ' I decided to be bolder with him.

'And in real life?'

'Don't know – fifty, sixty, seventy . . . '

'Hareram! Hareram!' he giggled wailingly. 'She doesn't even remember their number! So you mean you make love for fun.'

'What else? – not to produce children I hope.'

'And you don't even remember the names of your partners. So does that mean that if you made love to someone tonight, you'd forget in a few weeks who it was?'

'Well, not if it were you, Mr Chief Minister.'

He gazed at me, as though perplexed by the illusion and reality of life twinkling before his eyes.

'She's not an actress this woman,' he mumbled to himself, 'she's a sorceress.'

* * *

'Good news, good news, Madam,' announced Shahid on the set today, handing me a crumpled envelope. It was Tanhai's reply to my letter – as bizarre as her reputation.

Dear Miss Scott,

Begum Tanhai, Queen of the Free Women's Utopia of Auratabad, has directed me to convey to you her sense of great delight at reading your letter in which you claim a common descendance from Bibi Humra. That the two sad fragments of Bibi Humra's womb should be reunited after a lapse of 160 years is indeed a matter of joy, and the Queen would feel honoured to receive you with due ceremony at her Auratabad temple.

On reading your letter, it appears that you are not fully aware of the circumstances under which Bibi Humra lost her infant whose illustrious progeny you are. I might take this opportunity to clarify that Charles Rousseau, the French perfume-dealer who was Bibi Humra's contemporary, did not buy the infant from her, but snatched it from her arms, and fled. Years later, it was established that he had fled with the child to France. On being informed of this, Bibi Humra was so grieved that she lost her mental stability. For some unknown reason, she then began to believe that only Lord Shiva, the Hindu Snake-God, could return her lost infant. So, on every full-moon night, she began to hold night-long prayers before a twin idol of Lord Shiva and Charles Rousseau, imploring them to return her child.

In homage to her adoration for Lord Shiva and the well-being of her spirit, Bibi Humra's descendants organise, on each full-moon night since July 1850, the year of her demise, a prayer at a nearby snake temple that was built in her memory.

The Queen of Auratabad would feel honoured to celebrate her family reunion with you over the next full-moon night prayers at the snake temple. The Queen has instructed me to reassure you that the snakes at the temple, though seemingly frightening, are harmless and friendly. I may also add for your information that the next full moon will appear on the 13th.

Looking forward to receiving you.

PUBLIC RELATIONS SECRETARY
TO THE QUEEN OF AURATABAD

I showed the letter to Awaara in the evening. He read it carefully several times over and then without uttering a word, wandered off into the bungalow garden. After a while, he returned to the room, still wordless.

'She does sound crazy, doesn't she?' I remarked. Awaara didn't reply. 'Don't you find the whole thing too eerie? I don't think I can brave this appointment in the company of a million snakes.'

'That's quite immaterial,' said Awaara, with a mischievous glint in his eye, 'I was thinking of something else. I think it is a marvellous subject for a film.'

'What?'

'The story of two cousins coming together after nearly two centuries. You in your own role, Rani in Tanhai's, and I as the script-writer.'

Awaara was so excited by the prospect of turning the Tanhai affair into a film, that he forced me to call Rani. As luck would have it, Rani too seemed quite taken by the idea. Encouraged, Awaara picked up his pen and started working on the story-line.

* * *

TWELVE

(wrote the King breaking a silence of several weeks). It was about Murad and me, playing hide and seek at the palace. He looked quite grown-up, about thirteen: and I was not really that old, but old enough to envy his nimble-footed youth. At one point, Murad searched for me all over the palace, but without any luck. He was nearly in tears when my wheezing — I had some breathing problem I recollect — gave the secret away: I was hiding in the Florentine vase in the riverside garden. The moment he saw me, he burst out laughing, and shot an arrow at me. The arrow hit the rim of the vase, and fell right under my eyes — I saw to my sense of utter horror that it was tipped with poison. 'What are you doing, Murad?' I asked, unable to understand his game. He answered me with a jeering fit of laughter, and shot another arrow. 'Stop it, Murad!' I thundered. He laughed back again, and shot another arrow. Recalling Khan-the-barber's dream about my murder, I suspected foul play, and leapt out of the vase, and started running for shelter. Murad chased me all over the garden, shooting a string of arrows at me, laughing louder and louder. When I knew there wasn't much hope for me to escape his arrows, I plunged into the river . . .

With that I woke up. And do you know where?

Not in my bed, nor on land, but in the river! Yes, right in the middle of the tumultuous river! – about to drown, swallowing gallons of water through my mouth, nose, ears. Luckily, the palace guards arrived in time and rescued me. So you see – I have been nightmaring and dream-walking at the same time. Do you think these are the first signs of my madness, Ann?

So many people have of late been laughing at me in my dreams, that I don't like the sound of laughter any more.

God is great,
But I am afraid.

N

* * *

(The following pages are again from my diary, but unlike the preceding ones, they were written many months after the events described here.)

It had been a particularly hard day for my nerves. The King's letter had once again provoked unbearable cramps in my stomach, and his gory imagination seemed to augur the worst. Fears of miscarriage and still-birth ceaselessly haunted my mind. The more the King spoke of his dreams, the more I suffered from anxiety, from the unforeseenness of the unknown – I was terrified of the unknown. I wanted to see my destiny in a mirror.

Unable to catch a wink of sleep one night, I sent for Shabnam, the 'prophetic storyteller' in the harem, who was renowned for combining the art of story-telling with an acute sense of intuition. On many occasions in the past, she had predicted the future of many a Begum in the stories she recounted. Shabnam arrived and sat on the floor beside my pillow, asking:

What kind of story would Begum Sahiba fancy?

Something new, Shabnam, I said. Something prophetic, that can unravel the labyrinths of my destiny.

She reflected for a while, biting her nails, and then, began a story, commencing with the customary prologue:

Sleeps all the world —
Waking is God alone —
This tale is not so false.
Nor are its words so sweet.
Eyes of mine saw it not.
From hearsay I repeat it.
Of him who hath composed it.
False or true, the meed be his.

There was an ageing King who did not have any children, because his wife was barren. One day, he confided his sorrows to the Vizier, and asked him for advice. The Vizier said: In the middle of a great jungle, many hundreds of miles away, there lives a holy fakir, Your Majesty. He sits at the foot of a great mango tree, and sleeps and wakes for twelve years at a stretch. Spirits and ogres protect him from attacks human and supernatural. The mangoes from his holy tree can cure a woman's barrenness.

The King summoned all the nobles and army officers, and asked if anyone would volunteer to go and meet the fakir. Not one accepted to face the perils of the journey, until the Vizier, whose own wife was barren, himself got up and accepted the challenge. The King admired the Vizier's courage, and embraced him like a brother, offering him half his empire if his penance could give him a child.

So the Vizier set his house in order, and left for the journey. He journeyed for many days — crossing thirsty deserts, pathless forests, sky-high mountains and deep rivers raging in flood. Wearied, he sat one evening under a tree for some rest. As he was trying to sleep, he overheard a parrot and a maina talking to each other.

Great is the sorrow of the King, said the maina,

and great the valour of the Vizier. But alas! he will never reach the Fakir.

Who so, my sister? asked the parrot.

Because there is a deep wide river on the way, which no boat can cross, and no human traverse. On the yonder side, there are ogres and spirits that no man can confront.

The parrot laughed, replying, But forget not, my sister, the Vizier believes in God.

The parrot's words emboldened the Vizier's resolve, who got up to pursue his journey. Several months later, he reached the mighty river which the maina had spoken of. Seeing the stormy waters roll eternally on, the Vizier was overcome with fear, and wept and prayed. Be not afraid, and walk straight on, said a voice inside him. No sooner had he stepped into the turbulent waters, than an angel appeared before him, and bore him across to the other side. The Vizier recounted his story to the angel, who was pleased to meet a man as brave and God-fearing as him. The angel gave him two packets, one with fire and another with water, and told him to use them whenever he was confronted with ogres and evil spirits.

The Vizier at last entered the most dreaded jungle of them all. Spirits muttered in the trees, and sinister shapes danced before his eyes, but the Vizier braved them all. Then a mouth of fire, like the opening of an oven, yawned before him. He quickly took out some fire from his packet, and hurled it at the spirit. Fire vanished before his eyes, but only to engulf him from the sides. The Vizier now used the packet of water – the spirits dissolved as earthworms in salt.

Dawn was breaking over the horizon, when the Vizier spotted the magical mango tree, under which sat a frightful-looking fakir. Grass and shrubs grew all over his body, cacti sprouted from his ear-lobes, his eyelashes, as long and wide as palm-leaves, touched the earth, and his white beard was so long and meshy that swallows nestled in it. The meditating fakir took no notice of the Vizier's greetings, but the Vizier stood on one leg for four-and-twenty hours, and prayed before the holy soul. What do you want? the fakir enquired at last, with a voice that stirred a storm in the woods. The Vizier recounted his story. The fakir gave him his trident, and said, Strike the mango tree one blow. Whatever falls is yours. Take it, and begone, and don't disturb me any more. The Vizier struck the tree, picked up the two mangoes that fell, made his obeisance to the fakir, and hurried back to the King's palace.

Seeing the Vizier return with the magical mangoes, the King's joy knew no bounds. He kept one mango for himself, and gave the other to the Vizier. Within months, the Queen bore the King a son. Overjoyed to see his heir, the King ordered state celebrations, and opened his treasury to the poor for three days, and to the Vizier, he gave away half his kingdom.

The soothsayers and the astrologers were called in to prepare the young prince's horoscope. As bad luck would have it, the wise men predicted that the child would be heavy on his father's head for the first nine years, nine months, and nine days. The King was indeed distressed to hear this, but thought of bringing the child up for the ill-fated period in an isolated palace where the child would have every comfort, save the joy of meeting his parents.

Meanwhile, the Vizier's wife too gave birth — to a daughter, as beautiful as a fairy. When the King and the Queen learnt of her celestial charm, they saw in her an ideal match for the prince, though for the moment they kept this secret to themselves.

Once the ill-fated period was over, the young prince came and joined his parents in the royal palace. One day, riding through the bazaar he caught a glimpse of a beautiful girl looking out of a window, and fell in love with her. Her name was Biswa Lakhi.

Romance between the two adolescents was in full bloom, when the King arranged his son's marriage with the Vizier's daughter. The prince was dismayed, and confronted by a dilemma: he was too obedient to disobey his father, and too much in love to disappoint his sweetheart. But Biswa Lakhi provided the answer. She allowed the prince to marry the Vizier's daughter, though taking a promise in return that he would never face his wife without a cloth band on his eyes. The prince gave his word of honour, and for months after his marriage, he did not permit his spouse to look him in the eye. Behind the princess's back, the prince continued his romance with Biswa Lakhi, spending days and nights at her house.

A few months later, news reached the beautiful princess's ear that Biswa Lakhi was carrying her husband's child. Rather than give way to despair, she thought of a scheme to win her husband back. She disguised herself as a milkwoman, and carrying a pitcher of milk on her head, went to Biswa Lakhi's house and sang at her doorstep:

> Come, buy my milk,
> If good or bad;
> Come buy my milk,
> And make me glad.
> Nor rest, nor peace,
> Nor joy is won,
> Nor sorrow cease,
> Till work is done.
> Then buy my milk,
> If good or bad;
> Come buy my milk,
> And make me glad.

Enchanted by the melodious voice, the prince went

charging to the threshold to look at the milkwoman's fair countenance. But alas! It was veiled. Poetry rose to his quivering lips. He sang playfully:

> Come with joy and gladness,
> All gloom away we will chase;
> Here put aside your sadness,
> And unveil your pretty face.

The milkwoman answered coquettishly:

> My milk is sold,
> My work is done,
> My face I hold
> My lord's alone.

The milkwoman left, leaving Biswa Lakhi sulky and jealous, and the prince, pining with love. On the third day, the princess returned, once again disguised as a milkwoman. This time, the prince followed her a long way back up to her house, and addressed her again in poetry:

> Thy form is fair,
> Thy jewels rare;
> But what thy face
> I cannot trace.
> With envious fold
> Thy veil doth hold
> Its beauty hid,
> My glance forbid.
> Then be thou kind,
> And ease my mind;
> Thy home, thy name,
> Thy state proclaim.

The princess chuckled behind her veil:

Not now I reveal to thee,
Or disclose it at your call;
Return in the night to me,
And thou shalt hear it all.

For a while, Shabnam-the-storyteller's voice faintly resonated in my ears, and then I fell asleep . . .

* * *

Shabnam came back next day at bed-time. That was a very soothing story, I said, paying her a compliment. Thank you, Begum Sahiba, she said, bowing, but you fell asleep half-way through it. She began recounting the rest.

As soon as the light of day was gone, the prince slinked into the milkwoman's house. Noticing the gold-brimmed chandeliers and the Persian tapestry on the walls, he said to himself, Goodness me! This is not a milkwoman's house, it is a palace. A eunuch offered him a glass of juice, and said, Please take a seat. My Lady will be here soon. Meanwhile, I will send in a story-teller to colour your loneliness. The story-teller came and recounted a story that was nothing but the story of the prince and the princess themselves. As the prince understood the trick, the princess walked in, wearing her best costume. He got up and embraced her, and swore never to be unfaithful again. Then suddenly, caught in a storm of anger, the prince thundered:

Witch! Biswa Lakhi is a witch. She kept me away from my marital bed. Kneeling before the princess, he begged forgiveness and then asked, Now choose the manner of Biswa Lakhi's death, my love — shall she be buried alive, shot with poisoned arrows, or torn apart by wild horses?

Let the decision be yours, My Lord, replied the princess, smiling coyly behind the veil.

The prince had the pregnant Biswa Lakhi buried alive for four and twenty hours, at the end of which she was exhumed half-alive and tied to the branch of a keekar tree. The prince himself shot two poisoned arrows at her, one in each breast. She was then untied, and each of her limbs knotted to a wild horse. Her body was torn to . . .

Enough! Enough! I cried out in horror. What a terrifying story this is, Shabnam!

Why terrifying, Begum Sahiba?

Oh! It's blood-curdling — a nightmare in words. Why did he have to do this to Biswa Lakhi?

She deserved it, Begum Sahiba. She kept him away from his marital love.

But why should he have got enchanted in the first place?

Shabnam laughed clatteringly, adding, Now aren't such questions taboo in a man's world, Begum Sahiba?

I pondered over Shabnam's story for a while, unable to fathom why she had recounted it to me, and then asked:

Why did you choose this story for me?

Because you asked for a prophetic story, replied Shabnam, in a manner that had suddenly become peevish, as though she were teasing me.

And what is so prophetic about it?

Shabnam laughed, without answering my question. Her behaviour, which had nothing of the usual servility of a story-teller, was beginning to sound more and more petulant.

I asked again, a shade authoritatively:

But what was so prophetic about it?

Hints are there for the wise to take, she answered.

What do you mean? Her riddle frightened me.

You know, Begum Sahiba, said Shabnam, now using a soft, conspiratorial tone. Our King is renowned for immuring his pregnant women.

190

Immuring his pregnant women? Who? Which one? Who said that?

I am sorry to bring this to your notice, Begum Sahiba, but it is common knowledge in the palace. He immured Afzal Mahal, one of his wives. And before that, he had immured four other women. They say he has something against pregnant women. In fact, among the harem women, there is a saying: Cursed is she who conceives by the King.

Shabnam turned towards the wall behind her, and then leaning on me, she intoned girlishly, And do you know where Afzal Mahal was buried, Begum Sahiba?

Where?

Right here — in this chamber. Pointing to the wall, she said. There, in that wall. Her spirit has sobbed and wept here for years. We have all heard it.

Shabnam's story made me shudder with fright. I motioned to her angrily to leave the room, and got up to get a breath of fresh air at the window. On the window-sill sat the familiar pigeon, bleeding from its neck . . .

* * *

Is it true that Afzal Mahal was immured in my chamber? I asked Mumtaz-the-eunuch, who by then was the only trust-worthy friend left in the palace.

But who told you that, Begum Sahiba? questioned Mumtaz, looking stunned.

Shabnam — the 'prophetic storyteller'.

And how did she manage to reach your ear?

I called her for a story.

Oh no! Mumtaz bewailed. You invite perils to your doorstep, Begum Sahiba.

Why do you say that?

Oh no! lamented Mumtaz, slapping his forehead, as though reproaching me for a fatal mistake. Why Shabnam, Begum Sahiba? Why she of all the people? — she is Dulari's confidante.

He paced up and down the chamber, reflecting, and then

muttered, This looks like Dulari's plot. She is surrounding you from all sides. Outside the palace, she is conniving with the British, and inside, playing on your nerves. Her intention is clear: she wants to provoke a miscarriage. Oh no! Begum Sahiba, I fear the stars are on the devil's side — the barber has fled, the King is going mad, the astrologer predicts gloom. Beware, Begum Sahiba, I fear the stars are on the devil's side.

But is it true that Afzal Mahal was immured in my chamber, Mumtaz?

Yes, it is, he said, looking down at his toes.

Is it also true that the King punishes his pregnant wives?

Not wives, just one wife — Afzal Mahal was immured.

I am told he had four other women immured before her?

Yes, he did.

Mumtaz shook his head repentantly. Beware, Begum Sahiba, I fear the stars are on the devil's side.

He left, and I blew out the bedside lamp.

* * *

I had been feeling nauseous the whole day. It was a peculiar sickness, that had less to do with motherhood than with the state of my mind. I mentioned my sense of physical discomfort to Dhanno, the new maid at my palace. She promptly answered. I know what to get you. I know of a very effective neebu sherbet for such states of mind. A few minutes later, she returned with a glass in her hand.

Just then Mumtaz-the-eunuch entered my chamber. It must have been something in Dhanno's manner that made him interrogate her: What is that in your hand? The maid suddenly lost her calm, and stuttered, looking pale: Sherbet for my lady. With that, the cup fell from her hand, and broke, and she ran towards the kitchen to fetch a mop. It was when she failed to return, for she had fled from the palace, that Mumtaz discovered that the cup of sherbet was indeed poison mixed with lemon juice.

Beware, beware, Begum Sahiba. Never trust unknown hands.

* * *

A loud pounding woke me up at night. Is it a dream, or someone at the door? I wondered, still half-asleep. I heard the same sound again, like that of a blacksmith beating iron. Who is it? I asked. No one answered. Who is making this noise? I asked again. Oh! Forgive me. Did I disturb you? answered a feminine voice, breaking into a metallic laughter — it wasn't even laughter, more like the clatter of a brass plate rolling on the floor. Strangely, I couldn't figure out where the voice, or the laughter or the pounding came from. Who is it? I enquired, trying to fuse more authority into my voice. Forgive me, Begum Sahiba, said the voice with an obvious overtone of sarcasm. Forgive me, but I was just making room for you. She laughed again, louder, clearer, and uttering teasingly again. I thought I'd make room for you before the King sent you here.

What room? I retorted — who are you?

She didn't answer.

As I tried to get up to light the bedside lamp, a heavy, invisible weight appeared on my chest, immobilising me on the bed.

Who? Who — who are you? I screamed, wrestling with the weight.

Ouf! It's me. She intoned playfully. You know me, of course, you do. One guess — go on, guess who I am.

The weight became heavier and heavier, making breathing difficult. Leave me alone! — I protested — Get this weight off my chest! Who are you?

She released the weight, laughed again, but didn't say anything.

I jumped out of bed, lit the lamp, and dashed towards the door. It was locked from outside. I tried the other door, that too was locked. I rushed to the garden window — strangely, the window had disappeared. I screamed through the door. Help! Help! Mumtaz! Save the Queen! No one answered. Except the whirling echoes.

So you can't even guess who I am, said the voice through

the side-wall. Come, I'll give you a lead. I was once a beautiful young woman like you, but I made the mistake of conceiving a child by the King. So now you know who I am?

No – who are you?

Afzal Mahal, she said, adding, Aha! I see that you are a beautiful woman. Your child must be as fair and beautiful as its mother. She laughed again, and said in a slow, theatrical, drawling tone, Come, don't be scared of me. Now be a nice mother, and give me your child. A hand touched my waist. I shrieked, No, no, never.

Come, come, be a wise mother, and hand me your child.

No, no, never! I shrieked again, rushing towards the door that gave onto the courtyard.

Surprisingly, the door was now wide open. I charged out and cried, Help! Help! Save the Queen! Save! Save!

Women in the zenana raised alarm, children began to cry, and the guards, led by Mumtaz-the-eunuch, came running up to me.

Arrest her, arrest her, chain her immediately, I ordered Mumtaz.

Who, Begum Sahiba? he enquired, puzzled.

Stop gaping at me like that. Arrest her immediately.

But who, Begum Sahiba?

Afzal Mahal – she is in my chamber.

But she died many years ago, Begum Sahiba.

No, she is in my chamber.

I beg your pardon, Begum. Afzal Mahal was immured ten years ago.

No, she wasn't. She is very much alive, and in my chamber. She wants to steal my child. Arrest her! Quick! Have her locked up instantly . . .

Saying that, Mumtaz told me later, I fainted. Ironically, on coming back to life, I remembered most of what had transpired. I had had a hallucination I realised. But alas! Too late. The game is over, said Mumtaz, sobbing. Your enemies have destroyed you, Begum Sahiba.

194

                              * * *

Possessed! Possessed! The Queen is possessed by Afzal Mahal's spirit! – the rumour spread like wildfire. Afzal Mahal's spirit has avenged herself, remarked one priest. A possessed queen's child should be buried at birth, counselled another. For His Majesty's well-being, both the mother and the child should be immured, advised the King's Brahmin.

The priests had sealed my fate. I could see my destiny in a mirror, weeping.

                              * * *

Lucknow had had a passing shower that evening, cleansing the atmosphere of all the dust. The air smelt of wet earth, and a gentle, cool breeze was blowing through the palace. Through the terrace windows, I could see the birds dance and the clouds sail past the twilight sky. Despite the events of the recent past and threats of immurement, a peculiar opiate calm reigned in my mind, the kind I had not felt for a long time. Was it the lull before the storm, or was it the quiet of a martyr before his hangman? – the paradoxical harmony of my mind perplexed me.

I wandered off into the garden, savouring the small, imperceptible pleasures of life that I seemed to have almost forgotten – I picked lemons, shooed parrots off mango trees, and felt the fragrance of honey-suckle slowly sweeten the bitterness of my destiny. After a long stroll, I returned to my chamber and laid back on a rocking chair. I felt my belly – it was big and round, like the balloon Charles Bonnet had floated on the Gomti skies! Will fate smile on my child was the only question that mattered to me.

I must have dozed off to sleep, for I remember being woken by a trembling voice:

Begum Sahiba, Begum Sahiba.

It was Mumtaz, dressed in white, a colour he rarely wore.

Another letter from the King, is it? I asked.

No, Begum Sahiba, he whimpered.

What is it then? I snapped.

His — His Majesty has sent for you, Begum Sahiba, he mumbled.

After a heavy silence, I plucked up the courage to ask: So has he broken his vow of not seeing me until childbirth?

So it seems, Begum Sahiba, replied Mumtaz, looking down. I suspect the stars are on the devil's side.

Do you think he is going to obey his priests and have me killed? I asked with delirious boldness.

God forbid. God forbid. God forbid, Begum Sahiba.

Does he want to kill my child?

I pray not, Begum Sahiba.

What does he want then?

Allah! Allah! Allah! supplicated the soft-hearted eunuch.

The die it seemed had at last been cast. My first reaction was to flee — flee anywhere, somewhere where the King and the world would never be able to find me and my child. But then, palaces are like royal cages, it is often easier to kill oneself than to escape the gaze of their million spies. I went into another chamber to think of things that fate might hold in store for me, but I noticed that reason was the first victim of my predicament. I just couldn't think. Then, slowly, the haze of fear and confusion cleared, and I took a decision — if the King wanted to bury my child at birth, I would plead with him to kill us both together, which I felt was the best solution under the circumstances. As for the rest, I decided to face the turns of my destiny with a bold and honest smile, and to conduct myself before the King as though nothing had happened.

I mounted the waiting carriage and reached the palace. Running into the King's private apartments with fake exuberance, I called out, My Lord, My Lord. The King was nowhere to be seen. I called out again, he still didn't answer. Now where are you hiding, My Lord? I said louder. Look, look at your child, look how big he has grown, My Lord. I heard a faint sound, of someone sobbing. I looked behind the curtain — the King was still invisible, but his sobbing was more and more distinct. Then he mumbled from somewhere. Oh! Your delightful English accent. Ann! These gems of the King's English that I had almost forgotten. His light-hearted remark fortified my optimism. But where are you, My Lord? His sobbing turned louder, and he sighed. Oh God! How much I loved her! I picked up an oil-lamp, and followed the trail of sound into the secret passage which connected our bedroom to the main street behind the palace. As I was looking at the corridor wall, the King spoke from somewhere close by. Here, here, Ann, I'm just trying to get this slab of stone out of the way. A stone dropped with a thud, and the King sighed romantically:

Oh how beautiful you look, Ann!

The King astounded me by sticking his head out through a large rectangular hole in the wall. He looked very different – wrinkles lined his face, patches of silver hair shone in the translucent light, he appeared to have put on years since I last saw him. I noticed that he was in his pyjamas. Surprised to see him sitting inside a hole, I enquired with wifely curiosity:

But what are you doing there inside a wall, My Lord?

You don't know how much I loved you, Ann, he remarked without answering my question.

Why loved? Don't you any more. My Lord?

I do, I do, but that witch has ended up avenging herself on you.

Who?

Afzal Mahal.

Why?

She has possessed you. Her spirit has cast a spell on you.

Surely His Majesty does not believe such baseless rumours.

The King began to reflect, and with that, his soft, melancholic eyes slowly transformed into cold marble. Staring severely at me, he declared:

But this is not a rumour. It is the sad truth. That was your destiny.

That is not true, My Lord. I implored, hearing the change in his tone. I just had a hallucination, and that was it. Now I am out of it – I am not possessed by anyone. I am fine as ever.

197

If the possessed knew they were possessed, the King scoffed, there would be no possessed. It is for others to judge.

But I feel perfectly normal. Look at me — do I look possessed by anyone?

When the late King of England's spirit possessed me, even I claimed that I was normal. A mad man does not know he is mad — such is the law of the supernatural.

But there is nothing wrong with me, My Lord.

That's what you think, Ann. In fact, I suspected all along that your pregnancy would end up in disaster. The barber's clairvoyance had seen it, the astrologer had predicted it, now your madness has proved it. Let's not argue about such things — the plain fact is that you've gone mad. Your greatness lies in accepting your defeat before destiny with due dignity.

My womb rose to my gullet, and I said pleadingly, But what are you saying . . .

Don't argue, Ann, he cut in curtly. Respect the verdict of God. He will spring worse surprises if you insist on defying his orders. Let's face it. That witch of a Begum has ended up settling her account with you. She has finished you — it's all over for you.

Hearing the first line of the verdict. I went down on my knees, and begged, But what has come over you, My Lord? Have mercy on your heir — just look at him throbbing with life. He is dying to be caressed by his father.

Oh how much I had desired that child! How much I loved him! The King sighed, responding compassionately to my appeal.

You will still have him, My Lord, I said reassuringly.

But I don't want that devil any more, the King snarled, reverting back to his callous posture. The heavens have turned upside down, his parents have gone mad, and the bastard is still alive and kicking — how selfish could he get! Khan-the-barber was right — this child will be my hangman. Devil!

The King shook his head vigorously, and shouted, Go away from here, Ann, I want to be alone.

The King's unexpected rudeness shocked me. This was

perhaps the only time in my life that he had raised his voice to me. I walked into the adjoining room, that had once been our private salon and saw that the King had procured many an exotic object for his successor, including a dainty ivory cradle that was waiting to embrace my child. I was trying to hold back my tears, when the King called out, Come in Ann. You can come in now.

I returned to the secret passage only to discover that the King had completely changed the setting of his drama. He was still inside the hole but no longer in his pyjamas: he was now adorned with the ceremonial costume of the King of Awadh, and his diamond crown twinkled in the faint light. On the sill of the rectangular wall-hole that separated the King from me, a collection of sumptuous edibles was laid out – roasted almonds, salted pistachio nuts, fried peanuts, kababs, wafers, fresh pastries, and a large bottle of cognac. As I stood puzzled before the web-infested dungeon, the King recited a quatrain like a grace:

All dreams and fantasies are but an illusion,
For it is death which ends up winning.
Over, over, over,
Over like a night of illusory pleasures.

Pointing to the food before us, he then said to me:
Go on, try some. Try the walnuts, they are fresh from Kashmir.
But what is this, Your Majesty? I asked, bewildered once again by his imagination.
The Last Supper.
What does that mean?
It means what it is supposed to mean – your last drink and meal with me. After this, your destiny awaits you.
The King poured out two large glasses of cognac, and clinking his with mine, he said:
Before your destiny takes you away from me, let me ask you – do you want anything special from the King?

I have already taken too much to merit any more, My Lord.

But something — something for your family.

No, nothing.

Come, come, Ann, don't be angry with me. Ask for something — anything.

Can you efface my past, Your Majesty? I asked.

Why do you say that?

Because I want to be what I was.

Aha! You prefer being an ordinary woman to a queen, said the King, amused. But that's too late now. Even God cannot efface your past. You can ask me for anything material.

I have nothing to ask.

The King declared:

So here is my verdict.

My Lord?

I have decided to kill . . .

No! I shrieked spontaneously.

Yes! I have decided to kill . . .

You are going to kill me and my child?

The King burst out into an uproarious laughter, saying, Kill my heart's love? Kill the only woman I have loved in my life? No, never! — I've decided to take my own life.

What!

Yes, I have decided to take my own life.

What has come over you, My Lord? I asked, not quite believing him. You aren't going to kill yourself, are you?

Kill! Haha! the King said, chortling. Kill is not the word for it. It was a hard decision to take, you know.

But, what are you . . .

Please do not interrupt me — let me speak. I came to this decision because there was no point in being a doomed King. The only child I had ever desired was augured to be my butcher. The only woman I had loved had gone mad. And Khan, the only man I had trusted, had betrayed me. On top of this, the British are all set to lay a siege on the palace. So, before the enemy gets him, brave is he who takes his own life.

No, My Lord, you must live for me and your heir, I pleaded, suspecting that the King was being serious.

My decision is taken, Ann, declared the King in all seriousness. Nothing can change my mind. In fact, if you ask me, the great question before my mind was not whether to die, but how best to die? How to choose an original path of death which no King in history had treaded before? I contemplated wandering off into the woods like a sanyasi – but that was too common. I debated offering my life to Joe Manton, my lovely gun – but nothing could be more commonplace. So after much reflection, I thought of something that no King had done to himself before – to immure myself!

What are you saying, My Lord?

Yes, to confer on myself the same punishment that I had so unjustly meted out to others. So I am killing two birds with the same stone – absolving myself of all guilt, and dying with a touch of poetic originality. What an unusual life I would have had, my love! My father didn't know how I appeared on this earth, now my subjects won't know how I disappeared from it. Between God, me and you, my fair love, let this secret dissolve into the night.

But what are you . . .

The King desires no discussion, commanded the King like the King of Awadh.

He then took out of his pocket two keys, and handing them over to me, he stated, One is for the safe. Take all the jewels away – leave nothing for the British. And the other is for the secret passage. Vanish from the palace before the light of dawn.

What has come over you, My Lord? I pleaded, embracing the earth. What spirits have cast a spell on you? No, no, do not leave me a widow. Think of your child, My Lord. Think of Murad, think of that lovely balloon festival with which you celebrated his conception. No! No, My Lord!

There is no greater sorrow, Ann, the King said quoting his favourite line, than to recall the time when we were happy. Alas, sentiment has no place on the bed of death. Let us part in fun and laughter, for humour alone can triumph over death. Come, rise from the earth and offer me your lips . . .

* * *

I shut the book, slightly surprised by its abrupt ending.

'That was abrupt,' I remarked to Awaara, who was about to fall asleep.

'Ah, you've finished reading it.'

'But why did you end it so abruptly?'

'That's how Miss Walters ends her diary,' said Awaara groggily. 'I thought it'd be best to leave the book at that.'

'But what happened to the King?'

'He immured himself.'

'And did people get to find out where he had disappeared?'

'Not until the palace wall was destroyed by the British artillery in a battle. Out of the debris came some bones, a Joe Manton and a pair of tongs Khan-the-barber had once given the King. That's how they inferred that the King must have immured himself. He was reburied later.'

'And Miss Walters' child?'

'We know from a letter that her child was born exactly a week after the King immured himself. She named him Murad.'

'And what happened to her?'

'She fled from Lucknow, wrote her autobiography, and then went back to the life of an ordinary dancing-girl. But that's another story — let's leave that to another day,' said Awaara sleepily.

I switched off the lamp.

THIRTEEN

'TCH, TCH, TUT, TUT, HUTT, HUTT.'

I woke up with Awaara producing some strange sounds on the verandah. 'What is it?' I asked. 'Hutt, hutt, bhug-bhug, bhag, bhag sale,' resumed Awaara, without answering me. Then he dashed back into the room, picked up his bathroom slippers, and hurled them at something – I heard a crow flap away, cawing. Seconds later, the crow he was trying to shoo, returned with two others, each as vexatious as the other. Unusually agitated by the cawing, Awaara then picked up shoes, forks, knives, salt-cellars, chess-board pieces — whatever he could lay his hand on — and launched a string of missiles at the obstinate birds. 'Uh! They'll drive me mad,' he fumed. 'I've been up since four.'

A minute later, the crows were back on the terrace, cawing with reinvigorated fervour – earlier on, they were cawing for themselves, now they seemed to be doing it for an audience. Realising his futile mission, Awaara gave up chucking things at them, and tried to keep them away with a frantic motioning of hands; it looked as though he were guiding a helicopter-landing on a roof-top. Amused by his gestures, I remarked, 'Now, don't tell me, it's your turn to get possessed. Leave them alone, Awaara, you can't beat a crow.' He came in and sat beside me. 'On my first day here,' I said, 'I was so wild with a crow one morning that I asked Lingappa to do something about it. And do you know what he replied? "Madam, but, but, Madam, in my community, a crow cawing at home is considered auspicious. It announces a visitor's arrival".'

Lingappa's forecast might not have worked on the first occasion, but this time it did. Someone knocked at the door. 'Miss Valerie. Miss Valerie please,' squeaked a feminine voice. Who's that? I wondered, surprised to find a stranger at my bedroom door that early in the morning. Awaara, who liked to keep our relationship private, quietly slinked into the bathroom. 'Miss Valerie. Miss Valerie please,' spoke the voice again, with a rustic accent. 'Who is it?' I enquired. 'Tanhai. Your Indian cousin, Valerie,' she replied, beginning to tap on the door. 'Open, open the door. I have come a long way to meet you.' The voice persisted, 'It's me, me, your lost cousin, Valerie.' I opened the door. A woman leapt at me, splitting into peals of laughter:

'Fooled you, fooled you! I scared the hell out of you, didn't I?' screamed Rani-the-star, popping out of the blue, and embracing me like a sister.

'You really did,' I said, ecstatic to see her in Lucknow. 'Look at you, playing Tanhai even before we've discussed the film. But how did you land up here? I thought you were going to be shooting in Kashmir the whole month.'

'Well, I was so excited about the project that I took a couple of days off to come and see you. Let me get out of these silly shoes first.'

Rani flung her shoes and hand-bag off into the air in her characteristic style, and then came and sat on the bed, amazingly effusive and fresh for the early hour of the morning.

'But that was quick,' I remarked. 'I just called you last Sunday.'

'Yes, when something gets on my mind, I can't get it out of my system,' said Rani, visibly excited. 'What a wonderful story for a film, Val!'

'It is, isn't it? But let me be honest – the idea is not mine. It is his.'

'Whose?'

Awaara staggered out of the bathroom, schoolboyishly embarrassed.

'Pleased to meet you, Awaara,' Rani shook hands with him, adding with a twinkle in her eyes, 'Till now we had only read about you in the press. It's nice to be able to give a face to a name.'

We had barely sat down to discuss the film project, when Lingappa arrived with what was supposed to be our bed-tea. Looking at the feast of a breakfast he had promptly churned out — three varieties of fried chapaties, yoghurt, cheese, fried eggs and a host of south Indian dishes — I took a dig at his weakness for Rani. 'I see, I see, Linga, a miserly fried egg and toast for me, and a real feast for Rani.' 'Special Rani menu today, Madam,' he replied in telegraphic language, yelping, 'Rani and me both from the same town — Srirangapatnam.' Rani exchanged a few words with him in his local language, and that made his day. He went trotting back to the kitchen, humming a song from one of Rani's films.

'But aren't you excited about finding a cousin in Tanhai, Valerie?' Rani asked, sipping her tea.

'In a way. It's not easy though, to relate to a person who is not normal.'

'Why? Is she really nuts?'

'Not very normal anyway. She thinks she is founding a polyandrous monarchy on this earth. She considers herself to be the Queen of some Free Women's Utopian Kingdom of Auratabad . . .'

'God, she sounds completely nuts, this girl,' said Rani. 'Are you going to see her?'

'Well, that's my dilemma, you see. She has given me an appointment for the next full-moon day. And do you know where? — at a nearby snake temple, with crawling . . .'

'Stop it!' Rani placed her hand on my mouth, 'I've heard of that temple. Oh! It gives me the creeps, that place. So are you going to see her then?'

'If you accompany me, yes.'

'Me? No way!' Rani shrieked melodramatically. 'Snakes and me! No thanks!'

'It's not all that dangerous I am told. Apparently, it is a very frequented Shiva temple of this area.'

'Now don't you try and give me any of that rubbish about Shiva — I know exactly what it is. It's not my cup of tea. First, to see someone at a temple crawling with snakes, then someone who is completely bonkers — no thanks, I am quite happy with the three schizophrenics in my family. Anyway, if you ask me, your dear cousin is more fun in fiction than in reality.'

Rani poured herself another cup of tea, and then, turning to Awaara, asked, 'Shall we get on with the business then? What is the story?'

Awaara's story-line might have been inspired by my chance discovery of Tanhai in India, but it had a fair dose of fiction, so much so that my real story now seemed only a part of the whole. It started off with two women. Tanhai, an Indian living in India, and Juliette, a European living in Paris. Parallel dinner-table discussions with their respective mothers reveal that, a century and a half ago, an Indian child had been brought from India: the Indians believe that he was stolen by a childless, French *parfumier*, and the French believe that he was sold by a penuried dancing-girl to the Frenchman. For both sides, the child has had a pivotal importance — for the French, he is the beginning of their family tree, and for the Indians, someone whose loss caused his mother to go mad, thus laying the roots of some kind of a family ritual — the kind Tanhai had mentioned to me in her letter. Tanhai and Juliette, who are the only survivors of their respective families, discover through documents that a cousin from the other side of the family which had been separated with the child's coming to Europe, is still alive. Tanhai thus begins her search for Juliette, who is an actress in Paris. A messenger is sent to France in search of her. By the time Tanhai's man gets hold of Juliette's whereabouts in Paris, she has already left for a shoot in India. There, by chance, she comes across a reference to Tanhai in a press report. She goes to meet her, but Tanhai has just died of a cerebral haemorrhage. A shot showing Juliette at her cousin's funeral ends the film.

'Splendid, Awaara!' Admiration twinkled in Rani's eyes.

'Where have you been hiding all these days? Interesting plot, contrasting characters, lovely locations, a bit of Europe, a bit of India — smashing! What else do we need?'

'Marvellous!' I added my bit to the deluge of compliments. 'What I find most captivating in it is the twin plot. It's not just a European looking for her exotic roots, but an Indian too — which is what makes it original. Not just another European cliché.'

'That makes it truly international, doesn't it? Super!' Rani clapped her hands, like a schoolgirl cheering the home team, and then reflected, 'I have an idea. Why don't we make and promote this film as a completely female affair?'

'But that's nothing new,' said Awaara. 'There have been so many heroine-oriented films lately.'

'Yes, but I'm meaning something different. Let's make our film into a totally female show — A to Z. Female leads, as is the case, female director, a female cinematographer, a female editor, a female distributor, a female producer, a complete women's affair. Politically, it makes sense, and tactically, it will be the first of its kind. It will have a commercial appeal.'

'I know a superb female Director of Cinematography in Paris,' I said, thinking of Linda White.

'Usha, Usha, that woman in Sydney — what's her name?' Rani clicked her fingers to recall a name. 'Yes, Usha Khurana. Let's ask her to direct the film. She will be ideal. And for the screenplay, let's ask Geetanjali Singh — she's marvellous.' She turned to Awaara. 'You know her work, don't you?'

'Yes, I do. But, my fair megalomaniac ladies,' Awaara said, realising that his dream of doing the scenario was being swept off by the feminist storm, 'what do you think I am going to be doing in the film?'

Rani and I glanced at each other, and burst out laughing.

'Oh! It's so difficult to get rid of these men,' Rani moaned jokingly. 'But I have an idea. Why don't you use a female pseudonym, Awaara?'

'Done,' Awaara accepted unhesitatingly. 'I haven't been

able to make much of a name with my real name, so why not try with a pseudonym.'

'Great! The ball is in your court now — get cracking on the script,' said Rani to Awaara.

'But who is going to pay the poor fellow?' Awaara looked relieved to hear me raise the question.

'I put fifty thousand rupees on the table,' said Rani, slapping the table like a professional gambler.

'I'll put another fifty.'

'Is that okay to begin with?' Rani asked Awaara.

'I haven't earned that much in my whole life,' he replied, laughing.

Behind Awaara's laughter lay the story of a writer's misery. Although Awaara rarely talked about himself or his past, from our conversations I gathered that he had spent fifteen years in the film industry without being able to make two ends meet. The autobiography of Mrs Walters he had edited, had fetched him five hundred rupees for a year's work, while most of his translations were done for a song, and his job at the Bombay Poets' Guild was honorary. In the madhouse of Bombay, where every crook and smuggler seemed to have won the benediction of one Goddess of wealth or the other, Awaara lived in a tin-roofed tenement in the company of thugs, prostitutes, criminals, flies and mosquitoes. I asked him in Bombay once, 'Where do you live?' He replied, 'In Chembur until this morning.' 'And now?' His hand rose, curling fatewards, 'God knows. We were all evicted this morning — someone is putting up a sky-scraper there.' Life had taught Awaara this principle — if reality is cruel, then let life be a dream . . .

* * *

Rani left for Delhi by the evening flight. After dropping her, Awaara and I, making the best of our day off, went for a long stroll to the Baradari Gardens. On our return to the bungalow, we found Deboo waiting for us, looking tense and washed-out.

'I need your help, Awaara,' Deboo, sounded unusually pathetic.

'What kind of help?' enquired Awaara, with a tinge of disbelief, for Deboo was hardly the kind to demand favours of his foe.

'Tomorrow's balloon scene is in a real mess. Charles Bonnet's assistant is down with malaria, running 104–105. Can you replace him?'

'Well . . . ' Awaara lit a cigarette.

'It's a very decent role, damn it,' remarked Deboo impatiently, 'and it doesn't involve much. You know the scene. The King and Miss Walters are on the banks of the Ganges for the balloon show. The Frenchie, Charles Bonnet, and his assistant come winding down the river with the smoke-balloon, and then take off into the air. Bonnet handles the balloon, while his assistant prepares the banner. Then Bonnet takes over the banner, and his assistant handles the balloon. I think you'd be the ideal person.'

'Let me give it a thought,' said Awaara.

'But we have no time, Awaara,' Deboo spouted. 'Do you realise we have to be in Chunar tomorrow morning? So it is yes or no. You'll obviously be paid for the job.'

'That's not the problem,' said Awaara, half-persuaded. 'It's just that I haven't even rehearsed the scene.'

'Leave that to me. I know you can do it. Good, and see you in the lobby at seven.'

We slept early that night. I hadn't seen Awaara that happy ever.

* * *

'Aren't you sleeping?' I asked Awaara, hearing him laugh softly to himself in the middle of the night. 'Can't get over this day. Asked to write a scenario, then act, then paid for all these jobs – it doesn't look like a day out of my life.'

'Sleep, you silly,' I said, poking him in the waist.

'Aren't you asleep?' This time, Awaara asked me, a little

209

later the same night. 'Oh! I had this curious dream,' I said, stubbing out my cigarette. 'You and Miss Walters were making love in a river,' Awaara quietly lunged forward, lifted me by my waist and hurled me violently over to the other side of the bed. Madness stormed Awaara, and he stormed me: bottles broke, glasses cracked, mirrors laughed, pillows flew, our bodies refined the geometry of love. 'Don't,' I pleaded, 'Don't bite so hard – I have close-ups tomorrow.'

'Then let the camera immortalise my love-bites.'

In the morning, I said jokingly to him, 'I can't decide if you are a bull or a poet, Awaara.' 'Bull,' said the poet.

* * *

The balloon scene was easily the most challenging sequence of our film, the main reason for this being Deboo's love of realist fiction. He was adamant that this scene be an exact screen-replica of what had happened. Crowds, colours, games, camels, horses, carriages, he wanted all the paraphernalia of the early nineteenth-century village festivals to be on the screen. So rather than creating the effect of a spectacle, as some other directors might, Deboo had actually opted for organising a live event. This obviously posed many problems, not the least of which was the actual mustering up of two to three hundred thousand volunteers on the banks of the Ganges. The producer tried seeking the help of the state administration, but all they could promise was a couple of thousand of people. Then the million-dollar idea came from the sweeper at the set. He suggested, 'Advertise in the papers that a Grand Balloon Fair will be held, and take it from me that millions will flock to it.' That did the trick.

As publicity cars and jeeps went about the country, blaring on loud-speakers that a Grand Balloon Show was going to be held in Chunar, the villagefolk were more than enchanted. The drum-squads did the initial spade-work, the rumour-mongers did the rest. Within days, the entire Chunar country was abuzz with the sauciest of rumours – one even said that it wasn't a fair

that was being organised, but indeed a film shooting featuring
the Prime Minister and Lady Diana . . .

The unit met at the hotel in the morning. Deboo was
understandably tense and irritable. He spoke to all of us about
the sequence of events, ending the meeting with a stiff warning.
'Get it clear in your heads, there will not be any retakes. The
first shot will be the final. So think about your moves.'

We left for Chunar. Deboo sat in his own car, while Serge,
the Frenchman playing Charles Bonnet's role, and Awaara, his
assistant, came in mine. For most of the journey, the ambience
in the car was serious, each concentrating on his role. Spotting
the cemetery near Chunar that Awaara had taken me to, I
whispered in his ear, 'Hey! Remember the blond bushes in that
cemetery there!' 'Shut up – let me concentrate,' he rebuffed, his
eyes glued to his script. We were about to take the turning to
the Ganges, when Deboo spoke from his car, crackling on the
walkie-talkie:

'Alpha, Alpha, Valerie? Awaara? Can you catch me?'

'Yes, yes, go on,' answered Awaara, speaking into his set.

'Slight change in programme – the police say a massive
crowd has gathered on the south bank – they cannot guarantee
police protection for the bank scenes – hullo! hullo! alpha! alpha!
– can you hear me?'

'Go on. I can hear you quite well,' said Awaara, amused
to hear Deboo talk like an army wire-operator.

'Okay. So the King and the Queen shots on the bank are
out – Valerie should proceed to the PWD Rest House on the
cliff. And Awaara, you and Charles Bonnet – drop Valerie, and
rush to your spot on the Ganges – is that clear?'

'But when do we begin?' Awaara blared into the set.

'The cameraman tells me the conditions are ideal – wind
– light – balloons – everything is perfect – so drop Val at the
PWD Inspection Bungalow and rush to your spot – first the
camera and I will go up in our balloon – the moment we take
off I will inform you – then wait for my second signal – get
that clear, your cue is my second signal – and not the first.'

'Got it,' Awaara repeated the whole message back to Deboo

to confirm that he had got it right, and then said, 'You haven't answered my first question – when do you expect us to sail in with the boat? Can you give us a time?'

'In about an hour from now.'

'Okay,' Awaara put the set away.

As the car drove up the Chunar fort driveway towards the PWD Rest House, I recognised the familiar surroundings – the unforgettable hill-top view of the Ganges, the minuscule Hindu temple on the cliff, and the twin rocking chair on which Awaara and I had spent a whole day reading, and listening to Keith Jarret. 'Won't you spend another night with me at the Rest House, Awaara?' I said, nudging him with my elbow. 'Stop it, Val! Let me concentrate,' he snapped, irritated. 'Don't you see I am nervous?' The car dropped me off before rushing to the location on the river, and I climbed up the cliff to get a good view of the shooting.

An amazing crowd had gathered on the banks of the Ganges. For miles, one could see nothing but people, people and more people. And this wasn't obviously the end, for a large crowd was still on its way, their bullock-carts slowly creaking towards the holy shores. People bathing in the river, praying before the sun, fluttering saris drying in the wind – far from being a crowd scene for a film, it looked more like a religious festival. The fiesta of colours, sounds and sentiments brought Miss Walters' description of the Balloon Show to mind.

Action began sooner than I had expected. Deboo and the cameraman took off first, positioned on a large platform beneath a white balloon. The sight of a gigantic bubble in the skies abruptly cut short all the religious rituals and everyone's eyes turned upwards, more in wonderment than excitement – a sudden lull descended on the Ganges. Then gradually, surprise gave way to excitement, and the crowd began to gurgle. Deboo gave the cue, and Charles Bonnet and Awaara started sailing towards us. Reaching the platform on which the King and the Queen were theoretically supposed to be sitting, Bonnet bowed before His Majesty, and performed a few acrobatics. The moment their boat crossed the King, Awaara switched on the air-pressure, and the gorgeous yellow balloon rose upwards. The crowd burst out into a loud cheer. The balloon soared higher and higher, as did Deboo's in perfect symmetry to the other. Charles Bonnet, a superb mid-air Charlie Chaplin, took several bows from the ecstatic crowd, doffing his hat and waving out to the crowd. Then Awaara passed the Murad banner to Charles Bonnet, who stuck its staff out into the wind, and unfurled it with an exquisite professional flourish. Holding the enormous, green and white banner in his outstretched hand, Charles Bonnet then started revolving on his toes. It seemed as if the banner was caught in a whirlwind. As the crowd cheered louder and louder, whistling and clapping, Bonnet spun faster and faster, carefully varying the angle of the banner to lend a superb colour effect to the spectacle. Our heads were spinning, when I heard a blast. 'Help!' I shrieked, 'Awaara!' A bundle of fire dropped from the sky. People roared in excitement, thinking it was a shooting stunt.

'Awaara!' I cried from the cliff, but he was already dead.

* * *

'Death is the last laugh of the dead on the living. It reveals our ultimate wordlessness, our thoughtlessness: death can be lived, but not contemplated or composed. It is beyond language, beyond thought, perhaps even imagination.

'If anything, it is a sensation of stillness — like that of a flame which burns without shedding any light. Call it pain, call it sorrow, it is the sentiment that nothing is, for nothing was, and nothing shall be.

'After the storm is over, death is reborn as memory. In that form, it is the painful birth of remembrance in the cradle of time.'

Awaara had written these words the night before, in memory of his mother.

* * *

Awaara arrived at the bungalow a few hours later. Immaculately wrapped, like a gift of life to death.

He was enveloped in a spotless white sheet. There were strings round his chest, arms and feet. Strangely, he smelt of fresh jasmine.

His friends placed him on the floor, and stood around him. One of them touched him gently on his arm. Let me sleep, said Awaara. I've never been so peaceful before.

Someone uncovered his face then. It was blue, ink-blue, bruise-ink-blue, like a poem recalling a dream. Another friend touched his cheek. Let me sleep, said Awaara, it's a beautiful dream. Valerie is in mourning.

A wicked Awaara-smile lay frozen on his face, a pearl of water twinkled on his eyelash, a fly buzzed in his ear — let me sleep. I've never been so peaceful before.

I uncovered him to his chest, and touched the hair he loved to have caressed.

I held his hand and pressed it gently. He didn't press it back — so unlike him. I pressed it again, hard. He still didn't react. It was then that I heard death knock at my door. Come in, I said. I am yours.

I climbed up to the terrace.

The sun was setting on the Ganges, when mine had already set. Cranes, storks, dolphins, wind, rain — nothing could colour the blackness before my eyes.

Someone came and whispered from behind. 'I am sorry, Val,' and burst out crying on my shoulder. I shrugged his head off.

'The funeral is tomorrow,' said Deboo, recovering his nerve. I didn't answer.

'The funeral is tomorrow,' he repeated.

'If you don't mind I'd like to pay for the body to be flown to Bombay,' I requested, knowing Awaara had no family.

'It's not in Bombay, it is here.'

'Why here?'

'Because he belonged here — all of Miss Walters' family is buried at the Chunar cemetery.'

'What does that have to do with Awaara?'

'You know he was a direct descendant of Miss Walters, don't you?'

Like all beautiful people, Awaara died a riddle.

* * *

As though to mark the end of a fable, he was laid to rest next to Miss Walters' grave. The epitaph on his tomb, which he himself had chosen, read:

And when I shut my eyes to catch the birds of sleep, I hope above all to capture the marvellous paradise of total rain.

* * *

A year after his death, I returned to his grave and started writing the story of my life. This book is dedicated to his memory.